DEADLY RAIN

DEADLY RAIN

LAWRENCE McNALLY

A Critic's Choice paperback
from Lorevan Publishing, Inc.
New York, New York

Published by arrangement with the author.

ISBN: 1-55547-273-7

First Critic's Choice edition: 1989

From LOREVAN PUBLISHING, INC.

Critic's Choice Paperbacks
31 E. 28th St.
New York, New York 10016

Manufactured in the United States of America

POW

Jeff awoke at dawn. He'd been dreaming he was sitting in a big oak tub in the middle of a field. Valerie was pouring warm water over his head. An acrid stench filled his nostrils and rage tensed his body.

"You stinking yellow bastard," he screamed at the grinning guard who stood slightly to his left.

"What the . . ." Hefley jerked awake.

"That fuckin' gook just pissed on us."

"Why you motherfuc . . ."

"Don't," Jeff cautioned. "Just sit still. He'll kick your brains out just for the hell of it."

Jeff knew the humiliation and physical indignity were the least of their worries. *Somehow* they would have to survive. Somehow they *would* survive. *Somehow they would escape!*

Chapter One

It was hot. Damn hot! The giant rubber trees held the heavy air in a windless vacuum beneath their high crowns and the plantation floor, blotting out the sun except for an occasional beam here and there creating a weird lighting effect among the even rows of trees.

Earlier, a brief hard rain had pelted the thick trees. Now the sun beat down unmercifully. Droplets of rainwater and sap mixed on the broad leaves, dripping to the underbrush ninety feet below.

It was quiet except for intermittent animal sounds and splattering raindrops. Small birds flittered through the dank air, flashing momentarily as they shot through a sunbeam. Monkeys chattered in the distance and lizards grunted as they scrambled through the damp undergrowth.

Sergeant Jeff Spencer crouched beside the fat trunk of a tree. He squinted, his dark eyes trying to pierce the dim atmosphere in front of him. A fat lizard streaked from a bush on his right, stopping about six feet from him in the middle of the trail. It's beady black eyes rolled, looking for any sign of danger. Jeff shivered at the sight of the green foot long body. It's eyes rotated and locked onto Jeff, it's prehistoric brain trying to determine if he were some kind of a threat. The lizard's throat bloated as it made a low obscene sounding grunt then scurried across the path and out of sight. God, Jeff thought, as a chill swept his body, how he hated the slimy bastards. A bird screeched to his left causing him to tense. His ears strained for any unfamiliar noise. He heard the heavy breathing of the lieutenant behind him. It had a rasping, gurgling sound. He must have some internal bleeding, Jeff thought. His finger tightened on the rifle trigger as a flash of movement caught his eye. He stared, blinked, and stared again, watching the low figure of a man dart between the trees about forty yards away. He relaxed as the man approached.

"Hey Sarge. There's someone out there," he heard Hefley whisper behind him. " 'Bout thirty yards, eleven o'clock."

Jeff nodded without taking his eyes off the moving man. He made a circle of his right thumb and forefinger holding it up for the squad behind him. He felt them relax. Jeff waited until the man was ten yards away then snapped his fingers twice. A wide smile gleemed on Creeper's black face as he angled toward Jeff.

Private First Class Huey "Creeper" Jarvis trotted to Jeff and slumped against the tree, facing him. He pushed the heavy helmet back and wiped his glistening face with his sleeve, then took a long drink from Jeff's offered canteen. A concerned look came into his eyes as he glanced at the Lieutenant on the stretcher. "How's he doing?"

"He's not," Jeff said flatly. "What about the clearing?"

"It's there Brother Spence," he said. "But I don't like it."

"Why?"

" 'Cause I don't. Man, it's just too pat. Look Bro, we've been stomping around this mother plantation for three days and we ain't seen hide nor hair of no Viet Cong. This is the first place we've come across that could possibly be used for a landing zone. Right?"

Jeff nodded knowing what Creeper was getting at.

"Ya damn straight," Creeper continued. "So the Lieutenant just happens to get zapped by a Charlie booby grenade a thousand meters from the only decent LZ within twenty-five miles. Bullshit Bro, and you know it."

"Yeah Creeper," Jeff nodded. "Charlie has set us up but good. We know it and he knows it. It's three days back the way we came, two days straight ahead and ten minutes to a chopper ride. How big is the LZ?"

"That's another beauty," Creeper answered. "It's about the size of two football fields. Big trees all around it. A chopper's gonna have to drop in. There's no way he can swoop in and out. He'll have to come down like an elevator."

"Did you see anything?"

"No man. Look, except for this trail and the clearing this place is overgrown with heavy underbrush. A man could be one foot from the clearing and still be completely concealed."

Jeff suddenly felt hopelessly lost. He knew what the

3

score was. The Viet Cong had purposely let them wander around the plantation. There was no doubt the trail was being used as a supply route. It stuck out like a sore thumb.

The plantation hadn't been worked in years, yet the trail was the only place not covered with jungle growth. Yeah. Charlie was running supplies through here all right. Now the Americans knew it was here. So what?

Jeff knew the answer. Some smart VC had already sent word this trail would be unusable for a month or two. Yeah, and he'd dug into the bush on the other side of the clearing knowing someone got zapped by his booby trap, and was just waiting. 'Cause he knows I need a chopper and that little gook bastard would sure like to shoot up a chopper or two, along with a long range recon patrol.

Jeff turned to the medic bending over the Lieutenant on the makeshift stretcher. "What about it Doc? How long can he make it?"

Corporal Bill "Doc" Kenton wiped a trickle of blood from the corner of the Lieutenant's mouth. He turned to face Jeff. "I wasn't sure before, but I am now. He's got a punctured lung. It's a matter of bleeding to death or drowning in his own blood. Either way, I'd say an hour at the most."

Jeff turned back to Creeper. He shrugged his shoulders in despair.

"That ties it Huey. We got to get him out."

"Yeah man, but how? You know what Charlie's going to do."

"Yeah. I know. But maybe, just maybe, we can fake him out."

"How?" Creeper asked doubtfully.

4

"I'm not sure yet," Jeff said, turning to signal his radioman. He pulled a map from his pocket as Corporal Skip Douglas moved up next to him. He waited patiently as Jeff studied the map. Finally he made a circle on the map, marking the grid coordinates in the circle.

"Okay Skip," he said handing him the map. "Here's the LZ. Tell base we need two choppers. One stretcher wounded with four men for the first one. We'll switch to frequency baker baker, one, two, nine, for the choppers and mark our LZ with white smoke. Tell 'em we got a red target for chopper two and we'll mark with red. There'll be four souls for chopper two.

Skip nodded and moved away to start transmitting. Jeff turned to the rest of the squad, motioning them to gather round him.

"Okay troops," he began. "Here's the situation. We've got two choppers coming. Charlie's dug in on the other side of the LZ. So we might have to blast out. Maybe, just maybe, we can pull this off." He turned to Sgt. Chong, their Vietnamese army interpreter. "Chong, do you think they could use a tube?"

"No," he answered immediately. "Mortar no good. Too many trees. No room."

"Yeah," Jeff agreed. "I think so too, but I'd bet a months pay he's got some charges on the LZ."

"Yes," Chong agreed. "And maybe automatic weapons."

Jeff knew Chong was right. He knew the VC well. He'd been fighting them for ten years. Jeff valued Chong's judgment. He had been a member of Jeff's squad for over eight months. He was a tough little bastard. His knowledge of VC tactics had pulled Jeff out of more than one tight situation.

5

"Okay Chong. What do you think of this? Four men carry Lt. Davis into the clearing. They'll act like there's not a VC within a hundred miles."

"You mean just walk right into Charlie's sights Sarge?" Hefley asked.

"Yeah," Jeff gave the young soldier an annoyed look. "Now listen up. Four men carry the stretcher out about thirty yards. The rest of us will hang back, close to the edge of the clearing. We'll split up into two groups and stay about thirty yards apart. A team on each side of the trail. That way, when the shooting starts, the choppers won't be in the line of fire. Charlie won't be expecting us to split up. Now, who goes first?"

Jeff didn't wait for an answer. "Doc, you've got to go. Creeper, I'm depending on you to throw some red smoke on the VC position. And Chong, you've got all the information on this operation. Skip, I'll need a radio if the other chopper can't get in, so you'll stay with me. Okay now, that leaves Gains, Mayhew and Hefley. Who wants to go first?"

Jeff hesitated at their silence. He looked at their young faces waiting for a reply he knew wouldn't come. "Okay Johnny. You go first."

"But," Gains started.

"No buts," Jeff snapped. "You go."

After a few seconds of dead silence Jeff continued. "Skip, as soon as the choppers get on the radio, fill them in. Ask chopper two if he can establish a field of fire while number one is making his pickup. As soon as the choppers start firing we'll open up. I hope we can put enough lead into that tree line to make Charlie keep his head down. What do you think Chong? Will Charlie be greedy enough for a chopper to let us walk a stretcher into the middle of the clearing?"

"Yes," Chong readily agreed. "He'll wait for chopper. For sure. Maybe he even wait for two choppers, if he think they both come down at same time. I think maybe he see white smoke for one and red smoke for other."

"Yeah," Jeff nodded with just a glimmer of hope. "Okay," he signaled, "Let's move out."

The squad moved up the trail. Jarvis and Chong were up on point carefully checking for booby traps. Jeff didn't expect any but you could never tell. The Vietnamese, both north and south, were devious little bastards. He had seen too many guys get it because they had been careless.

It took them almost a quarter hour to reach the landing zone. Jeff halted the squad several yards from where the trail broke into the clearing. He motioned for Douglas and Hefley to join him.

"Skip. Take Hefley and follow the treeline down to the left about thirty yards. Stay about ten feet from the clearing. Now, we're going to mark for chopper one about forty yards straight out from this trail. When he starts down I want a white smoke straight out from your position. You'll have to move up to the edge of the clearing for that. I want the second chopper down on your smoke. Mayhew and I will be off to the right, and as soon as chopper one is boarded we'll break for your position. Don't wait for us. As soon as he's low enough, get on. Skip, I'm counting on you to get all this information to the chopper. You're gonna have to direct them. Any questions?" he paused waiting. "Okay then," he nodded. "Let's go."

7

He watched them thread a path through the jungle grass as he shrugged his shoulders and sighed. He was ready now. He'd made his decisions and there'd be no turning back. He just hoped to hell they were the right ones. He felt his biggest weakness was not knowing how many VC were dug in around that clearing. At least he could have figured his chances. If they had enough men for a crossfire Jeff knew he was in big trouble. A good automatic weapons man on either end of the clearing would be wipe out time.

In reality, Jeff felt they shouldn't be much larger in number than his own squad. There'd be no reason to operate a bigger force in this area unless it was a big troop movement going up or down country. If that were the case then he knew they'd never make it. But somehow, he felt it was just a small squad responsible for keeping supplies and troops moving or rerouted if the trail were discovered. His thoughts were interupted by the familiar sound of a chopper.

Jeff motioned to the four men holding the stretcher and they started into the clearing. He tapped Mayhew on the shoulder, "Come on kid," and started through the trees with Mayhew following. He cut through the underbrush about thirty yards then headed left towards the clearing. He heard the primer pop on a smoke grenade and eased up to the clearing as a thick cloud of white smoke rose vertically from the windless field.

Two helicopters soared into view over the tall trees at the far end of the clearing. Jeff turned to Mayhew who was leaning against a tree on his right. He pointed to the deadly M-79 grenade launcher in the soldier's hands and said, "Watch the far treeline about ten degrees to our left. Start popping rounds over there as fast as you can load. When you hear me yell go like hell for the second chopper.''

Jeff didn't wait for a reply. He turned to watch the four men carrying the stretcher. They were standing in position waiting for the helicopter. He saw it ease to a stop hanging like a giant spider. The downward wash of the rotors spread the smoke back to the ground as the chopper descended slowly. The four men set the stretcher on the ground and knelt next to it as Huey stepped away and pulled the pin on another grenade. He let the spoon snap out of his hand and casually threw the smoke grenade thirty yards toward the far edge of the clearing. It popped during the last ten yards of its downward arch burning a streaming red tail as Huey turned back to the stretcher.

Chopper one slid down an invisible shaft toward the waiting men as a red-orange cloud blossomed on the treeline. Jeff hoped it would keep Charlie blind for the few precious seconds they needed. As chopper one's rails bounced on the ground Jeff heard its door gunner open up with his machine gun on the opposite side of the chopper.

A white cloud of smoke bellowed forward of Hefley's position as Jeff and Mayhew started firing into the red cloud of smoke which was disappearing fast from the chopper's wash. He kept firing as the men hurriedly pushed the stretcher into the open side of the chopper and scrambled in after it.

Chopper two, on its let down, swung its nose toward the red smoke and Jeff heard the whoosh of the rockets spewing from the side mounted pods, as several sleek blurs burned a path into the dense foliage across from him. He was up and running along the clearing as the

9

rockets exploded into the treeline. Chopper two was almost down as Douglas and Hefley broke out of the clearing racing towards it.

Chopper one roared as it lifted. Charlie must have gotten wise about the same time because a machine gun opened up from his position. Luckily, his aim was at the chopper's ground position so the rounds chewed up dirt under the rising chopper. The VC were in the bush almost twenty yards from the point where the rockets hit, so they did nothing more than make him keep his head down during the explosion.

Jeff never heard the next explosion. He just knew he was in the air and looking up at the belly of chopper one. It had been thrust upward by the blast and concussion of a satchel charge. It hung momentarily at a crazy sidewards tilt as the big rotor blade fought for a hold. Suddenly, it righted itself and lifted away from the blast as Jeff hit the ground on his left side. He felt something snap in his shoulder as an immense wave of heat enveloped him. He shook his head, trying to clear his eyes as he struggled to his feet and looked around for Mayhew. He found he couldn't move his left arm. There was no pain, just a dull numbness and a hot flush over his entire body. He saw Mayhew about ten feet from him. He was lying on his stomach trying to push himself up. Jeff stumbled toward him thinking, this is a hell of a time to be doing push-ups.

Mayhew was half up as Jeff reached him. He snatched him by the back of the collar and pulled him to his feet. They turned towards chopper two as bullets whipped past them like angry hornets. They were still thirty yards from the chopper as it settled to the ground. He saw Douglas reach for the outstretched arm of the gunner and scramble through the chopper door. Jeff looked for Hefley and saw him down on his stomach about six yards from the treeline. Jeff started toward him when he felt Mayhew jerk and slam against him. They both went down in a tangle of arms and legs.

Jeff wanted to scream as searing pain shot up the left side of his body. He managed to raise his head as a second satchel charge went off to the left of the grounded chopper. It tilted sideways and the rotor blades dug into the ground and snapped. Douglas and the gunner fell backwards out the open door of the chopper as it lifted a few feet and fell on its side crushing the two men beneath it. He heard the steady clatter of a machine gun as spider web patterns stitched the bubble in front of the pilot and co-pilot. The blast popped his ears and an invisible fist smashed him into deep blackness.

Chapter Two

Jeff felt the numbness leave his body as pain and consciousness returned. The hot sun beat on his naked chest. He tried to clear his head, wondering why he didn't have a shirt on. He heard Vietnamese voices around him. One, very distinct, as if giving orders. Jeff groaned and felt a sharp pain in his shoulder as he attempted to move his left arm. He blinked into the sun and moved his right hand to shade his eyes. A shadow fell across him as he struggled into a sitting position.

He looked up as a rifle bore pointed into his face. He raised his eyes slowly, past the rifle, to the Viet Cong holding it. He saw the hatred in the VC's eyes and for a moment thought he was going to pull the trigger as the man tensed. A wave of despair froze him as he waited for the smashing bullet.

A sudden command in Vietnamese jerked the VC's eyes off Jeff for a second and Jeff saw him relax slightly. A flood of relief filled his body as he realized the VC was not going to shoot him. Moving only his head, he slowly looked around.

The chopper rested on its side. Fuel leaked from the punctured hull filling the air with its stink. Jeff could see the lifeless forms of the pilot and co-pilot through the nose bubble. Two VC were handing equipment out of the side of the overturned chopper. Yeah, he thought to himself. They'd take whatever they can use. He looked for Hefley and saw a VC stripping him of everything but his fatigue pants. Two VC picked up Hefley's body and carried it towards him. They dropped the limp form several feet from him and walked off. Jeff saw the rise and fall of the young soldier's chest and breathed a sigh of relief. He wasn't dead! Ted's right side was a mass of flaming blisters and his right pant's leg smoldered at a rip below the knee. He heard a groan behind him and twisted enough to see Mayhew laying a yard away on his back. He also had been stripped of everything but his pants. A large bloodstain covered his left thigh. He was still unconscious, but moaning and alive. Jeff turned back to the guard.

"Hey you, Charlie," he motioned back at Mayhew. "Let me look at him. He's bleeding. He'll die."

The guard looked impassively at Mayhew then back to Jeff and shrugged his shoulders. "*No bic*."

Jeff pointed at his own thigh back to Mayhew. "He needs help."

"*No bic*," the guard repeated.

"You understand," Jeff said through clenched teeth. "Don't give me that *no bic* shit." He knew it was useless to argue, as well as he knew the guard would shoot him if he moved.

Jeff looked around for the officer in charge. What he saw almost made him vomit. Three bodies had been dragged away from the chopper wreckage. Two VC's were dressing a decapitated corpse. As they held the body up to put on the fatigue shirt he saw an arm and leg were missing. They slipped on the shirt and one of them took a machete and chopped off the remaining hand. He picked it up and threw it into the door of the chopper. They picked up the body and pushed it into the wreck. The remaining bodies were prepared and shoved into the chopper. One of them looked like the gunner that had been blown out the door with Douglas. Jeff saw the foot and leg protruding from under the wreck and guessed it was the radioman. The stench of fuel was stronger and Jeff was amazed the chopper hadn't blown on impact or a VC bullet hadn't started a fire.

Jeff wiped his mouth with the back of his hand as seven VC approached him. They were dressed identical to his guard in black pajamas and rice hats. One of them wore a U.S. Army web belt and a holstered forty-five. He stopped before Jeff, motioning the guard aside.

"You fix friends," he said in broken English pointing to Mayhew and Hefley. "We go now fast."

He crawled over to Mayhew. Jeff could move his left arm but not without pain. He suspected his collar bone was broken. The fingers of his left hand tingled as he tore the pants leg of Mayhew's fatigues. It was a flesh wound. The bullet had passed just under the skin of the upper left thigh for about three inches. A dark bruise spread across the area and blood pulsed slowly out of each hole. Jeff felt Mayhew stir and his eyes fluttered open, looking at Jeff.

"Sarge," he muttered.

"Just lay still buddy," Jeff said softly. "You've got a hole in your thigh." He pointed to the VC over his shoulder, "and Charlie's got us." Jeff saw the fear slip into the young man's eyes. "Don't worry," he said quickly. "They're not going to kill us, at least not yet. So keep quiet and let me get a bandage on this."

Mayhew nodded and Jeff turned to the VC leader pointing to the first aid pouch laying in a pile of their gear. "Medicine," he gestured. "I need the medicine kit."

The VC leader spoke rapidly and another VC picked up the pouch with the red cross on it. Instead of giving it to Jeff he handed it to the leader. He opened it, checking the contents. Jeff waited as the VC picked out each item, peered curiously at it and returned it to the pouch.

"Come on," Jeff urged. "He needs medicine."

The leader handed the kit back to his man. "No medicine," he said. "Better for VC. Now you fix. We go," he said, nodding to Mayhew and Hefley.

Again, Jeff knew it was useless to argue. They could have all been in danger of dying and the VC would not have given up the valuable medicine. Frustrated, Jeff tore some strips from Mayhew's pants and bandaged the wound. He glanced at Hefley, who was coming around. He struggled to sit up. Hefley looked at him, then the VC. He made a gesture towards Mayhew and looked questioningly at Jeff. Jeff made an okay sign, but as he looked down at the wound, he had second thoughts. It wasn't a bad wound. The skin was rapidly discoloring and there was some noticeable swelling. With proper treatment it would have been a simple thing. But now,

15

with no medication or clean dressing, Jeff was worried about infection.

The VC leader gave some rapid orders and Jeff knew it was time to go. Any hope of stalling for a rescue party faded as two of the VC motioned with their rifles for the three prisoners to get to their feet.

Jeff got up, pulling Mayhew with him. "Can you stand on it?"

"Yeah Sarge," Mayhew grimaced as he put weight on the leg.

"You'll have to help me walk him Hef. My shoulder's banged up so put your arm around my waist. Hef, get on the other side of him. How's your side and leg?"

"Okay Sarge. It's just a burn," Hefley said with a weak smile. "We'll make it. Right, Ken?"

"Right on," he said unconvincingly.

The three soldiers watched as the VC divided the captured equipment. The leader picked up several G I dog tags and put them in a pouch. They were herded out of the clearing back to the trail they had discovered and were halted just inside the treeline. The leader barked an order and one of his men, armed with Mayhew's grenade launcher, stepped back into the clearing and fired at the chopper wreck. Jeff heard the grenade explode and the *whoosh* as the fuel ignited. He heard small popping sounds as rounds went off in the wreck. A louder explosion erupted as the fuel tanks blew. He knew the rockets would go any minute. Jeff thought of the bodies in the wreckage and prayed they were all dead. The fire was a loud roar. Then he heard several explosions as the rockets detonated. Anything left would be unrecognizable.

"What the hell they blowing up a wrecked chopper for Sarge?" Mayhew asked.

"They're destroying the evidence," Jeff said calmly.

"What evidence?" Hefley and Mayhew asked in unison.

"I'll tell you later. I'm not sure I understand it myself," Jeff muttered as the leader motioned them to move.

"We go now. You no talk," the leader said, very pleased with himself as the three barefooted Americans limped down the trail. A very good day, he grinned at their back. Yes, a very good day indeed. Yet, he thought to himself, if that other helicopter had not escaped, it would have been an exceptional day.

Chapter Three

Jeff's mind cleared slowly as they trudged along the trail. A dull, steady pain throbbed in his shoulder. They were moving north toward the DMZ. He could only guess at their destination but he was willing to bet a month's pay it would be well within North Vietnam. He tried to visualize a map in his mind.

The plantation was about a hundred thirty miles south of the DMZ, and some twenty miles east of Laos. A river flowed southeast from Laos into South Vietnam, curving south, then southwest into Cambodia forming a thirty mile crescent at the tri-border junction. The plantation's west border was almost in the middle of the crescent and well within the boundaries of South Vietnam.

Normally, it would have been about a day's walk to the river. In their condition it would take at least two days. It made sense. Their captors would head for the river and cross into Laos. There'd be too many friendly patrols in Vietnam.

Jeff knew the trail they were on ran north. If he were right, they'd be turning west in the next hour or so. They hadn't found any trails intersecting the main one, so that meant they'd have to walk through heavy underbrush. He shivered at the thought of walking barefooted in that stuff. Even with heavy combat boots it was hard going, but in their bare feet—forget it. It would be pure torture. Their feet would be a raw bleeding mess after a half mile. Also, Jeff thought reluctantly, there were deadly snakes, lizards, spiders and hundreds of bugs and insects. The mosquitoes had already started to feast on their exposed skin.

It started raining. Maybe, Jeff hoped, it would cool. No. There were still four hours of sunlight left. He knew the rain would pass in less than an hour and the sun would cook the trees again, baking the plantation.

In another week the monsoon season would be in full fury. Communist infiltration of troops and supplies would increase to a hectic pace. The heavy rains would slow allied patrols and operations to a snail's pace due to loss of air power. Jeff knew only too well how much the allied forces depended on air movement. So, for the next couple of months the war would be on an almost even basis for both the allies and the communists.

Charlie would take advantage of the deadly rain. He could move forces without fear of being detected by spotter planes. Rapid deployment of allied troops would cease to be a possibility. Fear of bomb strikes against his supply routes would halt because of bad flying weather. Yeah, Jeff thought, Charlie welcomed the hard rains and thick cloud cover. He would use it effectively to hit base camps and major installations. He also knew it would knock their chance of being rescued by eighty

19

percent. There was always the hope of running into an allied patrol but not if the rains increased. A deadly rain indeed, in more ways than one.

Any thought of escape at the present time was simply out of the question. In their physical condition, with no supplies or weapons, they wouldn't last a day. If the VC didn't recapture them the jungle was sure to claim them. No, escape would have to be put aside until they were completely ready. Also, their wounds needed medical attention. In this jungle climate simple scratches became rotting infections if neglected. So that had to be his primary concern. He supposed their captors would turn them over to a regular force belong long. He prayed their wounds would be taken care of then.

He was sure Hefley and Mayhew had the physical stamina to recover quickly. He was worried about their mental attitude. Right now they were in shock, but later, they'd start thinking about their predicament. It would eventually dawn on them they were POW's. How would they react? Jeff knew he had to hold them together and it was going to be damn difficult because he didn't have much hope himself.

It's funny, he thought, both of them had joined his squad about the same time, four months ago. They spent a lot of time together but Jeff realized he really didn't know much about them. He was a loner, keeping mostly to himself when they were in base camp. He knew they referred to him as a "lifer." A term given to anyone serving more than one hitch. Of course, there had been times when Jeff joined them for a beer or a bull session, but he always felt like an intruder. Socially, there wasn't a feeling of comradeship. His early orphan life was completely different from their background. Basically, they didn't have a common starting point. There was, of course, the Army. Typical of soldiers, they bitched and complained; cursed the Army, the war and Vietnam, but so did everyone else. In the field it was different. They were good troops. They did their jobs and he was certain he could depend on them. They had a common enemy while on an operation. Yet, he thought, he had seen them everyday for the last four months and still didn't know them.

Jeff's mind snapped back to the present as the VC momentarily halted their march, then went west off the trail into the dense underbrush. It was extremely difficult for three men abreast, supporting each other, to move in the thick growth. It was clear they were not making the headway the VC leader would have liked. Jeff felt a rifle muzzle jabbed in his back and knew he was being prodded to pick up the pace.

They walked for perhaps a quarter of an hour and Jeff was surprised to see a pathway as they emerged from the underbrush. It was narrow and seemed to come out of nowhere, but he noted it appeared to be well trod. The VC probably utilized it as an approach to the main trail, making sure they varied their paths through the underbrush so a link between the two trails could never be formed and detected.

Their pace increased as they continued west on the second trail. The track was muddy and Jeff felt relief as damp mud caked his scraped feet.

It was almost dark when they finally stopped. The guard motioned them to sit in the middle of the trail. When they were settled, the VC made themselves comfortable along the edge. They passed out the captured rations among themselves and started eating, offering

21

none to the prisoners. The leader said something, pointing at the Americans and they all laughed.

"The bastards," Hefley hissed in a low tone.

"Just relax," Jeff cautioned. "Conserve your strength. I've got a feeling you'll need it."

"What the hell Sarge," Hefley protested. "We've got rights as prisoners."

"Tell Charlie that," Jeff said, pointing to the grinning VC leader. "I'll bet he never heard of the Geneva Convention. Besides, I doubt if we are POW's officially."

"What'd you mean?"

"Well," Jeff said. "Do you remember that gook shooting at the chopper just before they marched us out?"

"Yeah."

"I'm just guessing but I think they were trying to make sure the bodies in that wreck weren't identifiable."

"Why?"

"Hell, who knows, but just think about it a minute. Our forces are going to recover that wreck and pick up what's left. Charlie switched our dog tags with three of the crew members on that chopper. I saw them do it. The way that stuff will burn in the chopper, there is no way they can identify those bodies. They'll collect the dog tags they can find and list them as killed in action. They figure the chopper got hit during the ground pickup and most of the crew got out and were captured."

"Yeah man," Mayhew said. "The Army will report us killed and those other dudes missing."

"But why?" Hefley asked. "Why would Charlie go through all that hassle?"

"Just think about it," Jeff answered. "The confusion. Army records, next of kin, insurance. Man, the whole orderly system is going to be all screwed up. Three families are going to receive death notices and three are going to get missing in action reports. Even after we get back," Jeff purposely avoiding the fact that they might not get back, "just think of the effect it will have on morale when the story gets out. Everyone would have doubts if there was any question of identification. How many times has this happened before? For all we know, this isn't the first switch. It's going to be one hell of a mess to straighten out. Just think of your own folks. How are they going to react to news of your death? Then later, you show up alive. Man, think about it. They've already had your funeral, collected your insurance and probably adjusted to the fact you're dead. Sure, they'll be glad you're back and alive, but Christ, what a fucked up hassle its going to be."

"Yeah," Mayhew and Hefley nodded in unison as their eyes reflected their deep thoughts of concern.

After a long silence, the VC leader gave an order and the three prisoners were bound, hand and feet, back to back. One guard remained on watch as the others slumped against trees to sleep. The cold night air brought shivers to Jeff as a light drizzle started. The night animal sounds stirred around them and mosquitoes feasted on their clammy skin. Jeff felt Mayhew sob. He pushed back and their hands touched and folded together in a tight grasp. They would escape and make it back, Jeff promised himself. They huddled together for warmth as a doubting despair settled over them like a giant emptiness.

Chapter Four

Ted Hefley shivered as his head bowed slightly. He felt the damp skin of Mayhew and Spencer's backs against his own. He relaxed, letting his chin drop slowly to his chest. He knew he wouldn't sleep; not tonight anyway.

Now I'll know, he thought silently to himself. POW Prisoner of War! He never thought the term would apply to him but it did now and he was scared. So scared he wanted to cry. He wanted his mother. To have her hold his head against her breast and sooth his fears. For her to reassure him in a soft loving voice that everything would be alright. He thought of her and hated himself for being so weak. Why her?? They had never really been close. Even when he was a small child there had always been a substitute: a nurse, a teacher, a tutor. But now, for some reason he wanted her. He tried to rationalize. To sort out his feelings.

After a while he decided it was the uncertainty of the situation. Too many doubts were in his mind right now. What would the VC do with them? Would they be killed? Could they escape? A hundred questions ran through his head. He realized he couldn't answer any of them. Not yet anyway. He knew this would be his test. This ordeal would be the ultimate test of his life and somehow, someway, he vowed silently to himself, he'd endure it as a man.

Ted eased the thoughts of war and captivity from his mind, recalling the look in Mr. Chandler's eyes, as they shook hands at the Tucson airport. He remembered the man's firm grip and had detected a slight wavering in his deep voice as he spoke.

"You know son, this is one of the reasons I'm glad I never had a son. I wouldn't have wanted to see him off to war like this."

"Yes sir. I understand."

"No Ted. I don't think you do. You see, I'd be proud. Like my Pa was of me, when I went into the Army and later overseas during World War II, but now I know how he felt. He sent away a boy, a young man, and four years later I came home an old man. Not old physically, but old and worn out inside. I saw enough of war to last several lifetimes. I did what I was told and it made me sick knowing what man can do to man. Now some of those fellows that shipped out with me, it never bothered at all. A few even enjoyed it but most of them hated the war and only fought because they were fighting for a cause they believed in. I suppose you could use that rationalism and apply it to either side in any war. Well, I guess what I'm really trying to say is

25

this. You already have a hate in you son. I've seen it in your eyes. Just don't let it get a hold on you. Ted, you're a bright young lad and my daughter loves you. You've spent some time with my family and we've welcomed you into our home. We all feel you are part of the family already but Ted, I don't want your hate to infect Kathy. Get rid of it boy. Get it out of your system once and for all. If you can't, then I don't want you to marry her. I'll do everything in my power to stop it. Maybe she won't respect my wishes but I believe you will."

"Yes sir. I would."

"Good. Now take care of yourself and write to us."

"Yes sir."

"Uh, Ted. Have you let your parents know you're on your way to Vietnam?" Ted paused wondering what to say. For some reason he felt ashamed of the truth. He shook his head slightly, "No."

"Well son, I suppose you have your reasons but at least think about it. You just might feel better. You could call them from Oakland. It would probably mean a lot to them. Well anyway, think about it and take care of yourself. You know you have one big advantage I never had in my war."

"What's that sir?"

"You only have to do a year over there."

"Yes sir," Ted said. "Goodbye Mr. Chandler."

"Goodbye Ted."

Ted remembered how his mind had fought with his conscience as he boarded the big jetliner. It had been over a year since he'd seen his parents. He and his father had quarreled because Ted had quit school. He had tried to explain his feelings to his father but it had been useless.

"Two years of college wasted," his father had screamed. "The goddamn money I spent on you goes right down the drain because, as you put it, you can't find yourself. Bullshit, you kids today are all alike. All you want is dope. Don't think I don't know what's going on."

Ted remembered staring out the window as his father raved about the younger generation and what the world was coming to. That was the last time he saw his father before going into the Army.

The flight to San Francisco was uneventful and Ted was one of the last passengers to leave the airplane. He was standing in the baggage claim area waiting for his duffel bag when he felt a tap on his shoulder. He turned and looked directly into his father's eyes.

"Uh, hello Ted."

Ted was surprised. His Dad looked older as he stood uncertainly with his arms hanging limply at his sides, as if he wanted to do something with his hands but didn't know what. His eyes, which Ted always thought to hold a hard stern look, were dull. His father's face brightened as Ted reached out and shook his hand.

"Hi Dad. It's good to see you."

"It's good to see you Ted. I hope you don't mind me coming down here to meet you?"

"No Dad. I'm just kind of surprised. I suppose Mr. Chandler must have called you."

"Yes. He did. You're not mad, are you?"

"No. In fact, I'm glad he called you." Ted released his father's hand and glanced over his shoulder at the baggage conveyer. "Let me get my bag before they put it on another plane." Ted snatched the heavy duffel as it swept by him and dropped it at his feet.

"Well Dad, I'm glad you could get away and come down here. How's Mom?"

"She's find Ted. Oh, she's out of town right now or she'd be here too."

Ted sensed the uneasiness in his father, aware that it was completely out of character for the man. "Look Dad. I've got to be at the processing terminal in Oakland in three hours. Why don't we go to the coffee shop and get a sandwich?"

"Sure Ted. How are you going to get to Oakland?"

"A cab, I guess."

"Why don't you let me drive you? I drove down from the office."

"Yeah. That'll be great."

"Good," his father beamed. "Now let's get that coffee."

Ted was silent as they found a booth in the restaurant and ordered. He pulled a pack of cigarettes from his pocket offering it to his father. He accepted one, searched his pockets for his lighter and gave Ted a light. Ted felt uneasy.

"You look great Ted."

"It's the uniform," Ted said as he took off his hat and placed it on the seat, running his hand through his close cropped hair. "And the haircut."

"Yeah," his Dad grinned. "You're hair hasn't been that short since you were eight or nine. But really, you look great and you've put on some weight too. What's the medal for?" he said indicating the marksmanship medal on Ted's jacket.

28

"Oh, just a shooting medal. The guy next to me was shooting at my target." Ted was glad for the interruption as the waitress brought their order. He recalled they didn't say much as they ate. Both of them were uncertain of what to say or do.

It was during the drive to Oakland, he finally opened up, after his father asked him about the past year. He was going to pass it off with more small talk but detected the concern in his Dad's voice and decided to tell the story.

"Well Dad," he began. "After our argument I just wanted to get away. As you know I packed a few things, got on my motorcycle and split. I really didn't have any particular destination in mind so I rode east into the mountains and bummed the old trails and mines. I went from town to town getting a job here and there and earned enough money to cut out again. I did that for eight months. I saw some beautiful country in those months and also the life of the people. You know, the real people of this country. The ones that are struggling just to make it from day to day. It really surprised me. I guess it opened my eyes quite a bit. Kind of made me appreciate what I had."

His father nodded, feeling the pride rise in his chest, and a closeness they never shared before. "So then what happened?"

"Well, I was heading for Tucson and I stopped at a roadhouse on the highway. A group of motorcycle guys came in. They decided to have a party and that was the place they'd picked. To make a long story short, I got drunk with them. One of the girls with them kept handing me beer and the next thing I knew we were all headed into the desert to make an overnight camp and continue the party. I guess I must have passed out or got knocked out because the next thing I remember was waking up in a bed and Kathy running a wet cloth over my face. Kathy is Mr. Chandler's daughter.''

"I see."

"Anyway, those cycle freaks must have used me for a football. I was bruised and cut and a couple of ribs were broken. I must have really been bombed out because I don't remember any of the beating. Kathy told me her father found me in the desert while he was out looking for rocks. He's retired and loves to roam the desert. He took me back to his place. He and his wife run a small motel and restaurant on what used to be the main highway before the interstate was built. So I stayed with them until I got better. I helped them run the place and really got to like them. Mr. Chandler retired to the desert because of his health and bought the small motel to keep him busy, but he spends most of his time scrounging around the desert. His daughter was visiting on vacation from college. We got to be pretty close during my stay there. In fact, I'm in love with her.''

"How does she feel about you Ted?"

"The same."

"Yes, I gathered that after my conversation with Mr. Chandler. He thinks highly of you Ted."

"Yes sir. I know."

"Well, how did this Army thing come about?"

"I knew if I wanted to marry Kathy, I'd have to find a job. So I went to Tucson to look for work. Every place I went they asked me if my service commitment was over. Of course the minute I said no, they'd say come back when it was. I finally got the message. They didn't want to train people in a job and have the Army snatch them up. Well, I tried for three more days, then I gave up and enlisted. So, after four months training and twenty days leave, here I am.''

"But why go to Vietnam right away Ted? I'm sure you could spend some time in the states.''

"I volunteered," he said, offering no other explanation.

His father nodded slowly. He silently prayed his son would find what ever it was he searching for and come back safe. When they said goodbye, his father shook his hand. Ted detected the wetness forming in the corners of his father's eyes. They clasped each other's shoulders and embraced.

Ted felt his eyes burning as the memory of their parting filled his head. He snapped out of his reverie as Mayhew moaned. Ted twisted his head as far as he could and whispered. "You okay Ken?"

He felt Mayhew move slightly as he turned his head. "Man," he sighed heavily. "My fucking leg is throbbing. How's the burns?"

Ted didn't answer as the guard moved away from the tree he was squatting against. At first Ted tensed, as the guard walked over to them and stared down, but then he moved over to a sleeping VC and shook him. They talked, pointing and nodding toward the prisoners, then the second VC assumed guard duty as the other went to sleep. The three men waited several minutes until the guard was settled, then found they could talk in low whispers.

Ken asked again about Ted's burns. "They're all right. This drizzle is cooling them down but I'm freezing my ass off."

Ted knew it was about sixty degrees. It always amazed him how cold it felt at night, especially during the monsoon season. The high temperature in the daytime made the nightime drop in degrees seem like going from a steam room into an ice cold pool. Back at base camp he could sleep comfortably at night with two covers, but during the day his bunk would be soaked in sweat with no covers at all.

"How's your shoulder Sarge?" Ted asked.

"It's okay. Numb as hell but I guess that helps," Jeff answered.

"Man," Ken breathed. "We need a medic or we're never going to make it."

"I think we'll get some medical attention by tomorrow," Jeff said. "They know we can't travel too far in this condition. I'm pretty sure they've got a base camp within marching distance of the trail, probably up river in Laos." Jeff purposely disregarded the thought that the VC might kill them and bury their bodies in the jungle. He was aware the possibility existed but he sure the hell didn't want to bring it to the attention of Mayhew and Hefley. The only way to get out of this was to keep their hope of escaping alive.

"This rain is soaking in pretty good," Jeff whispered. "Try to rub some mud over your feet, it will help protect the skin. If we can flick some up on our backs it might help against the bugs.

The three men squirmed and twisted at their bonds as much as possible trying to turn their hands and feet to smear the mud. Jeff felt bits of mud cling to his back as he dug his hands into the muck flinging it with his fingertips. Even though his left arm was numb, a sharp pain shot across his neck and shoulder and down the arm when he moved his fingers. Ken was having a similar experience with his left leg. When he put too much pressure on the leg he felt the muscular contractions of his thigh sear with pain. He stopped when he felt blood oozing from the wound.

The three men settled back, each in their own thoughts as the night wore on. Ted's mind drifted back to the Chandler's and Kathy. So far away right now, but her image formed in his mind, especially the first time he saw her.

He remembered waking up slowly, sort of piece by piece. The numbness in his legs. The sharp pain in his side as he breathed and the heaviness throughout his entire body. He was one big ache. He felt the coolness of a damp cloth on his forehead as he opened his eyes. A face blurred over him, then slowly came into focus.

Her honey colored hair was pulled back and tied with a red ribbon in a pony tail. She wore tinted wire rim glasses set on a straight nose that was slightly long for her face. Her lips parted in a smile showing even, white teeth. Her skin was clear and free of make-up and she had a fresh wholesome look that most people would probably pass off as plain. Her smile and round blue eyes glowed with a warmth and true friendliness that hinted at the hidden beauty of her face which was easily missed at first glance.

He remembered trying to smile as he drifted off again into unconsciousness. Several times he awoke to hear other people in the room. He later learned a doctor had been called for his cuts and bruises and had taped his ribs. The girl fed him some broth and made him take some pills and sip water but he couldn't recall how often.

It was late in the afternoon of the third day, he slowly woke as a coolness swept over his body. He felt a damp sponge caressing his chest and he knew without opening his eyes he was getting a bath. He could also feel the sheet had been pulled down and he was nude. He opened one eye slightly and saw the girl. She was concentrating on the sponge and didn't know he was awake.

She wore a light blue sleeveless blouse and matching shorts. Her left hand rested lightly on his upper chest as her right hand held the sponge and wiped carefully around his bandaged ribs. She bent over him to wash his hip and he saw her blouse was scoop necked as it fell away revealing the full mounds of her breasts. A tightness formed in his groin as her breasts wobbled slightly with her movements. He could see she wasn't wearing a bra and he pretended to sleep and struggled to control himself.

He heard her rinse and wring out the sponge. The coolness of it returned to wash his waist and hard flat stomach and slowly down to his pubic hair. He tensed as she wiped past his groin and down his left leg. She rinsed out the sponge again, then did his right leg. She sponged up his thigh and pushed his legs slightly apart to wash inside. Ted felt his penis stir as she paused momentarily and sighed. "Oh well. She held his penis out of the way and gently sponged his testicles. His penis grew under the soft touch of her hand. Blood swelling his thickening member, he opened his eyes. Her hand grasped it at the base as it stood erect and she wiped it with the sponge.

He noticed the hardened points of her nipples poking at the material of her blouse and felt a rush of desire pour into his loins. His eyes traveled from her breasts to his hard erection and slowly to her face. She was looking at him and she broke out in a wide grin. "At least we know it isn't broken," she said releasing her hold on him and rinsing the sponge.

"Now turn over so I can get the other side."

It was an effort for him to turn over but he finally did it and fell exausted onto his stomach. As the cool sponge wiped his back he drifted back to sleep.

The next morning he was sitting up when she came in. He had been awake for an hour and had gotten up to use the bathroom. He discovered he was in a motel room as he limped about the place. He had spent a half hour examining himself in the mirror. His six foot body was covered with cuts and bruises. His left side was sore but he could breathe a deep breath without too much pain. He was exhausted when he finally got back into bed.

"Hi," she smiled as she walked across the room and sat by his side. She still wore her hair in the same pony tail style and she had on matching yellow shorts and blouse. He could see the dark smudges of her nipples through the thin material. "I'm glad to see you're back among the living."

"Yeah," he grinned. "So am I. How long have I been here?"

"Almost four full days. Today is Friday. My Dad found you Tuesday afternoon."

"Wow! Those guys must have really done a job on me."

"Well, whoever they were, they certainly weren't friends of yours."

"Yeah. I guess I better learn to choose my drinking buddies more carefully."

They talked for over an hour. He told her what happened as far as he could remember. He learned about his discovery by her father. His bike, money, and other belongings were gone, evidently ripped off by the motorcycle gang. He felt like a fool as he fought off the thought of calling his Dad to ask for help. He'd gotten himself into this mess and he made up his mind he'd get out of it by himself.

The girl picked up the phone next to the bed. "Mom," she said after a short pause. "Our patient is alive and probably could stand something to eat."

She hung up the phone. "My name is Kathy Chandler. My folks own this motel."

"Hi," he smiled taking her offered hand. "I'm Ted Hefley. Thank you, and your parents. I guess if your Dad hadn't found me I'd be buzzard bait by now."

"Well, I'm glad he did."

"So am I."

She left to get his breakfast and returned with a tray of soft eggs, toast, juice and coffee. She helped him sit up with the tray on his lap and told him about herself as he ate. She was a third year art student at the University of Nevada in Las Vegas. She was home for summer vacation. He found himself liking her even more as she talked. Her voice was mature and somewhat husky. A throaty sexy voice and she smiled a lot as she talked. Several times her hand rested lightly on his arm when she laughed. Her light touch was reminiscent of her

36

tenderness the day before. He began seeing her as a young woman instead of a girl.

The next day he left the room with her after breakfast. He met her parents. They lived in a front building that served as an office and their home. There were twenty rooms in the motel complex with two small cottages for families. Ted liked the Chandler's as soon as he met them. Mr. Chandler was in his sixties. He was tall and lean, and Ted felt the strength in his grip and knew instinctively he was a tough old dude. His white hair was cut close like the military style and Ted had the feeling he'd worn it the same way for the past thirty years. His gray eyes showed a warmth of understanding, yet could not quite hide a piercing harshness.

Mrs. Chandler was the image of Kathy thirty years from now. She wore more conservative glasses and her hair was slightly darker. She wore it pinned up off her neck in a tight bun. She held herself erect and proud and shook his hand warmly. She possessed the lingering beauty he had detected in Kathy. She wore a light blouse and shorts that displayed her shapely legs and firm arms. Ted guessed she was about ten years younger than Mr. Chandler. She had the same husky quality in her voice as Kathy's.

They sat on a shaded patio, talking for over an hour. Ted told them about himself. He told them the truth and answered their polite questions honestly. He felt himself warm to them as a family. They didn't pry but let him talk freely. When he was through, Mr. Chandler asked Ted if he wanted to call his parents.

"No Sir," Ted replied. "I'm alright now. Thanks to you. I'm just not ready to talk to them yet." He wanted

37

to explain to them why but he wasn't sure himself, so he let it drop.

"I see," Mr. Chandler said. "Well son, what are your plans? You've lost all your money and your bike."

"I don't know yet," Ted paused. "I'll probably get a job in Tucson. I want to repay you for all . . ."

"Forget it," Chandler cut him off. "We've got plenty of room here. Besides, I could use some help around this place for awhile. Business is picking up and I think Kathy needs a friend her own age around here," he smiled, winking at Kathy. "She's supposed to be on vacation and she's been working her butt off."

"Come on Dad," Kathy protested. "Ted doesn't want to be stuck out here in the desert."

"Now hold on you two," Mrs. Chandler cut in. "The boy's hardly back on his feet and one of you wants to put him to work and the other wants to run him off. Ted," she smiled leaning forward to touch his arm. "You're going to rest here a few more days, then you can think about what you're going to do."

"Yes, Mrs. Chandler," he laughed.

"And," she added. "Please call me Bonnie."

"And I'm Paul," Mr. Chandler grinned. "Now, you women get busy. Ted and I are going to relax here awhile. After all, I am retired."

So Ted stayed on helping with the motel although there were never more than a few units rented at a time. The small restaurant was going pretty good. A cook and a waitress were hired for it. Mrs. Chandler took care of the motel office and supervising a cleaning woman for the units. Ted had the feeling that the Chandler's didn't have to depend on the place for their livelihood. It was just as Paul Chandler had said, something to keep him busy.

Ted regained his strength quickly and found himself doing jobs around the place. It had a small pool and Ted cleaned it thoroughly every day. He scrubbed the tile decking and painted the small fence around it. When he asked for some paint for the small cottages Mr. Chandler just laughed and ordered him to slow down and enjoy himself.

Several times in the next few weeks he and Kathy drove to a nearby drive-in movie. She had her own car and insisted Ted drive all the time. He found himself growing more and more fond of her each day. It was during a trip to the drive-in that Kathy had grabbed his shirt front in her fist, pulling him to face her. Her face was inches from his.

"Ted Hefley," she hissed. "If you don't put your arms around me and kiss me, I'm going to scream bloody rape."

Ted was taken back as he stared into her fiery blue eyes. Her jaw was set hard and her nostrils flared as she breathed. Slowly a grin crept across her face and they both roared with laughter. As their mirth subsided, Ted pulled her into his arms and softly kissed her waiting lips. He heard her moan as she relaxed in his embrace.

Their kiss was gentle at first. Lips brushing lips, several times with just a slight pressure. Finally, he pressed harder and forced her mouth open as his tongue sought hers. He recalled the warmth enveloping him as her breasts crushed against his chest. He broke the kiss, hugging her, and smelling the clean fragrance of her hair. His lips gently touched her neck and ear then back to her parted lips. This time her tongue sought his with a hungriness of want and desire. His hand caressed her right breast and he felt the nipple harden against his palm. She moaned and pushed against him as a familiar hardening stirred in his loins.

"Oh Ted," she sighed, breaking the kiss and resting her head on his chest. "I've wanted you to hold me like this for so long."

"I've wanted you too Kathy," he whispered, "but I wasn't sure. I knew I was falling in love with you but I was afraid of your rejection."

"Oh darling," she kissed his face softly, "Don't ever feel that way again."

"I won't Kathy. I love you. I love you so much."

They left the drive-in and drove slowly back to the motel. She sat close to him holding his hand draped around her shoulder. Her left hand rested lightly on his thigh inches from his aching hardness. At times she'd kiss his cheek and look thoughtfully at him as he tried to concentrate on driving. When they arrived at the motel, they sat in the car kissing and caressing for half an hour. Finally, he could no longer stand the growing need for her. He reluctantly kissed her goodnight and went to his own unit.

When he reached his room he tore off his clothes and stepped into the shower turning the cold water on full blast. He managed to shove his thoughts of Kathy to the back of his mind as he lathered his body carefully avoiding his shrinking member. After ten minutes he shut off the water and dried himself. He wandered into the bedroom and flopped onto the bed. The light from the bathroom partially lit the small room. Visions of Kathy drifted into his mind. The way she smiled. The huskiness of her voice. Her long tanned legs and smooth thighs moved behind his closed eyes. The saucy bounce of her breasts flooded desire back into his groin. His penis rose again, throbbing for release at the thought of her. His hand traced down his hard chest to his flat belly, trailing across the dark coarse hair to wrap around his thickening member. He stroked it slowly knowing he had to have some relief. He squeezed it almost to the point of hurting.

Ted froze as the door to his room opened slowly. Kathy entered closing the door behind her. She wore a short terry cloth robe belted at the waist. Her thighs gleamed in the soft light. She unbelted the robe as she approached the bed, letting it part and shrugged it from her shoulders. She stopped beside the bed letting him enjoy the nakedness of her body. Her full breasts were tipped with dark brown nipples, tightened into hard nubs with her excitement. They rose high on her ribcage as her breath quickened. Her concave stomach was stretched taut and flowed invitingly to her small waist and flat belly. Ted's eyes bathed in the lovliness of her as his breath quickened and he reached for her.

Without a word she slid onto the bed next to him. He turned sideways pressing the full length of his body against hers as their lips touched softly. Her legs parted allowing his hard erection to nestle between them against the moist warmth of her vulva. She tightened the muscles of her thighs and her breasts flattened against his chest. They kissed deeply and pushed their bodies together. She rotated her pelvis slowly around his stiffness and felt a tensing in his thighs as his tongue probed her mouth. He finally broke the kiss and panted hotly in her ear, smelling the muskiness of her skin. "I love you Kathy. I love you . . ."

"Yes darling," she smiled looking deeply into his eyes. "I love you too."

Ted grinned in spite of the cold drizzle that soaked the three men as he remembered how he and Kathy had explored each other's body. They had stayed awake all night loving and being loved. He remembered how ashamed he was when he penetrated her and climaxed immediately. She had laughed it off as she held the hardness of him deep within her. "Don't worry darling," she had smiled, tightening her hold over his stiffness. "You're not done yet."

Fading pictures of Kathy filled his head as he drifted off in an unrestful sleep.

Chapter Five

Jeff awoke at dawn with a start. He and the others had finally dozed off sometime during the night. He'd been having a dream he was sitting in a big oak tub in the middle of a field and Valerie was pouring warm water from a bucket over his head. A stench filled his nostrils as anger tensed his body. "You stinking yellow bastard," he screamed at the grinning guard who stood slightly to his left, shaking his penis.

"What the . . ." Hefley jerked awake. "What happened Sarge?"

"That fucking gook just pissed on us," he nodded toward the guard.

"Why you motherfuc . . ." Ted started but the guard kicked out quickly catching Hefley on the side of the neck. He groaned and slumped against Jeff and Ken.

"Don't," Jeff cautioned. "Just sit still. He'll kick your brains out just for the hell of it."

The commotion woke up the rest of the camp. Jeff watched the leader shrug out of a poncho and stand up. He looked around and barked an order. The other VC got up and slowly started to break camp. The leader disappeared into the bush and returned a few moments later. He approached the three bound prisoners glaring down at them. He gave an order and one of the VC came over and untied them. When they were free he motioned for them to stand.

Jeff felt needles of pain stabbing through his entire body as the circulation returned. Mayhew was still sitting. "I can't move my leg Sarge," he cried. "It's stiff and won't move!"

"Come on Ted. Let's get him on his feet." They positioned themselves on each side of the young soldier and raised him to a standing position.

"Oh," Ken moaned. "I can't put any weight on it." His chest heaved and tears rolled down his face as he gulped for breath and a searing pain shot through his leg. "I can't," he sobbed. "I can't make it!"

Jeff and Ted struggled to support him between them. Jeff say Ken was keeping the legs slightly bent so not to put any weight on it.

"Just hold on Ken," Jeff whispered. "I know it hurts buddy but you're going to make it. Ted and I can support you. Just don't give up. Okay?"

"Yeah," Ken sighed. "I'll be all right in a minute."

"Good."

The VC leader gave another order and two guards motioned the three men toward the bushes. Mayhew hobbled painfully on one leg as Jeff and Ted helped him out of the small clearing and into the bush.

"What now?" Ted asked hesitantly. "Are they going to shoot us?"

Jeff looked at the guards standing four feet away with a bored expression on their faces.

"No," Jeff said finally, as he realized what they wanted. "I believe this is a latrine break."

After relieving themselves they were herded back into the clearing and motioned to sit on a log. The VC were eating the American rations and jabbering among themselves. The leader walked over to the trio and handed each of them a small packet. It was a folded piece of banana leaf and Jeff knew it contained cooked rice. The VC traveled light and they could exist for days on these rice packets and water.

He opened it and discovered he was right. In the dim light the brown rice looked like something less than food. "Eat it," he cautioned the two other men. "Eat every bit of it, then eat the leaf."

Jeff held the open packet and sucked the rice into his mouth. It was tender and had probably been cooked with some kind of fish. The stench almost made him gag.

"I can't," Mayhew said.

"Me neither," Ted echoed.

"Damnit," Jeff hissed. "Eat it! We don't know when we'll get fed again. We've got to keep up our strength."

Jeff watched as Ted licked a few grains of rice into his mouth. Ken brought the packed to his lips and gagged as the smell filled his nostrils. "I can't Sarge," he whimpered. "I'm not hungry anyway."

"Okay. Okay," Jeff sighed. "But don't throw it away. Fold it up and put it in your pocket. Maybe you an eat it later."

It was getting light and Jeff could see patches of dull morning sky through the tops of the tall trees. Animal sounds filled the air as the plantation came alive. What would this day bring, Jeff thought to himself and suddenly felt scared as he realized he would live one day at a time from now on.

They were handed a canteen and were each allowed a few sips. The water was stale and heavy with the taste of canvas. A VC approached from the bushes and handed Hefley a crudely made crutch hacked from a tree limb. The VC leader took the canteen and stood before Jeff. "See," he said pointing to the crutch. "Vietnam people good. Help sick soldier."

Jeff was surprised and decided to play it for all it was worth. "You are number one Vietnam soldier boss," he praised. "This man," he pointed at Mayhew, "is very sick. He needs medicine for his leg. And him," Jeff nodded at Hefley, "needs medicine for burn. You're number one soldier and can help them. If they must walk to your camp they must have medicine."

Jeff waited tensely for a long moment as the VC leader looked at Mayhew, then Hefley. Finally, he gave an order and another VC brought the medical kit and handed it to the leader. He held it toward Jeff.

"You look."

Jeff quickly opened the kit and removed some bandage packets, a tube of burn ointment, a tin of sulfa, and two vials of morphine. The VC leader checked each item as Jeff removed it from the kit. He picked up the small morphine syringe in its plastic vial and placed it back in the kit leaving the other on the ground. He handed the medical kit back to the other VC and walked away.

Jeff hurriedly opened the remaining vial and jabbed the needle in Mayhew's thigh before the leader could change his mind. He handed the tube of burn salve to Ted.

"Here. Dab this on your burns as thick as you can. Use all of it. They'll just take it back if we leave any."

Ted took the tube as Jeff opened the sulfa tin. He untied the old bandage on Mayhew's leg. It was soaked in blood. He looked at Ken and saw the glassiness of his eyes. Well, he thought. The morphine is taking effect. Jeff poured sulfa into both small holes of the wound noting the swelling. The bleeding had almost stopped but the entire thigh was discolored. He opened the bandage packed and wrapped the wound with clean gauze.

It was fully light now and the VC were getting ready to move. Jeff tore off the bottom part of his pants leg and wrapped the material around the fork of the crutch to pad it. Mayhew's eyes were closed and a silly grin was on his face.

"How do you feel now Ken?" Jeff asked.

"Oh, wow man," he droned. "This shit is outta sight."

"Jesus Christ!" Ted exclaimed. "He's fuckin tripping out."

"Yeah," Jeff grinned, "but when that shit wears off he's gonna be one hurting mother."

The VC leader gave an order and motioned them to their feet. Jeff and Ted somehow got Mayhew between them and the crutch propped under his arm. They started slowly down the trail again. The crutch turned out to be useless because of Ken's ecstatic state so Jeff pitched it aside. Ken started mumbling as they trudged on.

"Hey man," Ken slurred. "That was really a good bag, Dina would flip over this shit. Dina's my wife. Man, what a chick. An absolute fuckin', foxy chick. I ever tell you about Dina, Jeff?" he asked. "No man. Never did. I mean, she is a stone fox. Long silky hair . . . big tits. You know, like I really dig big knockers. Man, she's got 'em. I mean really big . . ." his voice trailed off incoherently.

Several times as they walked Ken would mutter a clear word but mostly he ran his words and inflections together. Jeff and Hefley lost themselves in their own thoughts. Their walking became automatic as they trudged on, each motivated by his own desire to live, pushing one foot in front of the other.

Several times in the next couple of hours they stopped as choppers flew high overhead. Although there was no chance the small group could have been seen through the tree tops, the VC leader would stop them and they'd stand quietly until the chopper faded in the distance.

About mid morning the morphine started to wear off. Mayhew cried out several times when his wounded thigh bumped against Ted's leg. He was almost completely dead weight as they half carried, half dragged him along. They fell and all three cried out as pain racked their bodies. The VC leader ordered them up and after a few steps they fell again. The leader screamed at Jeff and kicked him in the side. Jeff doubled up, waiting for the next kick but the leader turned sharply, screaming at his companions.

Two VC scurried into the bush and returned after a minute with two long tree limbs. They made a stretcher with two ponchos and placed Mayhew on it. Jeff's shoulder would not support the full weight of one end of

48

the stretcher so he and Hefley carried the back end and a VC carried the front. Jeff felt a certain satisfaction when he saw it was the VC that had urinated on them. His satisfaction was short lived, after a short trek the VC pretended to trip and dropped the front of the stretcher.

Mayhew screamed when his legs slammed into the ground. The VC recovered quickly as Jeff moved toward him. The muzzle of his rifle stabbed painfully into Jeff's chest bringing him to a stop and Jeff watched his finger tighten slowly on the trigger. The VC leader spared Jeff's life by stepping between them knocking the rifle aside. As it cleared Jeff's chest the rifle went off and the deadly round roared into the trees.

The VC leader backhanded the guard, shouting at him. Although Jeff didn't understand, he knew the leader was making it clear it would be unhealthy for the VC to be so clumsy again. The man scrambled to pick up the front end of the stretcher and glared hatred at Jeff. He knew he'd pay dearly if the man ever got a chance to get even. They started out again. Mayhew was unconscious but Jeff was reassured as he watched the even rise and fall of Ken's chest.

It started raining sometime in the afternoon. Ken was delirious and cried out several times. His body was hot, yet he shivered almost constantly as chills racked him. He was burning up with fever. Jeff didn't think he would make it. He was continually moaning and thrashing about on the stretcher. They finally had to use their belts to tie him down. His ramblings were incoherent and then he lapsed into deep unconsciousness.

Both Ted and Jeff were physically exhausted by late afternoon. Their bodies were a solid aching mass. Jeff knew they'd have to stop for a rest pretty soon or collapse from weakness. Ted was about to give up when the VC halted them. He and Jeff were blindfolded and allowed to sit down for a short rest. Both men were puzzled by the blindfolds but after they were on their feet and marched down the trail a few hundred yards, Jeff guessed the answer. He could hear the water. They had arrived at the river. The VC leader wasn't taking any chance of them identifying the location where they departed the plantation or who was transporting them.

It was still drizzling when they were led aboard a boat and pushed into a shelter of some type on the deck. Evidently Mayhew had been placed on board before them because when Jeff and Ted were seated their hands were tied behind their backs to the stretcher poles. Jeff on one side and Hefley on the other. Jeff guessed they were aboard a river sampan. Usually they were covered amid-ship with rice mats tied across an arched framework. The bow and stern of the craft would have about four feet of open deck. The shelter they were under not only hid them from view by anyone on the shore or river, it provided the VC the opportunity to disguise themselves as fishermen or cargomen and blend in with the hundreds of other sampans on the river. They heard the VC come on board and the craft was pushed away from the bank. Jeff heard the sound of cloth rustling and knew a drop cloth had been lowered at each end of the shelter. Another precaution against prying eyes.

Wordlessly, the two soldiers slumped against their knees getting as comfortable as possible. The steady patter of rain lulled them into a dazed rest. Jeff strained to feel the movement of the craft, so he'd know which way the boat was headed. His mind fought for a sense of direction but he couldn't decide. Yet, he was willing to bet they were headed up river toward Laos. He could barely feel the movement of the craft as exhaustion overcame him and he dozed off.

Jeff didn't know how far or long they had traveled but he snapped awake as the prow of the sampan slid onto the riverbank. He and Ted, still blindfolded, were herded ashore and roughly pushed into a sitting position. Jeff heard the sounds of the stretcher being moved and it was placed near them. The rain had stopped and it seemed to be cooler now. Three or four minutes passed before they were hauled to their feet and their blindfolds removed. The sampan was gone. The fading daylight told Jeff it was early evening and he blinked several times as the area came into focus.

They had arrived at a small fishing village. Some twenty ramshackle huts were built along the outer treeline of a rain forest about forty feet from the river's edge. He guessed the village would be just about impossible to see from the air because of the tree overhang. A light aircraft or chopper flying low over the river could see it, but what would they see—a peaceful fishing village. A few small sampans were beached on the bank and a group of children played at the water's edge.

The VC leader motioned for Jeff and Ted to pick up Mayhew. They reached for the stretcher and were stopped as the leader shook his head. Yeah, Jeff thought silently to himself. The stretcher had served its purpose. They had reached their destination and there was no longer a need for it. Besides, the VC leader didn't want to appear soft before the villagers, or his superior, so he'd make Jeff and Ted carry Mayhew between them. It would also make the Americans appear humiliated and defeated.

The VC led them down the bank in front of the huts as the women and children gathered around them. A few old men were present but not many. The villagers shouted as the Americans stumbled past. Jeff suspected the reason for the screaming and curses. Their young men had probably been forced to fight for the VC.

Jeff eyed the villages as several of the women lunged forward to spit on them and swat angrily with sticks. Some of the children threw handfulls of dirt, splattering the weary GI's. One of the children, a young boy about eight, spit on Jeff and struck him on the leg before a VC pushed him away. Jeff couldn't understand their taunts and cries but he had a pretty good idea what they were saying.

Jeff felt the humiliation. He knew his enemy only as a battlefield adversary. An efficient fighting man, knowledgeable of guerrilla tactics, jungle warfare, and dedicated to his cause. Here was part of the war he never expected to see. The enemy's home ground. His family and children. Jeff felt sick to his stomach. They were paraded past half the huts, then turned and led toward the back of the village. Jeff looked up, almost stopping from surprise. Behind the village, hidden by the towering trees, was a fully operational VC base camp. Jeff stumbled open mouthed as a rifle prodded his back. The rain forest had been thinned out to provide several large clearings. Huge stacks of supplies were scattered throughout the trees. He looked upward and saw the clearing was screened from the air with vines and rope holding a giant network of branches and foliage. Damn, he thought to himself. They had used the natural greenery to camouflage the whole damn camp.

Several bamboo buildings had been built throughout the camp along with numerous smaller huts. Viet Cong soldiers squatted around cooking fires. Hammocks were strung in clusters around the huts for the single soldiers and children, while the huts were obviously for the married couples. Jeff knew it was a common practice for Viet Cong families to be at a secure base camp. The prisoners were herded toward the largest of the bamboo structures. Again, women and children stopped to stare with curiosity and amusement at the captured Americans as several VC joined their trek across the camp.

Jeff could hear truck motors laboring behind the larger buildings and saw several vehicles being unloaded further back in the clearing. So this was it, he thought. The Laotian side of the Ho Chi Minh trail. Probably the end of the motorized part of the supply line. Supplies were trucked into here for staging, then shipped out on sampans to various trails down river. Jeff's mind recorded the activity as they were pushed along, not even sure why he bothered. If they got out of this mess, his chances of finding this small village were remote. He was pretty sure he could come within thirty miles of it on a map, but that wasn't going to be too much help. There were probably ten such villages along the river in that distance.

They halted in front of the largest building. The entire structure was built on pilings, approximately three feet above the ground, as were all the other buildings and huts due to the floods of the raining season. Jeff guessed this to be the command building. A wide porch ran the width of it. Two armed guards flanked the porch steps. They eyed the prisoners as the VC leader spoke to the sentry nearest Jeff. He nodded several times and watched as Jeff and Ted eased Mayhew down to a sitting position. Jeff stood up as the sentry said something to the leader. He answered as the sentry brought the muzzle of his AK-47 rifle to bear squarely on Jeff. The sentry looked down at Mayhew and spit on him. Jeff's body tensed as the sentry grinned at him. His eyes daring Jeff to make a move. Jeff fought to relax as he watched the man's finger caress the trigger of the weapon. He stared at Jeff, then laughed as he turned and went up the steps into the building. Jeff eased the breath out of his tight chest and knew it would only be a matter of time before they suffered worse humiliations.

Several minutes later the sentry came out and resumed his post at the foot of the steps. He was followed by a middle aged Vietnamese man dressed in dark slacks and a white shirt. Probably the area chief, Jeff guessed, indoctrinated in North Vietnam and charged with running the local supply depot. No doubt when the supply camp was fully operational he would be replaced by a North Vietnamese regular officer. It was one thing to let a southerner run a hit-or-miss operation but once it became a high priority depot the authority would be placed in more efficient hands.

The chief stood at the top of the steps, looking down at the prisoners as the VC leader stepped forward to make his report. The chief silenced him with a wave of his hand. Pointing to each prisoner, he asked questions rapidly. The chief acknowledged each answer, then barked an order to the other VC standing around watching the proceedings and they hurried off. His gaze swung to Jeff. ''Your injuries will be taken care of,'' he said in accented english. He motioned the VC leader to follow and went into the house.

Jeff was dumbfounded as a new group of VC picked up Mayhew and led the prisoners toward an adjacent bamboo building on the left. He hadn't expected this kind of treatment and it caught him off guard. As soon as they entered the building Jeff saw it was a field hospital, or at least the VC version of one.

It was about sixty feet long and twenty feet wide. The walls ran up about four feet and mosquito netting served as screens for another three feet where it met the overhanging thatched roof. Rice mat pallets were spaced evenly on the floor on both sides of the wide room with an aisle running down the middle. At the rear end of the building an enclosed area of mosquito netting formed a cubicle for the last ten feet of the room. It stretched from wall to wall, ceiling to floor.

There were eight or nine patients lying on the mats to the right of the room. Two women, probably nurses, moved among the patients. One of the nurses looked up as they entered and a man emerged from the netted area. He was wearing a white smock and Jeff knew he was the doctor.

The doctor and the nurse approached them and one of the VC guards spoke directly to the doctor. He nodded and directed the VC carrying Mayhew to place him on the nearest mat. The doctor knelt next to the unconscious soldier feeling for a pulse and glanced at Jeff's and Hefley's obvious wounds. He pulled a pair of surgical scissors from his smock and cut the bandage off of Mayhew's leg, looking at the ugly discoloration and the small holes oozing pus and blood.

The doctor pointed to the netted enclosure and Mayhew

was taken into it. He then looked at Hefley's burned side and the swelling in Jeff's shoulder. He said something to the nurse, then turned and went into the netted cubicle.

"Come," the nurse motioned for Jeff and Hefley to follow her and a guard trailed them outside the building to a small area adjacent to the hospital. A makeshift shower had been built using old basins supported on overhead poles. In halting english the nurse told them to strip and wash themselves. Jeff looked at Ted, then shrugged as he removed his pants and shorts, his last two articles of clothing. Ted removed his clothing and they stood naked before the nurse and guard. Ted could imagine what a sight they made. Both of them had a four day beard and their skin was caked with mud. The insects had left their marks along with the scratches and welts from the jungle brush.

"Not the best bathing facilities I've ever seen Sarge," Ted said.

"No," Jeff agreed. "But I'll be glad to get some of this grime off. I guess they don't want us to dirty up their hospital."

Ropes were attached to the basins and Jeff stepped under one and tilted it with the rope letting the water splash down on him. He had to stoop because the makeshift shower was built for the small statured Vietnamese. Ted stepped under the other basin letting out a loud yelp as the cold water ran down his burns. They rubbed themselves with their hands during several more dousings then were led naked back into the hospital. The nurse pointed to two mats on the left side near the netted area away from the other patients and the two Americans settled on them. She went into the draped enclosure as the guard made himself comfortable squatting against the opposite wall.

Jeff looked at Ted. "I guess we sit here and drip dry."

"Yeah," Ted grinned. "What do you think that is Sarge?" nodding toward the netted area where blurred shapes moved around what appeared to be a table.

"Probably their operating room," Jeff answered. "The Doc seems to have assigned priorities, and Mayhew is first."

"Yeah. Man, did you see that swelling and the color of his leg? Christ, I hope he ain't got gangrene."

"Me too. How's your side?"

"It hurts likes hell. Some of the blisters have popped but the water seems to have cooled them off a little. Your shoulder looks twice as big as it should and it's the color of the rainbow."

"I know. It's throbbing like a fucking jackhammer."

Ted was silent for a moment as he looked around the building. Jeff could feel his question coming even before he said it. "Where are we Sarge?"

Jeff sighed, thinking for a moment. "I don't know for sure Ted but I'd guess somewhere in Laos, northwest of our operational zone and smack in the middle of one of their supply staging areas."

"Damn," Ted hissed. "We'll never get back."

"Don't even think about it Ted. We need to get our strength back and some medication. We need that VC Doc and his hospital now. We'll worry about the rest later. Just keep your head and don't panic."

"Okay Sarge, but I think we bought the farm this time."

"We'll see."

A rumble of thunder broke the late afternoon calm and in a few moments rain pelted the matted roof. A wave of silence swept over both men as they huddled quietly with their thoughts of the uncertain future afraid to think of what it might bring.

Jeff looked around the hospital and at the other patients at the far end. Pretty efficient operation for a field hospital he noted. Not the most comfortable setup he'd ever seen but it appeared to run smoothly. No doubt it would be operating at full capacity once the North Vietnamese offensive got under way. By then, he knew they would be expendable if hospital space was needed.

The other patients seemed to be asleep except for the two near the farthest end. They were talking in low whispers and nodding toward the two Americans. One of them had a bandaged stump where his left forearm and hand should have been. Even at their distance Jeff could see the hatred in the eyes of the man. His voice hissed with anger as he talked. Well, Jeff thought, I'd better get used to the tone. I'll probably be hearing a lot of it.

The Doctor and nurses finally came out of the netted area. Jeff watched silently as they treated Ted's burns. He moaned several times as they hovered over him. Finally, the Doc turned to Jeff. His fingers probed lightly over Jeff's shoulder and collar bone. The Doc eased him back, so he was laying flat. Jeff cried out as the Doc poked the bone itself. He closed his eyes and gritted his teeth as a sharp pain seared through his shoulder. He knew the bone was being set as the Doc positioned his arm and applied pressure. A wave of nausea flooded over him and he lapsed into unconsciousness.

58

Jeff woke up sometime during the night as a torrent of rain beat on the roof. The entire hospital was dark expect for the dim glow of a lantern at the far end of the building. Jeff started to move into a more comfortable position and felt a stab of pain in his shoulder. His left arm was strapped to his chest and he felt his shoulder throb with each heartbeat. He shivered slightly against the damp night air and looked over at Ted. He was just a dark shape but Jeff could hear his even breathing and knew he was sleeping. Sleep, he thought silently to himself and sighed. It would be their only escape if their dreams would give them peace.

Chapter Six

Jeff awoke to the sound of trucks outside the hospital. He looked around and some of the other patients were stirring, disturbed by the noise. Ted lay quietly, staring at the ceiling. Tears ran down his cheeks and he blinked several times. He turned his head slowly and looked at Jeff. His hand wiped his eyes.

"Morning Ted. Burns really hurting you huh?"

"Yeah Sarge," he smiled, thankful for the excuse of his tears. "But that salve really helped. I'll be okay now."

"Course you will. When did they bring him out?"

Ted looked at Mayhew lying next to him and watched the even rise and fall of his chest. "I'm not sure. Sometime during the night. I've been awake a couple of hours and he hasn't moved. I guess they gave him something to make him sleep."

Jeff raised up and looked at Mayhew noting with

relief the clean bandage on his thigh. At least he hasn't lost the leg, Jeff thought. Now he prayed it wouldn't become infected.

"They were giving him some blood but the nurse took it away when the bottle was empty and didn't replace it," Ted said. "I guess he must have lost a lot."

"Yeah," Ted nodded.

He was surprised they had even bothered but didn't mention it to Ted. For some reason the VC wanted them alive and that reason bugged him. Jeff's thoughts were interrupted as three VC entered the hospital followed by a nurse. They carried containers and started serving the VC patients at the far end of the room. The nurse came directly toward the three Americans as two more VC entered the hospital. One was armed and the other carried some bundles in his arms. They followed the nurse to the prisoners. The armed guard positioned himself against the opposite wall facing the prisoners, squatting in typical Vietnamese fashion while the other VC dropped a bundle at the feet of each American and walked out.

"Put on clothes," the nurse ordered, pointing to the bundle and turned away going to the other patients.

Jeff watched her squat next to the man with one arm and feed him. He had detected the bitterness in her eyes as she looked down on them. They were the enemy that had bombed her country and killed her people. She hated them equally. He'd bet a month's pay she didn't even know why the Americans were fighting them, only that they had invaded her country with their awesome weapons of destruction. He watched her a moment. She was young, probably in her late teens. Her long coal black hair was pulled back and knotted to hang down her back. Her shapeless black pajamas concealed the contours of her body. Her only symbol of status or station was a red cross patch pinned on her left sleeve. Jeff felt a sense of admiration for her knowing that her formal education and training was nowhere near her American counterpart but her dedication and devotion was probably just as strong.

The VC, both male and female were deadly foes, fighting fiercely against what Jeff thought were insurmountable odds. He wondered why they fought, especially when he saw their lifeless forms in the paddies and fields or pulled from blown tunnels.

He recalled the story of an old man ordered to carry a medium rocket round some seventy miles to a VC attack position and have it there on the third day. The old man ran for two days and nights to get the ammo in position and collapsed and died after reaching the site. The part he was carrying was only the tailfin assembly, not even the explosive or guidance system. A North Vietnamese general used an analogy comparing the Americans to an elephant and the Vietnamese to a tiger. The tiger knew he could never win a direct confrontation with the huge beast. So he'd lie in ambush and each day strike the lumbering elephant one blow with his powerful claws. Each time the elephant would turn to retaliate, the tiger would slip away into the jungle unharmed. Eventually the mighty elephant bled to death.

Well, so much for motivation, Jeff thought unrolling the bundle. It was a dark shirt and pants, pajama style, and a bowl and cup. He and Ted slipped into the garb. Ted helped Jeff button his shirt over his bad arm and shoulder. They struggled to pull the pants on Mayhew and drape the shirt over his chest. He didn't stir and Jeff was glad whatever the VC Doc had given Ken to make him sleep was still working.

They settled back on their mats until the food bearers finally approached them and filled their bowls and cups. Jeff watched wordlessly as their guard pointed to Mayhew's cup and bowl. They were filled and Jeff felt relief until the guard said something and one of the men handed the cup and bowl to the guard. He grinned at Jeff after sipping from the cup.

"Hey Sarge," Hefley started but Jeff cut him off.

"Forget it Hef. We'll save him some of ours."

Hefley nodded and sat looking dumbly at his cup and bowl. Jeff sipped the warm bitter tea then picked up his bowl. He smelled it and knew it was rice cooked with fish broth. Awkwardly, with his good hand he placed the bowl on the floor and leaned over it to scoop the rice into his mouth. The bland goo caked in his mouth and he had to sip tea to wash it down. He watched Hefley poke into his bowl then taste a few grains of rice on his finger. He made a sour face and started to put the bowl down.

"Eat it Hef. Forget the taste and smell. Just close your eyes and eat it. Chew it slowly, take your time. We don't know how often we're going to be fed. Eat everything they give you. We have got to build up our strength."

Hefley nodded.

Jeff felt a glimmer of hope when the food bearers returned and distributed a short stalk of sugar cane and a banana to each patient. However, his hopes were short lived as the Americans were bypassed.

Jeff watched sullenly as the Vietnamese consumed

the sugar cane. They savored it as a candy. Pounding an end of the stalk on the floor until it split then peeling it with their teeth exposing the middle pulp. They'd chew and suck the pulp finally eating the entire stalk. He recalled how he laughed the first time he watched some Vietnamese squatting around a pile of cane, jabbering as they banged and ate it. They had reminded him of a bunch of monkeys during feeding time at the zoo. Well, he thought wryly, he wasn't laughing now. Sugar cane was a tremendous source of energy that he and his companions dearly needed.

A groan from Mayhew caught his attention and Jeff moved around next to him after a wary glance at the guard. Ken moaned several times and his eyes blinked open staring at Jeff without recognition. Jeff placed his hand on Ken's forehead feeling the hot stickiness of his skin.

"Where am I? What's going on?" Ken asked as he looked around at his surroundings. For a moment he seemed disoriented. "Where are we Sarge?" he asked, finally recognizing the Sergeant.

"Quiet Ken," Jeff cautioned. "Lie still! You'll be alright. We're in a VC hospital of sorts but just be quiet a minute and listen to me. Okay?"

"Yeah," Mayhew nodded.

"All right," Jeff said after a few seconds then filled him in on their arrival at the camp. "You've still got a fever but your color looks a lot better so I guess the Doc did the trick. You were pretty well under last night. How's the leg feel?"

"Hurts likes hell," Mayhew grimaced, "but I'll make it now."

"Sure you will," Jeff reassured him. "Relax and let Ted and me get some chow into you."

Mayhew nodded as Jeff held up his head and Ted brought the cup to his lips. Ken slurped the bitter liquid and made a grim face.

"Hey now," Ted admonished. "Don't knock the grub. You need it man. Here," he scooped some rice with his fingers offering it to Ken.

Ken accepted the rice and made another face as Ted grinned.

"Sorry 'bout the fingers pal but Charlie don't set too good a table."

Ken attempted a weak smile and took another sip of tea. They were silent as Ken finished the meager meal. Jeff swore to himself that he'd make sure they were all awake when the next chow came so they would all get their share. They helped Ken get his shirt on and made him lie back.

"Now rest soldier," Jeff ordered. "Get your strength back and we'll figure a way to get out of here."

The roar of the trucks increased and Jeff noticed there seemed to be a lot more of them now than when he'd first heard them. He wanted to find out what was going on. It took him about five minutes to make the guard understand he wanted to go to the latrine. When he finally understood he led Jeff and Ted out of the hospital to a field latrine about twenty yards from the building.

Jeff couldn't believe his eyes once they got outside. Deep in the clearing some three hundred yards from them, a North Vietnamese field camp was being set up. Trucks were parked everywhere and regular soldiers were pitching tents and stacking supplies.

Trucks were still rolling in and Jeff watched a command car peel off from the convoy and head for the large building in the main compound. There were four men in the car and it passed within fifty feet of him. Jeff saw an officer in the car looking at him. The car braked to a halt in front of the building and the men got out. Three of them were North Vietnamese regular officers. As they entered the command building Jeff saw the officer that had noticed him, look back before he disappeared inside.

Their guard noticed Jeff's interest in the activity, decided the latrine break was over and led them back into the hospital. They settled down on their mats and Jeff had an uneasy feeling about the officer that had looked them over. He knew the North Vietnamese Army was the hard core of this war and he had dreaded the thought of being in a North Vietnamese prison camp from the first minute of their capture. He even hoped they might stay in South Vietnam under the control of the southern forces but now it seemed highly unlikely.

It was over sooner than he expected. Jeff heard a commotion of loud voices coming toward the hospital. Their guard jumped up as the village Chief stumbled through the door followed by two NVA officers. The Chief's mouth was bleeding and the front of his white shirt was bloody. One of the officers kicked the Chief sending him reeling toward the startled Americans. The Chief ran several steps forward before he lost his balance and sprawled on the floor rolling almost to Jeff's feet.

"Join them!" the officer screamed. "Join the American pigs you waste our precious medicine on."

The enraged officer grabbed the rifle from the guard and slammed the butt savagely into the Chief's back several times. Jeff clearly heard some bones crack as he and Ted tried to back away from the furious officer.

"Pigs! Pigs!" he shouted stepping over the prone Chief and raised the rifle over Jeff. "American Pigs!"

Jeff crossed his good arm across his face as the rifle butt came down squarely on his forearm taped to his chest. He knew he tried to scream as the force of the blow knocked the wind out of him. He turned sideways. Again it struck him, on his side below the ribs, causing him to retch violently. He tensed, waiting for another blow and heard Ted scream and the sounds of the rifle butt driven into yielding flesh and bone, and again, as Ken was struck several times. The officer was still cursing, "Pigs! Pigs!"

The officer's rage subsided as a third officer led six regular soldiers into the hospital. The officer with the rifle threw it back at the guard and pointed to the four beaten men.

"Take them out of here," he ordered. "Chain them together and throw them in the latrine pits. Let them wallow like pigs in the slime. If they don't drown by nightfall, I will personally shoot them in the morning."

Chapter Seven

Valerie Spencer stared unbelieving into the eyes of the young officer. They sat facing each other in her small apartment. Her eyes watered as she tried to concentrate on his words. Her mind reeled with the realization of what he was saying. His voice was soft and calm as if he were reciting a poem from memory. Yet, it had the warmth and tone of sincerity that triggered the unbelievable truth in her mind. Still, her love persisted, not wanting to believe. It had to be a mistake. Not Jeff! Not her life! She looked up at Cal Banner standing a few feet away and then to his wife Penny, seated next to her on the sofa. She saw the look in their faces and hot tears rolled down her cheeks as her heart pleaded.

"It's not true Penny," she tried to smile. "He's not dead. It's a dream. I'll wake up in a min . . ." Her voice trailed off as Penny slipped an arm around Val's shaking shoulders.

"I'm sorry Val," she whispered, cradling Val's head on her shoulder. "It's true."

"No. No," she sobbed. "I don't want him dead. I . . . I . . ." she couldn't finish and broke down in Penny's arms.

Penny felt the tears slide down her own cheeks as Val sobbed against her, repeating whispered protest. She could feel the grief overwhelm them as she looked at the Officer and her husband. She hated the uniforms they wore. The shiny gold buttons, the even rows of ribbons on their chest.

"Your war!" she hissed as she helped Val up and led her toward the bedroom. "Your goddamn lousy war!"

"Whew," Cal breathed as the bedroom door closed and he sat down on the soft. "That was tough."

"Yes," Lt. Mimms agreed. "And it's not over yet. I've got this whole week to get through, until the funeral is over and possibly a few days more if she needs me."

"You've been appointed casualty officer, huh?"

"Yeah. I've been assigned to Headquarters company as personal affairs officer for five months and this is my eighth case. I don't think I'll ever get used to it."

"I know what you mean. I wouldn't take your job for all the stripes in the Army."

"Are you and your wife close to her?"

"Yeah. Jeff and I were in training together. We got orders to the same unit here at Fort Campbell which kind of surprised us. You know how guys get scattered around the Army. I guess I was about the closest friend Jeff ever had. He was a quiet kind of guy. You know, keeping to himself. Did you know he grew up in an orphanage?"

"No. I didn't. I haven't checked his records yet other than to see his wife listed as next of kin. Come to think of it, I did feel it odd when I saw there were no parents listed."

"Yeah. Well you see, Jeff's parents were killed in a car accident when he was eight. There wasn't anyone except an old aunt, so he was put in an orphanage in Dayton, Ohio."

"Oh. I see."

"Jeff was a loner but we got to be pretty good friends. I was married and had a couple of kids. Jeff liked to talk about my family. He wanted a wife and kids. He had met Valerie about three or four months before he went to Vietnam. So, about two months after they met they were married. In fact, Penny and I stood up for them. Valerie decided to stay here because of her job. She and Penny work together. So that's about it. We see a lot of Val and as far as I know we're her closest friends. She misses Jeff and doesn't go out much, except once in awhile with us to the NCO club or a movie. I guess she feels if Jeff can't enjoy himself why should she."

"They didn't have any children?"

"No."

"Well Sergeant Banner, I'd appreciate it if you and your wife could be with her as much as possible. I'll get in touch with your commander if you think you'll have any problems getting away."

"No sir. He already told me to help her get settled."

"Good. Then I'll start making the arrangements. There are some things I have to know. Like, funeral home, burial place, type of services and such. The remains arrive here late tomorrow, so I'll be needing some

70

information by then. She's in no condition to discuss any of it now. If you could be here at noon tomorrow, I'd appreciate it. I'm sure you are aware of survivor benefits, therefore maybe you could talk to her. Perhaps, it would be easier coming from a friend. Is there anything you need to know?''

"Well sir, not about that, but do you know what happened?''

"Yes. Well, I don't have too much information, but it appears he was on a long range recon patrol. They called for choppers to make a pick up. Half the squad got out on the first chopper. The second one took a hit from enemy fire and crashed at the pickup zone. That was three days ago on the 23rd. A rescue team found the wreckage the next day and recovered the bodies. Right now that's all I've got. I'll get a detailed report when the personal effects and remains arrive.''

"At least she'll get a body to bury. Some don't get that,'' Cal said.

"Yeah. I know. I've handled two empty caskets. It's a bitch. In fact, I've only had two where the caskets could be opened. So,'' he said getting up. "If you need to get in touch with me, just call my office.''

"Fine,'' Cal said, shaking the Lieutenant's offered hand. He walked him to the front door.

"Tell your wife I agree with her. It is a lousy god-damn war.''

"Yeah,'' Cal agreed as he closed the door. He stood quietly for a moment listening to the muffled sobs coming from the bedroom and shook his head in despair.

Some four hours later that afternoon, Captain Russ Sanders was climbing the stairs of an old apartment building a few blocks from the Boston Common. Years

71

of decaying age assailed his nostrils as the creaks and groans of the stairs mingled with the sounds of an argument and the crying of an infant.

He searched the faded nameplates and paused before the second door on the fourth landing. He heard a muted feminine giggle and the deeper tone of a male voice. He shrugged his shoulders and tugged at the bottom of his Army blouse, then rapped on the door. After a brief pause he knocked again.

"Who is it?" a woman's voice asked.

"Captain Sanders, Maam. From the Army. I must talk to you about your husband."

"Just a moment," the voice said.

He heard scurrying movements inside as he waited. Finally a dead-bolt turned and the door opened slightly. A brown eye peeked at him through the crack.

"Are you Mrs. Mayhew? he asked. "Mrs. Kenneth Mayhew?"

"Yes," she answered and stepped back allowing the door to open. "Would you like to come in?"

"Yes. Thank you," he said stepping past her into the room.

"Please excuse the way it looks," her hand made a sweeping gesture of the unmade bed. "I was sleeping. I work nights," she added closing the door.

"I understand, Maam."

"Here," she pulled some clothes from a faded armchair. "Have a seat."

"Could we sit there," he indicated a small kitchen table and two chairs against a far wall. "I have some papers I must show you."

"Sure," she said walking to the table. "Just let me clear some of this stuff off."

He waited as she picked up some dirty dishes and beer cans, taking them into the small alcove kitchenette.

"What's Kenny done now?" she called out. "Run away from the Army or something?"

Sanders didn't answer as he waited for her. He saw a pair of jockey shorts laying under the side of the bed. He placed his briefcase on the table, snapped it open. She came out as he made up his mind on how to tell her.

"Well?" she asked.

He looked at her. Long light brown hair flowing to just below her shoulders. A pretty girl with big brown eyes that reflected more age than her actual years, which he knew was twenty-two. She wore a silver mandarin robe with blue dragons printed on the shoulders. It was a size too small, fitting her tightly and ending just above her knees. Probably a gift from her husband. He noticed the outline of her nipples under the thin material.

"Please sit down Mrs. Mayhew. I'm afraid I have some very bad news for you." He watched her eyes. Nothing.

"He's dead," she said, sitting down slowly, making it sound more a statement than a question.

"Yes," he answered. His eyes never left hers. "I'm sorry."

He waited a moment as silence enveloped them. She blinked and swallowed as her hand absently brushed her hair away from her face.

"Are you sure?" she asked softly.

"Yes. I have the message right here. Shall I read it?"
She nodded.

He extracted the notice from his briefcase and read the report. It was brief and precise.

"That's all the information I have right now. There will be more when the remains arrive."

"Remains?"

"Yes Maam. Your husband's remains are being flown home from Vietnam for burial. I will make all the arrangements but you must tell me what you would like."

"What I would like?"

"Yes. You are listed as next of kin. You have the legal responsibility of his disposition."

"But why me? We were only married a few months before he went into the Army. Let his parents bury him. They live in New Hampshire someplace."

"Yes. I know, Mrs. Mayhew. I was up there and talked to them. His father said he would make all the arrangements but, legally, you are next of kin. I told them I would consult you. His parents didn't know he was married, or even in the Army for that matter. He left home when he was seventeen and they hadn't heard from him since. I'm afraid it came as quite a shock to them."

He waited as a hint of hardness crept into her eyes, then added, "Therefore, as next of kin and beneficiary, it's your decision."

Interested, she leaned forward on her folded arms. The open neck of the robe parted slightly displaying the firm rise and crest of her breasts.

"What kind of beneficiary?" she asked.

"Well," he said, detesting her, "you will receive all survivor's benefits from the Army and Veteran's Administration to include for example, a lump sum payment of six times his base pay. I have a check here for just under two thousand dollars.''

"Two thousand dollars!''

"Well, actually it's," he found the check and handed it to her, "Eighteen hundred, twenty-three dollars and change.''

"Wow!" she exclaimed, looking at her typed name and the amount.

"And of course, there is the Serviceman's Group Life Insurance Policy, which I'll have later this week for twenty thousand dollars.''

"Twenty thou . . ." her voice trailed off as her eyes lit up. "Man, you're too much.''

"I assure you, Mrs. Mayhew," Sanders said fighting to control his emotions, "it's not me. Merely your dead husband's wishes," he emphasized dead.

Dina Mayhew tried to suppress her elation and attempted to sound remorseful. "Poor Kenny," she said unconvincingly.

"Yes, Mrs. Mayhew. Your grief overwhelms me. Now, about the funeral arrangements.''

Dina detected the sarcasm in his voice and cautioned herself to cool it. At least until that twenty grand was in her hands. Play the grieving wife she told herself, lowering her head and dropping her eyes. Her hand clutched the neck of her robe together as she asked about the funeral arrangements. Sanders spent a quarter of an hour explaining details to her, then waited for her answer.

"Well Captain," Dina started in an almost sincere voice. "I think Kenny should be buried in his hometown. He should be near his parents. And with a military funeral like you said. You can find out the place and things from his parents. I'd like whatever you think is best.''

"Fine," Sanders said closing his briefcase. "I'll complete all the details. My office is in the Fargo building. Do you think you could be there at eleven tomorrow morning? I have some papers you must sign.''

"Yes.''

"And if you need travel arrangements to New Hampshire I'll make them for you.''

"To New Hampshire?''

"Yes, of course, for the funeral.''

"Oh yes," she said almost starting to protest but cautioned herself again. For twenty grand she'd walk bare ass down Washington street on her hands. "Are you going to the funeral?''

"Yes, if that's what you want," he said, knowing what was coming and wishing he could get out of it.

"I'd appreciate it if you would take me," Dina said. "I don't know his family and I'll need someone to lean on.''

"Very well, Mrs. Mayhew. We'll plan the funeral for the twenty-eighth. Will you be ready to leave tomorrow about five?''

"Yes.''

"Good." He got up and started for the door. "Tomorrow at eleven?''

"Yes Captain," Dina followed him to the door. "And thank you.''

"Certainly," he said going out the door and muttered, "it's my fucking job.''

"What Captain?''

"Nothing, Mrs. Mayew. Nothing at all.''

Dina stood at the door listening to his fading footsteps. When she no longer heard them she crossed the room and sat on the edge of the bed.

"You can come out now, lover."

The bathroom door swung open slowly revealing a tall slim man in his middle twenties. He was completely nude and grinned at her. Dina grinned back as he leaned against the door frame puffing a cigarette.

Her eyes took in his long dark hair. His handsome face with a Fu Manchu moustache beamed at her knowingly as her gaze swept past his hairy chest and flat belly to his limp manhood. She smiled remembering how erect it had been when the knock on the door had interrupted them.

"Did you hear what he said, Mike?"

"Yeah Baby. I heard."

Dina giggled as her hands unbuttoned her robe. It parted over her nakedness and she shrugged it off her shoulders and down her back. She freed her arms and leaned back on her elbows spreading her long legs. She looked down between her jutting breasts to her dark mound.

"Come on lover," she taunted him. "You get to ball a frigging heiress."

Chapter Eight

Kathy Chandler entered the room just as her father hung up the phone. She stopped suddenly when she saw the ashen look on his face. Her mother was standing next to him shaking her head.

"Oh no Paul," she said. "It must be some mistake."

Kathy felt a chill pass through her body as her father looked up and saw her. She stood still as he crossed the room and placed his hands on her shoulders. She refused to believe what she saw in his face.

"Honey," his voice broke slightly as he took a deep breath, "I'm afraid I have some bad news. That was Ted's father on the phone. The Army . . ." he paused fighting to control his voice. "The Army notified him that Ted was killed three days ago in Vietnam."

Kathy looked at her father, her mother, then to the letter she held in her hand. She stared at it a moment then held it up for them to see as a smile formed on her lips.

"No Daddy," she grinned. "He's not dead. I just got a letter from him today and he couldn't . . ."

"Honey," he said softly. "Come and sit down with me and Mom."

He led her to the sofa and eased her down as her mother sat next to her putting her arm around her shoulders. Kathy held the letter up again.

"See," she pointed to the last paragraph. "He said to tell you both hello and he'll see us all in a . . ."

"Kathy," her father cut her off. "That letter was written several days ago. Honey, Mr. Hefley explained it all to me. Ted was on a patrol three days ago and the helicopter he was on was shot down. There were no survivors."

Kathy looked at the letter she held as tears filled her eyes blurring the lines of neat writing. She tried to clear her vision, straining to read the letter, as her mind finally gave in to the dreadful reality of her father's words. She collapsed against her mother sobbing uncontrolably.

Paul Chandler got up and went to the portable bar. He poured a small glass full of whiskey and gulped it down, fighting to get it past the lump in his throat. He stood staring at the empty glass shaking his head.

"What a waste," he muttered. "What a damn miserable waste."

Three days later, three funerals took place with full military honors. Though they were hundreds of miles apart they all bore the distinct mark of similarity.

The flag draped coffins, containing the remains of young men who had given their lives for a war they didn't understand, were surrounded by mourners wondering why it had to be these particular men to suffer the ultimate sacrifice. An Army Sergeant barked commands and seven soldiers in full military dress fired the traditional salute to fallen comrades.

As the echo of the last order faded across a mute California cemetery, one father wondered why it was his son being buried a hero while hundreds of young men burned their draft cards protesting the war and fled to other countries.

In a national cemetery in Kentucky, an Army honor guard solemnly folded the flag and handed it to a military chaplain. He executed a sharp about face, marched several paces and stood at attention facing a veiled young widow, placing the flag in her arms.

"A grateful nation . . ." he started his presentation and she knew silently that the nation was not grateful, nor did it express its gratitude as the chaplain was so reverantly stating.

The sounds of taps faded into the rolling country side at a small town cemetery in New Hampshire while another widow chewed gum impatiently and loosely held the flag presented to her. Next to her stood the parents of the dead soldier. The mother, heartbroken and bewildered, wanting to take the poor young widow home to share her sorrow and grief. The father would grieve the loss of his son for many years, and now secretly wished for the flag his daughter-in-law regarded so casually.

Captain Sanders stood at the rear of the mourners at the third funeral composing a letter of resignation in his head. At the very least, he would ask for an assignment to a combat unit. He did not intend to go through this again, he vowed silently to himself. He watched the mourners start for their cars and as Mrs. Mayhew turned to say something to her daughter-in-law, Dina turned away and headed for him, ignoring her completely.

"Get me the hell out of here and away from those two," Dina said grabbing his arm, leading him towards the car. "I can't stand their slobbering another minute. I'm sorry I ever let you bring me up here."

Russ Sanders let himself be pulled along until they reached the car. He stopped on the passenger side, opened the door and pushed Dina inside.

"Give me the flag," he said through clenched teeth, fighting to control his anger.

"What?"

"Just give me the flag," he said, pulling the bundle from her. "Stay in the car and shut up."

Sanders walked back to the grave site where the elderly Mayhews were standing alone. Mr. Mayhew had his arm around Mrs. Mayhew as she placed a flower on the coffin. He looked up as Sanders approached.

"She wants you to have this, Sir," Sanders lied, holding the flag out to the old man.

"Are you sure Captain?" he asked, taking the flag and holding it to his chest.

"Yes Sir, I'm positive."

The old man clutched the flag tightly as his eyes watered. "I ah . . ."

"Please Captain," Mrs. Mayhew interrupted, "bring her along to the house. Some of the family will be there and we want to make her feel at home. I have so much I want to talk to her about. The poor thing doesn't know which way to turn."

"Well, Mrs. Mayhew," he lied again, "I know she wants to be with you but right now she's so upset. I think she wants to go back to the motel and rest a bit. You know what I mean? Kinda pull herself together."

"Yes, I suppose so."

"I'll take her back there and give you a call later when she's feeling better. Goodbye for now."

"Goodbye Captain and thank you," she said, as he turned, hurrying to his car.

Sanders got into the car and sped out of the cemetery to the main highway toward the motel. His anger was almost to the boiling point as he ran a stop sign narrowly missing a station wagon loaded with kids. He slowed to a normal speed fighting to control his emotions. His knuckles strained the tight skin on the back of his hands as he gripped the steering wheel.

"What's the matter Captain?" Dina asked coyly. "Didn't I play the bereaved widow well enough for you?"

"Shut up Mrs. Mayhew," he said staring straight ahead. "Just shut the fuck up."

"Oh my, Captain. Now we're back to Mrs. Mayhew, huh? What happened to all that panting and grunting, and *Dina, my darling Dina*, like it was last night?"

"That should have never happened," he said defensively. "You ah . . ."

"I what? Seduced you?" she laughed. "Seems to me you participated just as well."

"Look Dina, I just don't want to discuss it now. So please be quiet and let me drive. Okay?"

Sanders was glad when she didn't answer and settled back with his thoughts as they drove along. How had he ever let himself get into this mess?

He remembered the anger he felt when he had left her apartment three days ago. Her attitude of indifference and pretended sorrow at the news of Ken's death irritated him. He knew all the time he was in her apartment someone was hiding in the bathroom. The money was the only reason she had even tolerated the burden of the funeral and the trip to New Hampshire. When he had gotten back to his office that day he called Mr. Mayhew and asked what arrangements he wanted, telling him that Dina would like whatever the family thought best. Sanders knew the Mayhew's were not financially well off, so he explained the benefits and allowances the Army and Veteran's Administration would make. The old man was relieved when Sanders told him that Dina would take care of the additional expenses of the funeral. He wondered why he'd ever made such a promise. He knew Dina would scream at every nickle she had to spend. He made several more calls including the mortuary handling Ken's burial and finalized the last arrangements. Mrs. Dina Mayhew was going to get a bill for just under two thousand dollars.

Later that evening, Sanders found himself in a topless club in Boston's infamous combat zone. Dina Mayhew worked there as a dancer but Sanders hadn't expected her to be working there that night. He found a booth in a far corner away from the stage and sipped a beer as a washed-out blonde wiggled to a rock record. During his second beer a slightly overweight redhead replaced the blonde. He was ready to leave when the redhead left the stage and was replaced by Dina Mayhew. She wore a feathered bikini top and bottom, and a beaded indian headband with a white feather in it. Her long hair hung straight down and was brushed to a shiny luster that glistened in the bright stage lights. Her skin gleemed from a thin coating of oil as she stepped onto the stage. She hadn't even started dancing and had outclassed every girl in the place.

Her music started and she moved sensuously to the pulsing drumbeat. Sanders felt a familiar gnawing in his stomach as she danced. Most of the chatter that had persisted while the other dancers were on was gone and every male eye in the place was on her. The bikini top pressed into the full crest of her breasts and the lights shadowed the deep crease between them. Her concave stomach flowed smoothly to her small waist and full hips. The small bikini pants were little more than a G-string, exposing her hips and buttocks completely.

She danced to the first record and Sanders felt his desire for her growing as she moved across the stage. He found it hard to believe she was even up there after the news she had received but, there she was, smiling and dancing, as if she didn't have a care in the world. When the second record started some of the customers were cheering and hollering for her to take off her top. She danced coyly as her hands played with the clasp on the front of her bra. She finally unhooked it but held the material against her, flashing one breast, then the other. When the roaring and clapping reached an overpowering din she turned her back to the crowd and slipped off the bra. She clasped her hands behind her neck and turned slowly, wiggling her shoulders. A cheer went up from the crowd as her breasts came into view. They were big, almost too large for her frame. The firm roundness of them, set high on her ribcage, made them look even bigger. Her nipples were tilted slightly upward as she struck a legs apart pose for the crowd with her elbows pushing against the sides of the heavy mounds.

Sanders stared at the beauty of the young girl and felt a desire his body wouldn't ignore. He wanted her and cursed himself for it. He knew he shouldn't have come here but now it was too late. He pushed himself out of the booth and hurried out of the bar, hating himself for being there, and her for what she was.

Dina showed up fifty minutes late the next day at his office. He had a stack of papers for her to sign. She listened as he explained the whole procedure and when he told her about the additional cost of the funeral she shook her head in protest.

"What?" she had asked. "I thought the Army took care of all that."

"Well not quite, Mrs. Mayhew. You see, most of the expense for a private funeral has to come from the family and . . ."

"Family," she interrupted. "Well then, let his family take care of the additional expenses."

"Yes, I'm sure they would but I happen to know it would be a burden on them to do that. So, I thought since you are the insurance beneficiary you would provide for your husband's needs."

She was quiet for a moment and he felt sure she was going to argue but she finally said she would think abut it and let him know. He had arranged to pick her up later in the day for the drive to New Hampshire. It had been after five when he pulled up in front of her building. She was standing outside waiting for him and jumped into the car as soon as he pulled to a stop. She was carrying a small overnight bag and her purse. She was wearing jeans, a blue blouse and a jeans vest. Her face was overdone with make-up and eye shadow. After a brisk hello, she turned up the car radio and lit a cigarette, settling back into the seat.

Sanders fought the evening traffic north out of Boston. It was just past Revere Beach before he attempted to talk to her.

"Mrs. Mayhew, ah, Ken's parents have made room for you at their house and . . ."

"No way," she cut him off, turning to face him. "Now look Captain, I don't know his family and I don't want to know them. So don't think you're going to take me up there and drop me off in the middle of a sobbing Mayhew clan."

"But they're expecting you. They want to get to know you."

"No chance Captain. No chance. Where are you staying?"

"I made reservations at a motel a few miles from town."

"Well, you can damn well make a reservation for me too."

They had arrived at the motel an hour later and checked in after he had managed to get a room for her. They met in the motel lounge later and had dinner. Dina showed up in a blue mini dress that had a plunging neckline and clearly showed she was braless. Sanders waited until dinner was over before he brought up the subject of her dress.

"You do have other clothes to wear to the funeral, don't you?"

She looked up with a hard bitterness in her eyes and a sigh of impatience. "Not unless I wear my jeans."

"Well damnit. You certainly can't go to your husband's funeral looking like a, a . . ."

"A what, Captain?"

Sanders bit his tongue fighting to control himself as she stared hotly across the table.

"Look," he began again in a softer tone. "Mrs. Mayhew, I apologize. I was rude and out of line. Let's start over, okay? How about a drink?"

"Okay," she conceded. "Why not. And quit calling me Mrs. Mayhew. You know my name."

"All right, Dina."

Sanders stopped a waitress and ordered two drinks. They were silent as their table was cleared and their drinks arrived.

"Dina," he began finally. "I think that dress looks very good on you. In fact you look terrific but it's just not appropriate for a funeral, especially your husband's."

"Yeah," she laughed. "I suppose I would shock hell out of all those New England prudes. But what can I do about it now?"

"Well, there's a shopping center a couple of miles from here. We could drive over there and pick something up."

"I don't want to go anywhere. I'm tired. I had to work last night."

"Yeah. I know."

"What?"

"Nothing. Never mind, listen," he paused. "Okay, give me your dress size and I'll go pick something up. Go back to your room and I'll drop it off. If it doesn't fit, we can exchange it in the morning."

"Sounds cool."

"All right then, I'll see you in about an hour."

Sanders ended up spending more time than he thought buying the dress. It was a little over two hours before he returned to the motel. He went directly to Dina's room and knocked on the door. After a few minutes of waiting he tried the door and found it open. He stepped inside turning on the light. The room was deserted. Her overnight bag was thrown on the bed where she had left it. He dropped the packages on the bed and looked quickly in the bathroom before leaving. He headed for the lounge and stood in the open doorway until his eyes adjusted to the dim light. The small room was jammed with people. A five man combo blasted out a rock tune. The tiny dance floor was packed with couples trying to dance. He threaded his way to the bar and finally spotted Dina sitting at a table with two bearded young men. The table was loaded with empty glasses and Dina was leaning against one of the men talking in his ear as her hand caressed his chest at his open shirt.

Sanders felt his blood boil as he approached the table. He stopped at the table edge facing her. He placed his hands on the table leaning forward as she looked up.

"Well," she slurred drunkenly. "If it isn't my long lost Captain."

"He didn't stay lost long enough, did he Ed?" the one receiving Dina's attention said.

"No. He didn't. Say Captain," he said placing a hard emphasis on Captain. "Why don't you go stay lost some more."

"Yeah Captain," his partner echoed, "get lost."

"Look," Sanders said, leaning further over the table toward Dina's companion as his voice took a hard edge. "We can settle this hard or easy. Now be good guys and say goodnight to Mrs. Mayhew and she and I will leave quietly or . . .''

"Or what?" the one named Ed asked.

"Or . . ."

Sanders placed his hand on Ed's wrist and pressed down trapping it against the table. "I'll start by breaking good old Ed's wrist and," he paused, looking directly into the other's eyes, "your neck. Now, what's it going to be?" he asked, leaning a little harder on Ed's wrist but still staring at his partner.

"Hey," Ed squirmed, trying unsuccessfully to free his wrist from under Sander's full weight.

"Come on Sonny, he means it. He's breaking my wrist."

Sanders watched the fear come into Sonny's eyes and he knew he had them. He eased slowly off of Ed's wrist, straightened up, towering over the table.

"Ready, Mrs. Mayhew," he smiled. "You've got a busy day tomorrow."

Dina looked at her two companions and pushed her chair away from the table, standing up.

"Creeps," she slurred contemptuously and turned and walked somewhat unsteadily toward the exit.

"Goodnight gentlemen," Sanders smiled tightly and walked out.

He caught up with Dina in the hallway and took her arm guiding her toward her room. They were silent until he opened the door to her room. She turned in the doorway and pressed her body against him as her arms went around his neck catching him by surprise.

"Stay here," she said, burying her face against his chest. "Please stay. I don't want to be alone."

"Dina," he said softly, maneuvering her into the

89

room and pushing the door closed, "get some sleep. You'll feel better in the morning. We have to get started about eight. Now come on," he pushed her onto the bed.

"Get some rest," he said turning for the door.

"Captain," she said as he reached the door. Her voice was hard now and without the drunken slur. He stopped and turned to face her.

"You know that little expense item you want me to pay for?"

"Yes," he answered, knowing what was coming.

"I'll sign the paper tomorrow," she said standing up as her hands reached behind her for the zipper of her dress, "I promise."

"Dina, don't," he protested, hearing the rasp of the zipper, seeing her full breasts straining against the fabric of her dress.

"Yes, Captain?" she smiled and shrugged the dress off her smooth shoulders and slowly down her body until it dropped in a pile at her feet. Her hands rested on her naked hips as she drew a deep breath expanding her lovely chest.

"I promise. I'll sign it in the morning and besides," she cooed, "you want me."

Sanders felt a lump in his throat as he stared at her inviting nakedness. Deep within his mind he lied to himself that he would do it for the poor elderly couple, so he could keep his respect. The growing desire in his loins showed his true feelings as he locked the door and moved silently toward her.

Dina had kept her promise and signed the check for the additional funeral expenses the following morning. In fact, the only problem he had was getting her to wear the black dress and small hat with a veil but she finally relented. Still, the dress was almost vulgar on her because of the fit and of course Dina didn't wear anything under it.

Sanders was steaming when they finally arrived back at the motel. He parked the car and got out, heading directly for his room. He started gathering his things as soon as he entered and finished snapping shut his bag as Dina entered without knocking.

"My," she said from the doorway, "in a hurry aren't we?"

"Look Dina," Russ said, looking up. "I'm not very proud of myself right now. So don't get cute. I'm in no mood for it. Now, if you want a ride back to Boston, I'm leaving. It doesn't make any difference to me. I really think you could have been a little more civil to the Mayhew's. They were only trying to be nice to you."

"Don't start that shit again," she said slamming the door.

"Okay. Okay," he said, walking to the door and stopping before her. "You've got the cash and no more worries, right? Well Dina, I just hope you can live with yourself. You're cold Baby. Cold!"

"And you're so righteous, huh? Well don't kid yourself either. You balled me and loved the hell out of it. But keep telling yourself it was for the old folks. Bullshit Captain, you wanted me from the start and," she paused, "you still do."

Sanders slapped her. The sound of it seemed loud in the small room. He raised his hand to hit her again and stopped it in midair as she glared at him. She hadn't uttered a sound. She just stood there and finally a small grin crept into her face. She was right. She knew it and he knew it.

He pushed her away from the door and went out, walking to his car. He angrily threw his bag in the trunk and paused beside the driver's side door. He turned and went back to the room. She was still standing by the bed. The side of her face was a red blotch.

Sanders closed and locked the door. He pulled open the buttons on his uniform as she watched him silently.

"Take off that dress bitch. I never want to see black again."

Chapter Nine

They spent the night in the latrine pit. It was a ten foot long trench about three feet deep and two feet wide. They had been shackled by the ankles to one another, dragged to the pit and thrown in. Since the trench was newly dug it contained only a couple inches of filth. Luckily, Mayhew had been chained between Jeff and Ted and they managed to keep him from slumping face down in the mucky waste. The unconscious village Chief landed face down and Jeff pulled him up and propped him against the side of the trench. They squirmed around in the pit until they were sitting with their backs crammed against one wall and their knees jammed against the other.

The stench of the rotting waste filled their lungs and Jeff and Ted began retching violently, throwing up what little food they had in their stomachs. Tears poured from their eyes as they finally stopped gagging and their exhausted bodies lapsed into unconsciousness.

A hard rain woke Jeff sometime during the night. Water was flowing into the trench and the level in the bottom had risen another couple of inches. Jeff quickly checked the two young soldiers and was relieved when he felt their breathing. The village Chief had slumped over and was lying face down. He wasn't breathing. Jeff leaned forward resting his head on his forearms and sobbed himself into a half-conscious sleep.

The rain stopped just before daybreak and it was shortly after that the camp started to come alive. A guard patrolled the trench unconcerned about the fate of the men lying in it. Several containers of human waste were thrown into the pit and the guard laughed and made some comment as it splashed on the men.

Mayhew regained consciousness only to start gagging and retching until he was exhausted. Jeff's body was on fire with the pain from the beating he had received and he knew Ted must feel the same. His hand touched Ted's arm and the young man glanced up with tears in his eyes and a hopeless look.

"I can't make it Sarge," he sobbed. "I can't make it."

For once Jeff didn't say anything because he wasn't sure he could make it either. Their eyes made brief contact and Jeff lowered his head again in despair.

Jeff fully expected the Officer to carry out his threat to shoot them. It was mid-morning when he looked up to see the Officer and several armed soldiers standing over the trench, their rifles pointed down at the prisoners. The Officer spoke and Jeff tensed, waiting for the bullets to slam into his body. A soldier leaned over Jeff, his rifle muzzle inches from his face.

"Out," he motioned with the rifle. "Captain say come out. Stand up."

Jeff struggled to stand up, pulling the half conscious Mayhew with him.

"Come on Ted," he grimaced as pain shot through his leg. "Help me get Ken up."

They struggled to crawl out of the trench and lay half in and half out because Jeff was being held back by the body of the village Chief. He pulled himself to a sitting position on the edge of the trench and grabbed the chain fighting to pull the body after him. Ted took hold of the chain and together the Chief's body was pulled from the ditch. The Captain and soldiers backed off several paces as the smell overwhelmed them. The three Americans sat exhausted on the edge of the trench covered with filth.

The Officer threw a heavy key to the ground near Jeff and pointed to the chains. Jeff understood and unlocked the shackles from their ankles, throwing the chains in a pile, next to the dead Chief. Jeff stood up glaring at the Officer and started unbuttoning his shirt as boiling hatred filled his eyes.

"Take off those filthy clothes Ted and throw them in the trench. We won't give them the satisfaction of dying like vile animals," Jeff said as he undressed and used the shirt to wipe the excreta from his body.

Ted's glazed eyed looked at Jeff as he pulled the clothing from his own body and finally helped Jeff undress Ken and wipe off his shivering skin. Jeff noted the bandage on Ken's thigh was still on tight. It was soiled but there were no bloodstains.

"Come on Ken," Jeff strained to help him stand up. "Face them like men. Show them we won't die like dogs in our own shit and vomit."

Jeff and Ted held Ken between them as they faced the enraged Captain.

95

"Pigs!" he screamed. "You will not be so insolent after you dig your holes. There," he indicated to the guards an area about twenty feet from the trench. "Have them dig the holes there," he said and walked off.

Jeff didn't understand the Officer but he knew what was expected of them when they were given three shovels and the ground was marked off where they were to dig.

"Sarge," Ted asked. "Are they going to make us dig our own graves?"

"I don't know Ted. I think they would have shot us in the trench if that's what they wanted and just bury us there. So I don't know. Just do what they want and maybe we'll still have a chance. Ken, do you think you can dig?"

"I, ah . . . I don't know Sarge. Maybe, if I sit, I can dig some."

"Just try. Don't aggravate them. Me and Ted will help you."

"Okay. I'll try."

They dug for almost four hours. The soil was soft from all the rain but their injuries made it almost impossible for them to work more than a few minutes at a time. The guards didn't protest when they rested as long as it wasn't more than a minute or two. Ken had only dug a couple of feet by the time Jeff and Ted completed their pits so they helped Ken finish his.

The pits were approximately three feet square and five feet deep. By the time they had finished Jeff had a pretty good idea how they would be used. He'd heard stories about how some POW's were kept. It turned out he was right when three cages were brought to the digging site by some soldiers.

The cages were made of bamboo poles lashed together to form a square. The top, or ceiling, was hinged to open like a box top allowing the person to enter or depart from the top after the cage was lowered into the pit. Once the prisoner was inside, the top could be secured with a bamboo pole threaded through two loops fastened to driven stakes. The pits always would be guarded even when the men were secured inside. Jeff knew escape would be impossible without help.

The Americans watched as the cages were lowered into the pits. The top of the cages were even with the ground after the soldiers stomped the corners to settle the weight. The only view from inside the cage would be between the tiny slits of the poles and then, only straight up. Dirt was thrown around the sides to pack the cages in and the prisoners were pushed in without a word. Jeff heard Mayhew cry out and the solid thump as he was thrown in.

Jeff landed hard in the cage and pain shot through his weary body. He collapsed on the hard poles. He was almost beyond the point of caring. His muscles ached and burned as a wave of dizziness settled over him. He had tried to say something to Ted and Ken just before they pushed him in the cage but his tongue felt so thick and heavy he couldn't form any words. He tried to clear his head as he lay on the bottom of the cage but his brain just wouldn't work. The last thing he heard were the soldiers laughing as the top was slammed shut and the holding pole slid across the top of the cage.

Chapter Ten

Jeff woke up with an intense pain in his stomach. He tried to slow his breathing and still the fire in his gut. He lay on his side feeling the hardness of the bamboo floor against his bare skin as he tried to collect his thoughts. He wondered what day it was as he eased his weary body into a sitting position. A wave of dizziness flooded his head when he moved and he knew it was from not eating. As far as he could remember they had gotten food only three times since their capture and they had been prisoners now for four days, or was it five? He tried to recall but couldn't.

He looked up and could see glints of light between the poles of the cage. The stench of the nearby latrine pit engulfed his cage and he fought back the urge to retch. He settled back against the poles and looked down at his filthy body in the dim light and thought of a clean white tub filled with steaming water. How long will they keep us like this, he asked himself silently? If they're keeping us alive for some reason they must know we can't survive like this. What good are we to them? What's their purpose?

He thought he knew part of the answer. This part, the humiliation, would break their spirit and attitude for resistance. Eventually, they would do anything to get out of the cages. In fact, Jeff had felt the hopelessness when he saw how they were going to be kept as animals. Already they were succeeding.

Jeff reached up and gingerly felt the bandage on his broken collar bone. He couldn't feel the bone because of the swelling but he thought it was still set properly. His wrist was tender and swollen from the blow of the rifle butt but it wasn't broken. He had another large bruise below his right breast and ran his fingers along the ribs, but didn't think they were broken or cracked. He slowly tried a deep breath and felt just a slight pain as his chest expanded. Well, he thought, I'll live if they don't starve us to death.

He wondered how Ted and Ken were doing and wished there were some way he could talk to them. He was worried about Ken. His wounds were the most severe and prone to infection. In his condition he would be the one to give up first. He knew it wouldn't take much for any of them to finally wish for death to ease their pain and despair.

Jeff snapped out of his thoughts as he felt several drops of water drip on him. It was raining again, Water, he thought, Good old rainwater. Hope flashed through his body as he squirmed to find the biggest gap between the poles. A thin stream was seeping into the cage and he opened his mouth directly under the gap swallowing rapidly. He drank for almost five minutes until his stomach felt full. Then he sat under the gap letting the stream dribble onto his head as the downpour increased. It was like a mini shower, he thought as he washed himself, rubbing his dirty skin and trying to collect water in his palms to rinse off the scum.

The rain lasted about an hour and Jeff rubbed his body inch by inch until he was satisfied he was clean. He drank some more and realized his bladder was full as cramps started in his stomach. He searched the bottom of the cage until he found a half inch gap between the poles and urinated.

Damn, he thought. What am I going to do when I get some solid food in my stomach? Someway he'd have to widen the hole and dig a pit. But how? Well, no sense in thinking about that until he got some food.

Jeff settled back in the corner of his cage thinking about food and feeling a gnawing in his belly. No, he thought. Got to keep my mind off food. Think of something else, anything but eating. Wonder if Ted and Ken had used the rain to wash? Cool water. Good for crops. Big red ripe tomatoes glistening with droplets of water. Taste so good. No. No. Can't think of food. His mind whirled. Valerie. Yes, that's it. Think of Val.

Valerie. Sweet Valerie. What was she doing? Did she think he was dead? God no! Somehow she'd know. A burning formed in his eyes as he thought of her. She won't give up. She knows I'm alive. But how could she? The Army will tell her I'm dead. She'd have to believe them. Tears slid down his cheeks. Stop it! Stop, his brain screamed. You'll drive yourself crazy. He shook his head trying to clear it, fighting for control. Get hold of yourself. Remember how you met? Remember the good things, his mind commanded. He let his body go limp as he drove his thoughts back to her and their first meeting.

It was a few months before Christmas in '67. He was processing out for his first Vietnam tour. She worked as a clerk in the personal affairs office of headquarters assignment section. He had spent most of the morning processing for his assignment and had been directed to her desk by another clerk. She hadn't bothered to look up from her typewriter as he stood before her desk. He shifted uneasily from foot to foot, waiting for her to notice him. The name plate on her desk read, Mrs. V. Grant.

"Sit down," she said, continuing her typing. "I'll be with you in a moment."

Jeff sat down silently, noting the impersonal tone of her voice. Her fingers were almost a blur on the typewriter keys as she concentrated on her note pad. He studied her smooth pretty features and the glossy sheen of her black hair which fell softly past her cheeks to curl inward at the ends just about her shoulders. She absently brushed a loose strand from her eye and Jeff saw she wore no wedding ring. His eyes swept casually down her soft neck to the firm swell of her breasts under her white sweater as she quit typing and looked up catching his gaze.

"Now, what can I do for you, ah," she paused to look at his stripes and nametag, "Sergeant Spencer?"

"The Corporal, over there," he nodded across the room, "said to stop here before I left. Something about insurance. I'm going to Vietnam in February and . . ."

"Let me see your records," she interrupted him.

Jeff handed her the folder and squirmed uneasily as

101

she opened it and flipped through the pages. He felt uncomfortable. He'd never liked the paper work part of the Army. He was an infantryman and felt more at home in the field than an office. Besides, this efficient woman was not helping matters any with her official attitude. He had always been ill at ease with women especially when they were pretty.

"Yes," she said finally, pointing to a form. "You don't have anyone listed as beneficiary on your servicemen's life insurance. Just give me the names of your parents or wife and I'll add it to the form."

"I don't have a next of kin. My parents are dead and I'm not married. I don't have a brother or sister."

"Oh. I see," her business like tone softened slightly. "Perhaps there's someone else. An uncle or aunt?"

"No," Jeff said flatly, looking directly into her dark brown eyes. "No one. I grew up in an orphanage."

"Well Sergeant. You can list anyone you want or a charitable organization. You really should list something but it's up to you."

"Could I list the orphanage I grew up in?"

"Certainly. Just give me the name and address."

Jeff furnished the information and she quickly typed it on the form. He signed it and rose as she handed him the record folder.

"Drop the folder in the box by the door Sergeant Spencer," she smiled for the first time.

Jeff grinned to himself as he recalled how he had mumbled a hurried thanks and nervously dropped the folder on the floor. He had scooped it up and rushed out of the office only to go about ten feet down the hallway before he realized he still had the folder. He walked back to the office and dropped the folder in the box and

102

saw her grinning at him. He made a hopeless embarrassed shrug and hurried out of the office.

He was sitting in the cafeteria a half hour later reading the newspaper and looked up to see her standing at his table holding a lunch tray.

"May I join you Sergeant Spencer," she asked. "There don't seem to be any tables left."

"Uh, sure," he said, quickly glancing around the packed cafeteria as he nervously half rose out of his chair.

"Thank you. Don't get up," she smiled as he awkwardly folded his paper making room for her tray.

She sat down letting her coat fall off her shoulders and over the back of her chair as she settled in the seat across from him. He thought of asking her if she wanted her coat hung up but decided against it.

"Normally, I try to get here fifteen minutes earlier and beat the crowd but no such luck today," she said taking a bite of her sandwich.

Jeff felt the uneasy flutter in his stomach and glanced around avoiding her eyes.

"You don't come in here much, do you Sergeant? I have lunch here every day and I don't remember seeing you."

"Uh, no," he quickly sipped his coffee and knew she noticed the clatter when he sat the cup back on the saucer. "I, uh, normally eat in the mess hall in our company area. We're pretty busy and it's too far to come up to the main part of the post."

"Mmmm," she nodded.

She had sensed his discomfort and chatted easily as she ate, making small talk about the post, the Army and

103

the weather. He had nodded and agreed, not adding much to the conversation.

"Well," she smiled, looking at her watch. "I've got to get back."

Jeff rose quickly and moved around behind her as she got up. He held her coat smelling the freshness of her hair as she slipped it on.

"Why thank you Sergeant Spencer," she grinned over her shoulder. "Chivalry isn't dead, is it?"

"I, ah . . ." he stammered.

"Goodbye Sergeant Spencer. Thanks for sharing your table," she said and walked away.

"Goodbye Mrs. Grant," he mumbled after her.

It started raining again as darkness settled over the caged prisoners and blackness flooded his hole. Jeff felt the chill settle over his body as he tried to relax his exhausted muscles. He refused to let the despair that tugged at his guts overcome him. Think of Valerie his mind urged. Think of Valerie.

He settled back against the bamboo trying to calm his tense body as he recalled the feeling he had after their first and second meeting. He had wanted to see her again but was uncertain of just how to go about it. He recalled several restless nights as images of her filled his thoughts the rest of that first week. It wasn't until Saturday night of that week that he learned more about her. He was at the Noncommissioned officers club and ran into another Sergeant. A buddy of his who worked at Headquarters, in the office next to hers. She was an Army brat—a term applied to children who grow up on Army posts because their fathers were career men. Her father was retired and living in Florida.

She had been married to an officer but word was she

divorced him over two years ago because he never quit chasing women. She had a small apartment near the post and her own car. His friend said she didn't go out with anyone on the post that he knew of. In fact, she turned down all offers for dates from guys at Headquarters, including one from him.

"She's cold man. Cold," his friend grinned.

So it was Jeff who was nervously standing at her table in the cafeteria the following Monday, asking her if he could join her. She had looked up, smiled and nodded to the empty chair across from her. She didn't seem to be surprised when he started joining her every day that week. They hadn't talked much except for small talk. Jeff was getting over his initial nervousness and by Friday it appeared she expected him to join her. By now, they were on a first name basis and he told her about his early life. She told him about her family but nothing about her marriage except that she was divorced.

During lunch on Friday Jeff had been rehearsing silently to himself how he would ask her out to dinner on Saturday. He was still trying to summon the courage to ask her when she glanced at her watch.

"I've got to get back Jeff."

He nodded dumbly, knowing he wasn't going to be able to ask her. He stood and helped her with her coat feeling a lost sickness in the pit of his stomach as she picked up her handbag to go.

"Jeff, would you like to come over for dinner tonight at my apartment?" she asked suddenly.

He was stunned.

"Uh. Sure," he answered finally.

"Good," she said opening her purse and handing him a slip of paper.

"Here's my address. About seven. Okay?"

"Okay," he grinned, feeling elated. "I'll be there."

And so the courtship had begun. Jeff feeling and acting like a school boy whenever he was around her. He had brought her flowers and candy for that first date and she seemed genuinely pleased by the gifts and the thought. Their relationship blossomed through the next month. He joined her daily for lunch and took her out about twice a week. He couldn't see enough of her but yet he didn't want to push for more dates. His advances were limited to goodnight kisses and those were more the innocent type, than lover.

She was four years older than his twenty-five but she never tried to mother him or play the older woman role. Their friendship developed quickly but Jeff was aware of a certain holding back on her part. At first, it wasn't anything he could pinpoint directly, but as he got to know her better, he sensed the feeling more and more. He felt she was holding back, afraid to let him get too close. He was aware of it but content to let the relationship continue as it was.

It was the week before Christmas and they had returned to her apartment after some shopping. Jeff had insisted on buying a small tree for her and was busily decorating it while she fixed dinner. He finished putting on the last of the ornaments and quietly slipped out to his car and retrieved an armload of gifts which he hurriedly stacked under the tree. He was standing with his back to the kitchen door surveying his work when she entered the room.

"Oh Jeff. It's beautiful!"

He stood grinning sheepishly, as she came up beside him, putting her arm around his waist and looking at the tree. His arm went around her shoulders and he kissed her lightly on the cheek.

"But who are all the gifts for?" she asked, nodding towards the brightly wrapped packages.

"You," he laughed, "but you can't open them until Christmas."

"Jeff, you shouldn't have," she admonished, as she turned to face him. Her eyes twinkled with joy when she looked into his eyes and her arms went around his neck.

"You nut," she said and kissed him quickly on the mouth. His arms pulled her against his body and the kiss developed into a passionate embrace. He felt her body relax against his as her lips parted slightly and her tongue lightly probed his lips. Suddenly she pulled away and he caught a glimpse of passion in her eyes but she dropped her gaze and breathed a deep sigh. Her cheeks were flushed and her mouth was forming an embarrassed smile. She turned and fled into the bedroom.

Jeff stood there, dumbfounded, cursing himself. He started to go after her but uncertainty held him back. After a brief moment she came out holding several wrapped packages in her arms. She smiled and knelt before the tree placing the gifts among the ones already there. She looked up at him and smiled.

"Well, so I'm a nut too."

They had dinner and he helped her with the dishes. Later, they sat on the sofa sipping spiked eggnog with only the lights from the tree illuminating the room. Both had been silent several moments, each lost in their own thoughts, as the radio softly proclaimed joy to the world and peace on earth.

"Jeff," she asked quietly. "Did you volunteer for Vietnam duty?"

"Yes," he said after a pause. "I've been in the Army seven years and war is what it's all about. What I was trained for."

She turned to face him drawing her legs underneath her.

"But you're an instructor here. Don't you think that's important? After all, training men to do their job is . . ."

"What Val? Just an excuse to stay out of Vietnam."

"No Jeff. I mean, somebody has to teach them."

"You're right. But do you know I'm one of the few instructors here that hasn't had a Nam tour. Possibly, I can come back and be a better instructor after I've gained the experience. Besides, the Army's been good to me. I walked out of that orphanage the day I was eighteen and joined the Army three days later. It's been my home. I'm a career soldier and I like it."

"Yes. I know. I guess I'm just being selfish."

"Selfish?"

"Yes. I was . . . I mean, I . . ." she paused searching his face.

"Jeff, I'm fond of you. I hate to see you go over there. I guess I'm afraid for you and . . . I don't know. It's just so hard to say Jeff. I've been alone for two years now. My marriage was a disaster and it hurt me deeply. That's one reason I've avoided dating all this time. My husband, or ex-husband, used me. He really didn't want a wife, but someone to help him get ahead in the Army. He was a swinger and he wanted me to go with other men, even some of his superiors. He made me do things I detested and I finally had a nervous breakdown."

"Val don't."

"No, let me finish," she said, taking a long drink. "I was bitter Jeff. I still am, I guess. I just built up a hatred in myself for men. Then, I met you and there was something about you. I guess the way you acted embarrassed around me. Like a little boy, I suppose. I was flattered and," she smiled, "amused at your innocence and your awkward attempts to be friendly. You were so sweet," she leaned forward and kissed him lightly. "Like now, you're blushing and well I . . . I guess I'm more than fond of you. I've fallen in love with you."

"Val, I ah . . ." he searched for the right words. "I've never had a girlfriend and I guess I really don't know what love is. I mean . . . I know how I feel about you. I want to be with you all the time. When I'm around you, I feel happy and relaxed and when I'm not with you, I feel lousy and can't wait till I see you again. I've never been with a woman before. I mean like in bed except for . . ."

"Hush," she whispered placing her fingertips on his lips. "I don't want to know."

"But I want you to know Val. I've read a lot of books and I know there is more to love than sex. I've had the rutting, sweaty sex with whores. What I want is the tender loving touches and the warm feeling laying next to a woman that really cares for me. I want children and a home for them."

"Oh, Jeff darling," she whispered softly, holding his face between her hands and pulling his lips to hers. They slipped into a tight embrace as her mouth covered his. Her tongue forced his lips open as they clung tightly to each other. They parted breathlessly. Thin streaks of tears dampened her cheeks and she looked deeply into his eyes.

"I love you," she whispered. "I love you."

He kissed the corners of her eyes and buried his face in her neck smelling the sweet fragrance of her.

"I love you too Val. So very much. You've made me the happiest man in the world."

He recalled how they sat there in the dim light holding and kissing each other. Necking like a couple of teenagers. She placed his hand on her heart so he could feel it thumping deep in her chest. He had hesitantly moved it to cup her breast and she moaned softly as she kissed his face tenderly.

After a few moments she got up and led him into the bedroom and they wordlessly undressed each other between kisses. He had marveled at her flawless body. Her smooth white skin contrasted by the darkness of her hair. Her firm breasts tipped with small hard nipples crushed against his muscled chest as she pulled his body down next to her on the bed. She lay on her back and spread her legs slightly. Her hand placed his fingers in the tight curls of her mound. She smiled up at him and snaked her other hand down to touch his erection.

"Be gentle darling," she whispered. "Be gentle."

Chapter Eleven

Ken Mayhew woke to the sound of dripping water. It was raining again. His stomach felt like it was on fire. He tried to remember when he had eaten something but couldn't. His leg hurt so much his only relief was sleep. He did remember during one of the rainstorms he had drunk rain water until he made himself sick.

He could see it was daylight now but he had no idea what time of the day it was. The cloudy sky and the trees covering the village blocked out most of the light anyway. It was hard to tell if it was noon or dusk. He wondered about Hef and Sarge. It was only because of them he was still alive. He wished he could talk to one of them.

He shifted around trying to get into a more comfortable position. There was an inch of water in the bottom of the cage and he prayed the Vietnamese would realize the water wasn't draining off. His entire body ached from sleeping on the hard bamboo. He examined his bandaged leg. The bandage was gray from dirt and filth but he was glad there weren't any bloodstains. At least the bleeding had stopped. The leg had swollen causing the bandage to pull tight around his thigh. He wondered if he should loosen it but decided against it. The wound seemed to throb with every heartbeat and the pain never stopped.

God, he thought, how long were they going to keep us like this? If they didn't get any food they'd die in a couple of days. Maybe that's what the VC wanted. To starve them to death. How long could a person live on only water? Wasn't it twenty-two or twenty-three days. Yeah, maybe for a person in top physical condition. But him, how long for him?

He felt a sudden craving for a cigarette. Man, he thought, I must have two cartons in my footlocker. And candy. Yeah man, there were some candy bars in there also. What else, his mind rambled? Some C's. Yeah, C-rations. The fruit cocktail or peaches he always kept. The fruit, peanut butter, and cheese packs for snacking later. C-rations. Damn, he never thought the time would come when he wished for C's. Even the Ham 'n Egg packet would go good now, and that looked like someone had eaten it and thrown it up in the can.

He cupped his hands under the dripping water until he had a handfull and sipped it slowly. He wondered if he should try to wash himself. What's the use, he thought disgustedly. I'm sitting here in an inch of water mixed with my own vomit and piss worrying about being clean. He splashed the next two handfuls of water in his face anyway.

The rain stopped and so did the dribble into his cage.

Now the sun would bake the earth and everything would be dry in ten minutes. In another hour or two it would rain again. In the meantime the temperature and humidity would go sky high. There was no way the air could circulate in the cage so he figured the temperature in it would be at least ten degrees higher than the outside temperature. That, and the odor of the latrine pit, plus the stench of his body and the muck in the cage would be unbearable. Damn, he thought. Why don't they let us out? Just a few minutes outside of this hell hole.

Ken moved around trying to find a position where his legs wouldn't hurt so much. He wedged himself against the back of the cage with his leg elevated about ten inches above the water. He put pressure on his foot to prop it against the side of the cage and it hurt like hell for a few moments then the pain seemed to subside. Not completely, but at least in intensity.

The temperature rose steadily and he started to sweat. The foul air in the cage seemed like a weight he could feel over his entire body. His mind drifted to meaningless thoughts for awhile then settled on home. What were they doing now, he wondered? His parents? Dina? Did they think he was dead? What had the Army told them? A hundred questions ran through his head.

How long had it been since he'd seen his parents? Over two years at least. Ken was the only child. His parents were in their forties when they married. His mother had such a hard time during his birth because of her age that the doctor advised against any more children. Ken had always felt their age difference caused a gap between them, especially in his teen years. He had struggled to get through his senior year in high school. After graduation the old man gave Ken a pep talk about his patriotic duty to his country. Since college was out of the question because of Ken's poor grade levels and lack of money, why not join one of the services? After all, his father said, he had been drafted during the big war and it had done him a world of good. He was proud to fight for his country and he couldn't understand why all these young kids were not willing to go do their duty. Yeah, Ken remembered the stories. His father had enlisted in the Navy and spent the entire war on an anti-submarine net tender guarding the bay to Portsmouth. The only time he was even more than sixty miles from home was during boot camp at Great Lakes Naval training center. However, to hear him tell it, they fought daily battles with German U-boats. So Ken promised he would join but he wanted to spend the summer on the beaches before he was off to beautiful Vietnam. That kept the old man off his back for the rest of the summer. His Dad even called his brother to get Ken a job. So Ken went to work for his uncle George. He owned a combination general store and bait shop with a couple of gas pumps on Route One, just south of Rye, New Hampshire. They did a terrific business during the summer, being right on the beach.

Uncle George was a confirmed bachelor and lived in a three room apartment in the back of the store. Ken bunked on the living room couch that made into the bed and worked his ass off from sunrise to sunset for two dollars an hour, but his uncle only paid him for eight hours a day. The other hours, his uncle contended, would cover Ken's room and board. Ken didn't argue that he was working for less than minimum wage because he felt the benefit of living on the beach was worth the difference. He met a lot of chicks at the store and would sneak off to the beach parties at night.

It was just after Labor Day weekend that Ken's mom called to tell him he had gotten his draft notice and was to report to the induction center in two weeks. Ken hadn't spent any money all summer; he had saved his entire salary. He cut for Canada with fifteen hundred dollars of his own money and another eight hundred dollars he stole from his uncle's cash box hidden in the bedroom closet. He had gotten as far as Old Orchard Beach, Maine when he realized he didn't have a birth certificate and couldn't cross the Canadian border. He decided to head for Boston and loose himself in the young college population.

Ken had no trouble getting along in Boston. He merged into the student crowd, made several connections and was soon pushing marijuana and pills to an eager clientel. He had a small two room apartment off Washington Street and that's where he met Dina. Her apartment was next to his and he'd seen her coming and going several times. She was always with a guy, so Ken never made any advances toward her.

He came home late one night and when he got to his landing, he noticed the door to Dina's apartment was partially open. As he turned the key in his door he heard a moan coming from her apartment, so he stepped to her door and listened. A light was on in the room but he couldn't see anyone through the small opening. He looked at his watch and it was a little after three in the morning. He heard the moan again and decided to knock on her door.

"Miss. Are you alright?"

No response.

"Miss," he knocked lightly again causing the door to open more.

He peeked around the door into the room. It was a mess. Clothing was thrown everywhere. The drawers in the dresser were all pulled out and what little furniture there was in the room had been knocked over or pushed aside. He heard her moan again and stepped into the room. She was lying on her stomach on the far side of the bed near the small bathroom. She was partially hidden by the bed and he hadn't seen her at first. He knelt beside her laying his hand on her bare back so he could feel her breathing. She was naked except for a pair of black panties.

"Miss," he shook her gently. "What's wrong?" Are you sick?"

"Ohhh," she moaned again and raised her head slightly to look at him. She brushed her long hair away from her face and Ken saw she had been beaten.

"Who . . ." she groaned. "Who are you?"

She was bleeding from the corner of her mouth and her bottom lip was starting to swell. Her right eye was puffy with a red welt and she had a small cut on the bridge of her nose.

"You need a doctor," he said.

"No, no doctor," she groaned. "Help . . . Help me sit on the bed. I'll be all right after I get my breath."

Ken reached her under the arms and lifted until she was sitting on the edge of the bed. She leaned forward with her arms resting on her legs cradling her head in her hands.

"Why don't you lay down Miss and I'll call an ambulance. You need . . ."

116

"No!" she snapped. I don't need anyone. Who are you anyway? What are you doing here?"

"I'm your neighbor. I was coming home and I heard you moaning like you were hurt. Your door was open and I . . ."

"The kid from next door?" she asked, looking up at him. "Oh yeah." She recognized him. "The kid from next door."

"Well, I was only trying to help," he retorted, offended by her calling him a kid. She was probably only a couple of years older than him. "I thought you needed help."

"Hey look," she gestured with her hand. "Thanks. I mean it. I feel like I've been hit by a truck. Would you wet a towel in the bathroom and hand it to me?"

"Yeah. Sure," Ken said, going into the bathroom. It was a mess. The medicine cabinet was torn apart and bottles of stuff were all over the floor. The lid of the toilet tank lay broken on the floor and clothes and towels were thrown everywhere. He found a reasonably clean towel and dampened it in the wash basin. He walked out of the bathroom and handed it to her. Standing uneasily in front of her as she wiped her face.

"Are you sure you don't want me to call an ambulance, the police, or somebody, maybe a friend?"

"No. I'll be alright," she looked up at him again. "Say, what's your name?"

"Ah, Ken. Ken Mayhew."

"Kenny huh? Well thanks again Kenny. I'll be okay now," she wiped her naked chest absently and winced as she touched one of the red blotches that spread over her bare breasts.

"Damn that son of a bitch," she said and got up

117

rather unsteadily brushing past him into the bathroom to inspect herself in the mirror. He watched her finger the bruises on her breasts and shoulders, not caring that he stood there and watched her. She touched the corner of her mouth and eye.

"That dirty bastard," she muttered again. "I won't be able to work for a week."

Ken felt it was time to leave and moved toward the door. The way she was standing there touching herself was getting to him. He stopped at the door and looked back.

"If you need anything miss just knock on my door."

"Yeah. Okay Kenny," she said, not bothering to look at him.

Ken went out closing the door after him and let himself into his apartment. Man, she was weird.

He wasn't in his apartment five minutes when a knock sounded on the door. He opened it to find her standing there. She had pulled on a man's white shirt which she left unbuttoned and Ken could clearly see her only other article of clothing was her panties.

"Hey look," she said. "I'm sorry, really, I want to thank you for helping me. You know most people wouldn't want to get involved . . ."

"Hey, don't worry about it."

"No, really. Thanks. Uh, do you have a drink or something? My head feels like it's coming apart. You alone?"

"Yeah." Ken smiled stepping back from the door. "Come on in. I've got some rum if that's okay?"

"Sure. Do you have any Coke?" she asked, walking by him as he closed the door.

"Yes. I think so. Have a seat." Ted indicated the

118

worn out couch and went into the kitchenette. He mixed two drinks.

"Do you think he'll come back?" Ken asked.

"Who?"

"The guy that did that to you."

"Oh. That bastard. God, I hope not but I wouldn't put it past him."

"What'd he want?" Ken said, coming back into the room and handing her the drink. He sat on the edge of the bed facing her. She took a long drink draining almost half the glass.

"I don't know." she shrugged. "Money probably or my stash. He's a junkie."

"Stash?"

"Yeah. You know, drugs or pot. He needed a fix. So he was looking for money to buy a fix or something to pop 'til he could get a fix. The creep took my jewelry and TV."

"That's too bad. Why not call the cops?"

"No fuzz," she drained the glass. "I don't need them crawling around my apartment. How about another one?" she handed him the empty glass.

"But you know who he is don't you?" Ken asked taking the glass and going back to the kitchen.

"Christ yes. I've been living with him for almost a year. He was a nice guy before he got strung out. I've been supporting his habit for a couple of months now and a couple of days ago I threw him out. I guess he came back tonight because he was desperate. When I wouldn't come across he just blew his cool. I thought he was going to kill me."

Ken handed her the drink and sat down facing her again. She pulled her legs up under her on the couch

119

and sipped her drink slowly this time. Her shirt had fallen open revealing the swell of her left breast and she leaned back closing her eyes.

"If I never see that fucker again it will be too soon," she said in after thought.

Ken leaned back on his side eyeing the smoothness of her skin and her long silky hair. She must have brushed it before coming over because it had a sheen in the light of the room. Even in her disarray she was attractive. He could see some of the bruises on her chest and they were turning darker. He got up and went back into the kitchen. He found a clean dish towel and wrapped some ice cubes in it. Returning to the bed he sat down.

"Here," he held out the towel to her. "It might help the swelling go down on your eye and lip. By the way, what's your name?"

"Huh," she said, opening her eyes with a startle. She looked at the wrapped towel in his hand. "What's that?"

"An ice pack."

"Oh. Thanks," she leaned forward and took it placing it against the side of her face covering both the eye and lip. Her shirt parted even more revealing the globe of her left breast. She didn't bother to cover herself and Ken felt a throb of desire as he looked at the firm mound tipped by a pink nipple. She settled back again and sipped her drink.

"Ah. What's your name?" Ken asked again, forcing his eyes away from her exposed chest and looking to her face.

"Dina. Dina Delight," she waited for a reaction and laughed at the look on his face. However, she cut it short and cringed, touching her fingers to the middle of her chest. "Wow, that hurts."

"Really," he asked, watching her fingers absently touch the bruises. "It's not really Dina Delight is it?"

"Well, that's my stage name," she said defensively. "My real name is Dianne McWilliams but even my family called me Dina. You said your name was Kenny?"

"Yeah, Ken."

"Ohhh. You don't like Kenny."

"No. Not really. Are you an actress?"

"I'm gonna be. Right now I'm a dancer but I'm studying drama two nights a week and in a couple of months my drama coach said I'll be ready."

"Are you dancing now? I mean dancing here with a show. A musical or something?"

"Well, I'm working right now at the Starlight lounge in the combat zone. You know it?"

"Yeah. It's a topless joint ain't it?"

"Yeah but it's a class place. Marty, the owner, he's the one that suggested my stage name. He used to be a Hollywood agent and he still has plenty of contacts. He said he'd fix me up with an agent on the west coast when I was ready. He's seen plenty of talent and he said I've got what it takes. So, as soon as I finish drama classes and save a little money, I'm off for Hollywood."

"Well, I wish you a lot of luck. I'd, ah, like to see you dance sometime.

"Hmmm," she smiled coyly over the rim of her glass. "I bet you would. Come into the club sometime but not for a week or so. I won't be doing any dancing with these bruises. Damn, that son of a bitch did a job on me. Just look at this," and she pulled open her shirt exposing both her breasts. They were large and full, set

121

high on her chest. She sucked in her breath sort of aiming them at him. He could see her ribs and her smooth concave stomach as it curved to her small waist. She ran her fingers lightly over each mound causing it to jiggle slightly. Then she half-heartedly closed her shirt and settled back against the couch.

"Don't you have to worry about getting cancer?" Ken asked dumbly. "I mean, I always heard that women were really sensitive there and if they got hit on their, ah, bosom, they could get it."

"Bosom!" she laughed. "Bosom! God Ken, where'd you grow up? In a convent? Honey, they're tits. See," she threw open her shirt thrusting them at him. "Tits! Boobs, even breasts for christsakes, but never bosom."

Ken felt his face turn red. He squirmed uneasily and hastily took a gulp of his drink as she taunted him with her breasts.

"I, ah, ah . . ." he stammered.

"My god," she grinned. "You're actually blushing. Wow, now I've seen it all. Just how old are you Kenny?"

"I'm twenty," he shouted getting off the bed and hurring into the bathroom closing the door behind him. He turned on the water in the wash bowl and splashed cold water on his face hoping she hadn't noticed the bulge in his pants. Damn, he thought, why'd he have to make a fool of himself. He shouldn't have shouted at her. He looked at his face in the mirror. It was still red. He took a couple of deep breaths and splashed some more water on his face. Could he help it if he was still a virgin? He wiped his face with a towel and flushed the toilet as he tried to slow his breathing. Finally, after a few moments he opened the door and found her sitting back on the couch. Her shirt was closed and she grinned up at him.

"Boy, are you touchy," she said. "Anyway, I'm sorry. Truce? How about another drink?"

"Okay," he smiled. "Truce."

He took her glass and went back to the kitchen. His hands shook a little as he mixed the drinks.

"Ken," she called after him.

"Yeah?"

"Do you think I could stay here tonight? That nut might come back and I've had all of him I can take. You've got a big double bed and I promise I won't take advantage of you. Okay?"

"I guess so," he said, coming back into the room, handing her the drink. "How do you know I won't take advantage of you?"

"Sir," she lapsed into a southern belle drawl. "A fine southern gentleman like you, I do declare."

"Hey," he grinned, sitting down. "That's pretty good."

"Good," she said, her voice back to normal. "I wouldn't want to think I've been wasting all that money on acting classes."

"No. It was really good. I bet you're going to be a super actress."

"I hope so," she held up her glass. "Let's toast to it and you can be my number one fan."

"All right," he touched her glass with his and they sipped the drinks.

"Do you need anything from next door Dina. I could get it."

"No, I don't think so unless . . ."

"What," he asked eagerly.

123

"Well, I would like to soak in the tub. Maybe it would help these bruises."

"Sure. What do you need?"

"Okay. Get my blue robe from the back of the bathroom door and if you can find it in that mess, there should be a big bottle of pink bath oil. Oh yeah, my purse, and also in the bathroom, a tan cosmetic bag. Okay?"

"Right. Is your door unlocked?" he asked going to the door.

"Yeah. Just turn out the lights and lock the door when you come out."

It took Ken about five minutes to find everything and return to his place. He closed and locked his door and heard water running in the tub. She was bending over the tub as Ken walked into the bathroom and set her things on the toilet lid. She still wore the shirt and panties and Ken glanced appreciatively at her rump as he backed out of the bathroom closing the door with regret.

"I think I found everything."

"Good," she said straightening up. "Don't close the door, I want to talk to you. You can sit in here if you like."

"Naw," Ken said, embarrassed again but pushing the door open. "I'll sit here on the edge of the bed."

"Suit yourself," she said, pouring the bath oil in the tub. Ken could see pink bubbles foam immediately in the water. He sat down on the bed as she recapped the bottle and grinned over shoulder at him. She shrugged the shirt from her shoulders and slid her panties down her long tapered legs. She bent over and tested the water with her hand, swirling around the bubbles. Ken's heart was thumping as he stared at her swinging breasts and the dark crease of her buttocks. She looked sideways at him and grinned, then slipped into the tub lowering herself until just her neck and head were visible above the suds.

Ken propped two pillows behind him and lay back on the bed. He reached under the bed rail and pulled out a small pouch he kept some joints in. He lit one up, pulled the acrid smoke deep in his lungs holding his breath as long as possible then released it slowly.

"Hey," Dina called out. "What'd ya doing?"

"Nothing. Just relaxing."

"Tell me about yourself. You a student?"

"No."

"Well what then?"

Ken told her about himself. His parents, school and finally working for his uncle. Then, how after receiving his draft notice he cut out for Canada but how he only got as far as Boston. Somehow he trusted her and told her everything. He lit another joint and asked her if she wanted some. When she said yes, he went into the bathroom and sat on the edge of the tub holding the roach to her lips. She had wrapped a towel around her head and it made her look older. Sexier, he thought. Her body was hidden completely by foam.

"Mmm," she exhaled. "That's some pretty good shit."

"I deal only in the best. These rich kids pay good but they want top stuff. I give them a good hit for their money and they're always back for more. I figure why blow a good thing by trying to cut it. I'm satisfied with the profit margin."

"Good thinking. Now," she stood up. "I'm about soaked through. You wanna dry my back?"

"Not just your back," Ken answered, looking at the puffs of suds clinging to her body.

"All right then." She lifted her leg, placing her foot on the rim of the tub so her crotch was level with his eyes. "Get to it."

The next day she moved in with Ken. At the end of the month they found a different apartment. Dina continued her dancing and still went to drama classes two nights a week. It was not hard for Ken to fall in love with her. She taught him how to love a woman and he was an eager student. They were both satisfied with the arrangement for a few months, then Ken started to pressure her about getting married. She kept turning him down because of her career. Besides, she always said, what more could they have by being married? So Ken would drop the subject for a week or so before bringing it up again. He was becoming more possessive and jealous. It was his jealousy that got him busted. He was so concerned about Dina he got careless and sold a couple bags to a Narc. Ken thought he was finished but it turned out the Narc wanted Ken's supplier. He gave Ken a couple of days to set up a buy. Ken knew if he set up his supplier for the cops he'd have to get out of Boston. The supplier was connected to a very powerful family and Ken couldn't stand that kind of heat.

It was Dina that came up with the solution. He had no choice with the cops, he had to make the set up. They would get married and Ken could join the Army. After all, where's a better place to hide from the mob than in the Army. A recruiter ought to be able to square it with the draft board and she would quit work and live

126

on her allotment check and what money he could send her. The idea of her quitting dancing appealed to Ken more then anything, especially since she would marry him. He could be away but he didn't have to worry about her being ogled in that cheap joint every night.

So everybody was set up including Ken. He joined the Army and was off to boot camp before he knew it. Dina wrote him exactly three times in the four months it took for basic and advanced infantry training and then it was to complain that her allotment check was late or hadn't arrived.

Ken received orders for Vietnam and ten days leave. The leave was spent with Dina, arguing because she hadn't quit her job. As a matter of fact, Ken was suspicious that she had been living with someone else while he was gone. Ken's blind love made him believe her promises and he was off to Vietnam for better or for worse.

Chapter Twelve

The rain water was almost a foot deep in the bottom of the cage. Jeff's greatest fear was he'd drown during his sleep. The horrible stench was almost unbearable.

He had used his fingernail to mark the days on one of the poles near the top of the cage. He ran his fingertips over the tiny notches counting eight of them. Now, time seemed to blend together and he wasn't sure when he'd last made a mark. With the darkness of the forest and the unevenness of his conscious moments he just wasn't sure any more.

He knew he was growing weaker due to lack of food. His captors hadn't given him anything to eat since he'd been in the cage. He assumed Ted and Ken were in the same condition. How long could he make it? And Ken? What about Ken? He was wounded the worst. Lack of nourishment would have the greatest effect on him. Jeff wasn't even sure Ken was still alive, or Ted for that matter. They hadn't had any contact since they'd been thrown into the cages. He'd thought he heard one of them cry out sometime in the past few hours but he wasn't sure. He may have been dreaming.

Jeff felt a wave of despair sweep over him as he sloshed around in the water. He managed to get to his feet, standing in a crouch because of the smallness of the cage. His body ached to stand upright and stretch his arms above his head. He rubbed his chest and arms. A gray scum covered his body; his skin was wrinkled and clammy. Sores were forming in his crotch and on his buttocks. He searched to find a handhold on the top of the cage to hold himself up but the poles were too smooth and offered no grip. He forced himself into a semi-erect position by planting his heels against the floor poles and locking his knees allowing his back to rest on the side of the cage. He was out of the water except for his feet and lower legs. He strained to lock the lower half of his body and let the upper half relax. After a few moments his legs started quivering and his thigh muscles involuntarily released, dropping him back into the water. He sat there numb as his whole body trembled. A hopelessness overwhelmed him, tears slid down his cheeks and sobs racked his body.

Damn them! Damn them, his mind screamed trying to form the words in his mouth. He panted and made a high pitched utterance that made no sense at all as he crouched in a corner. His breath came in gulps as he stared blankly ahead. He fought to control his breathing. He sucked in several deep breaths and slowly calmed himself.

"I'll make it you bastards," he whispered. "I'll make it. I'll make it . . ."

129

Jeff was awakened by the sound of the securing pole being removed from the top of the cage. He heard Vietnamese voices above him. This was the first time anyone had approached him since he'd been confined.

The top was slowly lifted away and even though the light wasn't strong, it overwhelmed him. He blinked several times as a Vietnamese face looked down on him then turned and walked away. He heard the top of the cage being tossed aside as he peered up toward the trees.

Jeff sat there perplexed. No one appeared and after a few moments he struggled to stand. He managed to grip the top edge of the cage and pull himself upright. He groaned, his muscles rejecting his movements, but somehow he managed to stand, his head and shoulders extended out of the cage. He rested his right arm on the ground outside the cage and looked around.

It must have been late afternoon. The light seemed to be fading into dusk. Jeff's eye caught the form of a VC guard sitting against a tree about twenty feet from him. He was armed with a rifle that rested casually in his lap and was watching Jeff, seemingly unconcerned. The guard didn't speak or make any movement and Jeff wasn't sure what was expected of him. Was it a trap? Would the guard shoot him if he tried to crawl out of the cage. Jeff doubted it. If the VC wanted them dead they could just leave them in the cages. It must be they were letting them out. They wouldn't help them out but they wouldn't keep the prisoners from getting out. It was just another example of the strange way the Asian mind worked.

Jeff looked towards the back of the camp. Several cooking fires were lit and the activity seemed normal.

Both VC and NVA regulars were moving about but no one seemed to be paying any attention to him. Soldiers were coming and going from the main buildings and he could see only one motorized vehicle in the entire camp, a small truck parked near the command building. The main force must have moved out because the large stacks of supplies were gone.

Jeff gazed back at his guard, then looked to the two adjoining cage pits. Their tops had also been removed and cast aside. There was no sign of life from either cage. Panic swept Jeff.

"Hef?" Jeff said in almost a whisper. His voice hoarse. He cleared his throat and quickly glanced at the guard, no reaction.

"Hef," he called slightly louder. "Can you hear me? Ken, can you hear me? Hef?" he tried again.

Jeff heard a movement in the cage next to him. A hand reached out and grasped the top of the cage. Slowly Ted Hefley's head came into view.

"Sarge?" he asked in a low voice. "Is that you Sarge?"

Jeff felt a surge of relief to see and hear the young soldier. Hef's face was pale as he pulled himself to eye level with Jeff. A thin smile creased his face and Jeff could see the relief in his eyes.

"Sarge," he repeated. "I, uh, thought, you were dead."

"I'm okay. I'm okay."

Ted looked around and immediately saw the guard. He hadn't changed his position.

"Are they letting us out Sarge?"

"I don't know. It looks like they want us to make up

our own minds. Can you hear anything from Ken's pit?''

Ted shook his head negative and moved to the other side of his cage closer to Mayhew's pit.

''Ken,'' he called quietly. ''Ken? Answer me? It's Hef. Ken?''

Ted looked over his shoulder at Jeff and shook his head again.

''Okay. Listen Ted. I'm going to get out of this pit. Don't you try it until you see how the guard is going to react to me. Understand?''

Ted nodded.

''Okay. Here goes.''

Jeff braced himself with his good arm. He knew he couldn't put any pressure on his bad shoulder. He took a deep breath and lunged upward. He flopped on his chest pinning his good arm under him. He was half out of the pit. Pain shot through his shoulder and lower stomach where the rough edges of the poles were digging into his skin. He paused momentarily and gritted his teeth for the next move. With all his strength he pushed with his good arm, swinging his legs upward and rolled out of the pit onto his back. A wave of blackness swarmed over him and he fought to maintain consciousness. He closed his eyes and took several deep breaths, forcing his body to relax. When his breathing calmed he opened his eyes. The VC guard was standing over him with the muzzle of the rifle pointing at his chest. The guard leaned over, touching the barrel to the hollow in Jeff's throat then agonizingly trailed it lightly up his chin to his mouth, until it brushed his lips. Their eyes locked for a moment, then the guard laughed. He laughed in an irritating high pitched thin voice, then turned and walked back to the tree and resumed his sitting position, still laughing.

"God, Sarge! Man, I thought he was going to blow your shit away."

"Whew," Jeff let his breath out. His body was trembling. He could taste the oil from the barrel of the rifle on his lips. He turned his head and looked at Ted. "Can you get out by yourself Hef?"

"I don't think so Sarge. I can't put any pressure on my burned side."

"Okay. Don't try. I'll help you in a minute. Just let me get my head together."

Ted nodded.

Slowly, Jeff eased himself on his hands and knees and crawled the couple of feet to Ted's pit. He pushed with his good arm until he was in a sitting position with his feet hanging into Ted's cage.

"All right Ted, grab my arm and push with your legs. We'll get you halfway out so you're resting on your chest, then slowly pull you all the way out okay?"

"Yeah," he answered. "Say when."

"Now," Jeff felt Ted grip his arm and he drew a deep breath and leaned back pulling with all his weight. The strain of Ted's weight spread across Jeff's back tugging the muscles of his wounded shoulder causing him to cry out. He felt Ted slipping and gripped him under the arm, throwing his upper body back. Ted moaned in pain as he was yanked half out of the cage. They both lay there exhausted trying to catch their breath. After a few moments Jeff sat upright and reached down, getting a grip on Ted's leg he pulled as the young soldier pushed with his arms and agonizingly inched out of the pit.

Ted rolled over on his back, looking up at Jeff, a weak grin creasing his face.

"Man," Jeff said. "You look like shit."

Ted's body was in much the same condition as Jeff's. The skin was gray and scummy except for the burned area on his side. It was red with puffy blisters, some of them broken and festering. Thin scratches down the front of his chest and thighs were starting to bleed where he had dragged himself over the rough edges of the cage.

"What are they going to do with us now Sarge?"

"I don't know. We couldn't have lasted much longer in the cages. I know one thing though. We've got to get Mayhew out. Can you move now?"

"Yeah, I think so."

Jeff looked at the guard. He was still sitting there seemingly unconcerned. The rest of the encampment appeared to be going about their normal routine equally unconcerned.

They crawled around Ted's pit and reached Mayhew's cage. The evening light was fading but they could see Mayhew slouched in the corner of the cage. He appeared to be unconscious and Jeff felt relieved when he saw the rise and fall of Ken's chest.

"He's still alive Ted. He's breathing. One of us is going to have to go in and get him and I don't think I can."

"Okay Sarge, I'll get him but let me rest a few minutes."

It took the two of them a quarter of an hour to get Ken out of the cage. He was unconscious and offered no help. It was a struggle for Ted just to get Ken into a position where Jeff could get a hold of him. They

134

finally had him laying on his back between them next to the pit.

"He looks bad Sarge."

"Yeah. I know and he's got a hell of a fever. I'm pretty sure his leg is infected. Man, look at it!"

Ken must have torn the bandage from his wound. His entire thigh was swollen, the wound itself was a dark blotch oozing pus from both bullet holes. There didn't seem to be any bleeding. Jeff could see the wound was dangerously infected and would get worse. He was sure if it wasn't treated Ken would lose the leg.

Nightfall was slowly settling over the compound. Jeff watched the soldiers moving about apparently indifferently to the Americans. Several of the village woman squatted before cooking fires serving small groups of soldiers. The situation here was not uncommon along the borders of Vietnam. The proximity of this small Laotian village had little bearing on the overall politics of Laos. The villagers were probably just as much Vietnamese as they were Laotian. The men could have been taken to fight for the VC or the Pathe-Laos. However, it seemed at the present time the VC were in control of this area and would remain so long as North Vietnam was using it as part of their line of communication and supplies.

Jeff watched a VC approach their guard. He spoke a few words and gestured toward the prisoners. The guards got up and walked toward them with the VC. Jeff watched their rifles and noticed they were being carried loosely, not menacingly. The guard stopped a few feet from them but the VC approached and squatted within arms reach of Jeff. He cradled his rifle across his thighs pointing it away from them.

He was young, maybe in his mid-teens. He wore the

135

familiar black pajamas but he had leather sandals not the cheap rubber type of makeshift ones usually worn by VC. He smiled at Jeff.

"How you doing GI?"

Jeff was taken aback by the English. This kid had spent some time around the Americans.

"No good," Jeff said. "Very bad."

"Yeah," the kid kept smiling. "I see. You and friends look like number ten."

It was common for the Vietnamese to grade a thing or situation. Something extremely good was a number one while something extremely bad was number ten.

"What's going to happen to us," Jeff asked? "Why have we been let out of the cages?"

"Oh you see soon. Boss man know I speak English. He say come get you and friends. I take you to hooch. Most soldiers are gone and there is plenty hooch now. You get clothes and food and drink tea. You not have to stay in number ten water cage. Come now, I show you."

The young VC stood and gestured for them to follow. Jeff and Ted struggled to get Ken upright and positioned between them. He was completely dead weight so their progress was slow. They half dragged him following the VC towards the back of the camp. Off to the left were a row of huts constructed with a bamboo frame, elephant grass, and broad flat leaves. They seemed to be vacant and the VC stopped before the opening of the first one and pointed inside.

"Here," the VC said. "You like new hooch. Very dry. You stay inside and not come until VC soldier say. Okay GI?"

136

"Okay," Jeff answered, "but my friend needs doctor and medicine. He will die if he doesn't get help."

"Okay GI. I talk to boss man. No sweat."

The guard remained outside the hut as the young VC walked off. Jeff helped Ted pull Ken into the hut. They managed to drag him to the center of the hut laying him on his back. It was almost pitch black inside. Jeff crawled around and found several rice mats probably discarded by the previous tenants. He scuttled back to Ted and placed two mats on the dirt floor next to Ken. They eased him onto the mats then spread two more mats for themselves on each side of Ken. They lay down next to Ken without a word, exhausted from the short walk across the compound. The lack of food had weakened them alarmingly over the days.

Jeff lay on his back staring at the ceiling. His eyes growing accustomed to the darkness. He could make out the structure of the hut. It was typical of these small villages. A bamboo frame about ten foot square with a peaked roof. Woven sheets of rice stalks or elephant grass mats were tied over the frame and a layer of banana leaves placed on the roof. Four or five VC or NVA had probably shared this one. They would sleep on floor mats or hammocks stretched between the poles. It was a hut pure and simple, not a hooch as the VC had said, although, he probably didn't know the difference.

A hooch was a term the GI's used for their barracks at a base camp. It normally was a wood framed structure on a cement slab with wooden sides coming up about four feet and screening continuing to the ceiling. The roof was corragated tin. They varied in size, housing from ten to thirty men. A ten man squad tent placed over a wooded frame and floor also was called a hooch.

At a fire support base a sandbag structure was built using any materials available for a frame, such as ammo cans and boxes, or crating. It was built over a large foxhole and held two or three men.

Jeff heard voices outside the hut. Someone entered holding a kerosene lamp before him. The light hurt his eyes and he sat up shielding his eyes trying to see past the lamp.

"Hey GI's," came the young VC's voice. "I bring you food and lady doctor." He moved into the hut and to the left wall. He was carrying two coffee size cans and a bundle which he placed next to the wall at his feet.

"Come here GI's. Eat, drink, let lady doctor look at friend."

Jeff saw a woman standing in the doorway evidently waiting for them to move away from Ken. Probably a nurse but he wasn't going to argue with the VC. He and Ted crawled weakly to the wall near the VC and sat quietly waiting for the next command. The nurse entered the hut taking the lamp from the VC and knelt next to Ken. She placed a small canvas medic bag on the floor and examined Ken's thigh.

"Here," the VC said squatting down and holding out one of the cans to Jeff. "Drink. Very good tea."

Jeff held the can to his lips and sipped a warm bitter tea as the VC handed the other to Ted.

"Eat," he directed Ted. "It is rice cooked with fish water. Good for you."

Jeff watched Ted gingerly scoop some of the rice paste with his fingers and put it in his mouth. He made a wry face as he chewed it slowly and swallowed. Jeff took another sip of tea and traded cans with Ted. He poked some rice into his mouth and fought to keep from gagging. The mushy rice had a strong fish taste but Jeff chewed and swallowed. He knew their bodies had to have some nourishment. He and Ted continued to eat and drink slowly as they watched the nurse.

She turned and called to someone outside and within a minute another VC entered with a bucket and a handful of rags. The nurse took the rags and dipped them in the bucket. Jeff saw it was filled with water as she wrung out the rag and wiped Ken's wound. The other VC left and the nurse worked quietly on Ken. She cleaned the wound then poured some kind of solution on it from a bottle she removed from the bag.

Jeff noticed the bag was a U.S. Army issue medic bag, probably the one taken from his team. She dabbed the wound dry and sprinkled it with sulfa, finally bandaging it with issued dressings. She felt his forehead and spoke to the VC without looking up. The VC took the can of tea from Ted and handed it to her. Jeff watched her take a pill from the bag and place it in Ken's mouth. She held his mouth open and forced some tea into him. Ken moaned slightly and swallowed involuntarily, coughing a few times. She waited and slowly gave him some more tea until she was satisfied he had taken the pill. She spoke to the VC pointing at Ted.

"You go lay down," he motioned to Ted. "She look at burns."

Ted crawled back to his mat resting on his back before her. She washed lightly over the burned area until it was relatively clean. Jeff could see Ted grimace even with her light strokes. She applied some clear gel from a tube smearing it over the area. Satisfied, she motioned Jeff to his mat. He moved, taking a sitting

139

position next to Ken and she moved around to him. Her fingers gently probed his swollen shoulder. He winced a couple of times as she pressed against the collar bone. She made a sling with a large bandage and slipped it over his head guiding his arm into it. She stood up, picking up her medical bag in one motion. She looked down at the three naked Americans, then turned and walked out without a word.

"See GI," the VC said, moving next to Jeff, setting the two cans by his side, and dropping the bundle near his feet. "She number one lady doctor. Fix you all up good. Now you put on clothes and eat. I come back in morning."

With that the young VC departed, taking the lamp with him, leaving them in darkness. Jeff sat waiting for his eyes to grow accustomed to the dark.

"Sarge," Ted asked. "What the hell is going on? Man, first they treat us like POW's, then throw us in cages to die, now we're back to being prisoners. I can't go back in the cage again. I'll make them kill me first. Just what the hell do they want? Are they trying to break us? Or what?"

"I don't know Ted. I'm as confused as you are. At least we're out of the cages, so maybe we're not supposed to die. I don't think that NVA Captain is around any more. I'm almost positive he would have let us die."

"So what's going on?"

"I'm not sure but I think the main force moved south and took most of the supplies with them. I didn't see that many NVA left in camp and hardly any of the big supply stacks. My guess is the soldiers left here are a reserve force to resupply the main force when they make contact. You know it makes sense. The main force can make contact and fight or hit and run, being resupplied and reinforced in either situation. Anyway, we're back to square one. What ever. We've got a chance to regain some of our strength and try to get Ken well. Man, his leg looks bad. I hope he won't lose it.''

"Yeah, I know. Should we try to feed him something?''

"No, he'd probably just choke on it. We can get these clothes on him and maybe he'll drink something. The nurse left the wash bucket so let's get him cleaned up first.''

Between them they managed to wash the young soldier and dress him in the thin VC pajamas. Ken was unresponsive to their touch but he did swallow a couple of mouthfuls of tea. His body was hot from fever but he seemed to be resting quietly when they finished with him.

Jeff and Ted cleaned and clothed themselves, then finished the rice and tea. Jeff was counting on the VC to keep feeding them from now on although he was sure it wouldn't be much more than rice and tea. They settled back on their mats giving their wretched bodies a chance to relax in the prone position for the first time since being thrown into the cages. Jeff had found two more rice mats in the darkness and used them to cover Ken. His breathing was regular and Jeff felt reassured. Tomorrow he'd try to get some food into Ken.

"How long we been here Sarge?'' Ted whispered.

"I'm really not sure but I think it's been about twelve days since our capture. We have to start marking one of the poles to keep track. Now try to get some sleep. Get your strength back.''

"Okay Sarge.''

141

Jeff closed his eyes as rain started beating on the roof of the hut. A wave of exhaustion swept over him and he tried to bring a picture of Valerie into his mind. Her image flickered in his head as he dropped off to sleep. She seemed to be standing on a lonely hill beckoning to him. He tried to climb the hill and just as he'd reach her he would slide back down.

It was the sixth day before they were allowed out of the hut. A routine had developed over the previous days so Jeff was surprised when the VC told them to follow him that morning. He allowed them a short walk around the compound returning them to the hut. It also surprised Jeff that they were allowed to sit outside the hut when they returned. Of course Ken was still confined to the hut. His condition had improved but he couldn't walk. He had gained consciousness on the second day. The nurse had returned to treat his wound and rebandage it. He was eating and drinking a little now but Jeff noticed a positive attitude towards his survival was lacking. He just didn't seem to care. Ted tried constantly to talk with him but Ken was withdrawn.

The young VC was named Nhang. He would bring them food and drink, in the morning and then again at night. He alternated guarding the prisoners with an old man during the daylight hours. Jeff didn't know who guarded them at night or if they were even guarded. In their condition it was certain they weren't going anywhere.

Nhang liked to speak English. He would sit in the hut doorway for hours asking about the United States. He had also told Jeff his life story. He was fourteen years old, an orphaned street kid living off the Americans in Bien Hoa. The giant airbase there and Army units surrounding it provided Nhang with an ample clientel for his business which was hustling GI's. Shoe shines, drugs, girls, or blackmarket activities—if you wanted to deal, Nhang would find a buyer or seller. He used the shoeshine boy front to move easily in and out of the hundreds of bars the GI's hung out in. However, he made the mistake of supplying one of his girls to an MP Sergeant who unfortunately caught a dose of clap. The Sergeant and two of his friends caught up with Nhang a few days later and damn near beat him to death.

Nhang spent nearly a month in a Catholic hospital in Bien Hoa. He swore he would get even with the Sergeant. One of the orderlies befriended him and became quite sympathetic to Nhang's revenge. They made a deal. If Nhang would help the orderly steal some medical supplies, he would help Nhang get the Sergeant. The night before Nhang was to be released they broke into the hospital supply and loaded themselves with as much as they could carry. Outside the hospital they were met by two other Vietnamese in a Lambretta cycle cab. They quickly left Bien Hoa and headed toward the military complex at Long Binh, which was where the Sergeant was stationed. The two installations are about four miles apart so the trip took less than fifteen minutes.

They hid the Lambretta in a rubber plantation just north of Long Binh. Nhang was given a backpack to carry and they worked their way through the plantation to the edge of the tree line stopping about two hundred yards from the perimeter of the base. There they assembled two mortar tubes and thirty rounds of ammo. Ten of which had been in the pack Nhang was carrying. They hid until about three in the morning, then started shelling the base. The fourth or fifth round hit an ammo storage area and there was a tremendous secondary explosion. They fired all the rounds and slipped back into the plantation to where the Lambretta was hidden. They stayed there the rest of the night then joined the normal flow of traffic back to Bien Hoa in the morning.

Nhang was told the National Police would know about his involvement in the robbery and the mortar attack, so he must leave Bien Hoa and accompany the orderly to a Viet Cong camp. He was given false identity papers and boarded a bus for Tay Ninh. The medical supplies were hidden in bundles they carried. The orderly whose name was Cuong escorted him to a VC camp west of Tay Ninh in Cambodia. Cuong was given a hero's welcome for the medical supplies and shelling of Long Binh and Nhang was given three weeks of indoctrination, lectures, and training. He was sent north through Cambodia and Laos to help bring supplies south for the monsoon offensive.

When he arrived in this camp, the NVA officer in charge found out he spoke English and assigned him to guard the prisoners. Nhang felt it was better to guard prisoners than be a VC in the south. He said he wasn't mad at the Americans anymore but he had to be a VC because the national police were looking for him.

Jeff listened patiently to Nhang during all their talks. He answered all his questions about America, painting elaborate pictures about the people and countryside. He felt Nhang was the key to their escape but right now he was the key to their survival. He knew it would be easy to win the boy over but he'd have to be extremely careful.

Jeff looked around the compound. It was virtually deserted now. All the supplies were gone and the only North Vietnamese Army soldiers left were three or four living in the command building. The vehicles had departed and there were six VC in the camp including Nhang.

The village people seemed unconcerned about the camp in their back yard and stayed out of it except for the children who would run through once in a while. Several of them would stop at the hut trying to get a look at the prisoners but Nhang would run them off. There appeared to be only four men left in the village and they were elderly.

"Ted, see if you can get Ken to eat something. I want to talk to Nhang." Jeff winked at Ted and motioned his head toward Ken.

"Uh, sure Sarge," he answered going into the hut.

Jeff waited a few moments, looking at Nhang who was sitting with his back against a tree about five feet away.

"Nhang, I didn't tell you I was an orphan like you did I?"

He looked surprised. "You. Orphan! I don't think so."

"Yes. I am. My mother and father were killed in a car crash when I was little and I went to a Catholic orphanage. I lived with the sisters till I was eighteen, then I joined the Army."

"Really?"

"For sure."

"How about that Sarge. You and me pretty much same."

"Yeah, but I didn't have to live in the street like you Nhang. I really admire you. You made it by yourself. Did you know your mother and father?"

"Yes, my mother very beautiful but she died when I

was five. My father was French paratrooper but he killed at Dien Bien Phu just before I born. My mother tell me all about him. I even have French name but my mother give me Vietnamese name because Vietnam people no like French people no more.''

Jeff had noticed the Caucasian features in the boy, especially the eyes. "What is your French name, Nhang?"

"Jean-Claude Veauthier," he said proudly. "Same name as father.''

"Then you're a junior," Jeff grinned.

"What is this, junior?''

Jeff explained what he meant by using both their names and writing them in the dirt with a twig. Nhang was pleased but he quickly erased the writing, looking around cautiously, he told Jeff he was afraid for anyone else to know he had a French name.

Nhang told him about the orphanage and how he was somewhat of an outcast because of his European features. His mother had been a French teacher so Nhang could speak French fluently, even at the age of five. His mother taught school at a large rubber plantation near Phuoc Vinh located about forty miles north of Bien Hoa. His father was a French Army Captain in charge of the local garrison securing the area from the Viet Minh, which is what the Viet Cong were called during the French occupation. His mother and father had been married a year before the French defeat and surrender at Dien Bien Phu. When his mother died Nhang was placed in an orphanage in Ben Cat. He ran away from the orphanage when he was eleven and managed to get to Bien Hoa some twenty miles to the south. The Americans were building up the big airfield and Army camp there, so Nhang learned English and how to hustle the

GI's. He had a good thing going until the incident with the MP Sergeant.

The older guard relieved Nhang and made Jeff go into the hut. Ted was feeding Ken and looked up as the Sergeant entered the hut.

"What was that all about Sarge?"

"I'm not sure yet but maybe we can use that young kid. I think he'd like to get out of here as much as we do. We'll talk about it later. How's Ken doing?"

Ted shook his head negatively and shrugged. "He won't talk to me. He barely eats anything. I told him he had to build his strength back up but he won't listen. Talk to him Sarge."

Jeff reached for the tea can and held Ken's head up. "Come on Ken," he pleaded. "Don't give up on us. We're going to get out of here."

Ken took a small sip of tea and lay back. He looked up at Jeff as tears formed in the corners of his eyes. "I can't make it Sarge. I can't. You guys are gonna have to leave me. My leg. It hurts. I'm scared Sarge. I don't want to die out here."

"You're not gonna die Ken. That's why you got to eat. In a couple of days you'll be walking around. Now just get some rest. I promise you that when we leave here it will be the three of us. You can bet on that."

Chapter Thirteen

Russ Sanders squirmed uncomfortably in the confining seat of the big airplane. The pilot announced they'd be landing in Las Vegas in five minutes. The stewardess' made a last minute check of the passengers. The four hour flight from Boston had been smooth but Russ was tired of sitting. He felt the plane gradually lose altitude and the thump as the landing gear was extended.

"Oh, look Russ. There's a lake and a big dam. Is that Lake Tahoe?'

Russ leaned forward to look past Dina Mayhew at the sparkling blue water off the right wingtip a couple of thousand feet below them.

"No Dina, that's Lake Mead. Tahoe is about five hundred miles north, near Reno."

"Oh yeah."

Russ settled back closing his eyes. Thoughts of indecision ran through his head. Well, it's too late now.

The Army had accepted his resignation and processed his discharge. Six and a half years of honorable service. What the hell, he could always go back in if things didn't work out between him and Dina. Still, he had a nagging guilty feeling about leaving the Army.

His service time hadn't been bad. The Army ROTC program had put him through college enabling him to graduate with a business degree. He pulled a couple of good duty tours including a year in Vietnam. His last duty assignment in Boston had given him the opportunity to pursue his law degree. He was about a year from taking the Bar exam.

His plans hadn't included a permanent relationship but Dina had gotten to him. Not that she persued him. In fact, he doubted she would have ever contacted him again after their return from New Hampshire.

After the funeral Russ had returned to work trying to push Dina from his mind. He drove himself relentlessly for a couple of weeks. At times his mind would wander, thinking of her. A haunting remembrance of her perfume, a flash of her supple body. The memory of her warm flesh against his. He'd catch himself day dreaming and force her out of his mind.

In the middle of the third week he relented. The thought of her was driving him crazy. He went to the club three times in a row to watch her dance, hoping that just the sight of her and what she was would stamp out his desperate desire for her. He sat inconspiciously amid the darkened crowd so she wouldn't see him.

He watched her glistening body as she danced. Her long flowing hair and firm creamy skin bathed in the spotlight. He knew he had to have her. The gnawing in the pit of his stomach overwhelmed all the reluctant barriers he had established against her.

On the third night he bribed his way backstage after her last dance. Dina didn't seem too surprised to see him. She agreed to let him buy her a late snack and he ended up spending the night with her. She was living alone because her boyfriend had stolen five grand from her and split. Most of the money from Ken's estate was still in her bank account. She was giving up her job and moving to Hollywood at the end of the month. Her boss had lined her up with an agent and a dancing job until she could get an acting job. Russ had never seen her act but he was willing to bet the boss was blowing smoke and Dina would never be anything more than a stripper.

Towards the end of the month Russ made up his mind and offered Dina a proposition. He would resign from the Army and go with her to the west coast. He wanted to finish his degree at UCLA. They could share an apartment and she wouldn't have to get a job dancing. She could devote all her time toward her acting career. Dina agreed and moved in with him at the end of the month while he waited for his resignation to be approved.

He was somewhat surprised she had accepted so readily, but the more he thought about it he realized she was using him. She wasn't so dumb after all. He could provide the security and protection she needed without having to worry about him being some creep after her money. All he wanted was her body and she could deal with that. Actually, he was doing her a favor and all she had to do was keep him happy.

It had taken three more weeks for his resignation to come through and they left for Los Angeles. Dina decided she wanted to stop in Las Vegas for three or four days since she had never been there. Russ had been there a couple of times and was glad for the diversion. Perhaps, the fast paced lifestyle of Vegas would firm up their relationship. Just relaxing and being together might improve their union.

They caught a cab to the hotel and Russ was glad to let the driver play tourist guide and answer all of Dina's questions. She was as excited as a kid with a new toy and didn't let up until the cab pulled up in front of the Dunes.

"Russ. Look, there's the MGM and the Flamingo, and, oh look, Russ. Wow. Caesars Palace. Are we going there? I've just got to see it. Can we?" she pleaded wrapping her arms around his neck.

"Yes Dina," he smiled. "We'll see them all. Now," he kissed her lightly on the lips, "let's get checked in so we can freshen up, okay?"

"All right," she beamed, giving him a little peck on the cheek and taking his arm and pulled him toward the hotel doors. "I'm ready."

The shock that one experiences the first time they walk into a major hotel casino in Vegas is unique. You find yourself stepping from the hot arid desert air through the massive glass doors into a cavern of refrigerated mass hysteria. It hits you all at once. The sounds, lights, decor and smell all combine to immediately overwhelm you. The entire scene is laid out in front of you, the size of a football field. Dina was no exception. She stopped dead in her tracks.

"Oh wow! I can't believe it. Man, I mean it's absolutely unreal. I can't believe it," she said as she stepped forward and stopped again at the top of three steps leading down into the casino area. "Unreal!"

"Nope," Russ said. "It's real alright but designed to hype you out of everyday reality into the Vegas style adult fantasyland. Kind of gets your blood boiling doesn't it?"

"I'll say."

"Go on," Russ grinned. "Wander around the casino. See where everything's at. I'll get us registered. Just stay in the casino area and I'll find you."

"Unreal," Russ heard her say again as she cautiously stepped down into the gambling area.

Russ registered and ordered a bottle of champagne and a dozen roses for their suite. He decided to have a drink at the bar and allow time for their luggage to be taken up. He managed to find a spot at the crowded bar and ordered a drink. The casino was full of people, probably due to the weekend and Russ had a hard time spotting Dina. He finally saw her as she casually walked through the gambling area, stopping now and then at a table to watch the action for a few moments. He knew she was fascinated by it all.

The barman brought his drink and Russ settled back in the bar chair listening to the buzz of the casino. The action was always fast and noisy, with the call of the stickmen and shouts of the players. Slots whirled and clanged as lights flashed. Winners yelled and losers groaned with every bet. The constant public address system paged someone or another every few seconds competing with the keno game calls of numbers. He scanned the milling crowd noting every type of dress imaginable. Some people looked like they couldn't afford to lose a dime and others looked as though they'd stepped from the pages of a fashion layout. The mix was unbelievable.

Russ nursed his drink for ten minutes, then set out to find Dina. He checked the gaming pit but failed to see her. He walked the rows of slots and finally found her playing a quarter machine.

"Having any luck," he asked, slipping his arm around her waist as he stood beside her.

"Yeah. Look," she pointed to the payoff tray. It was half filled with quarters. "The change girl told me to play this one."

"Good," Russ smiled. He knew it was not uncommon for a change girl to pick several machines in her area, hoping one of them would hit a big jackpot and she would get a tip from a grateful player.

The machine Dina was playing had a thousand dollar jackpot for a play of three quarters. Russ noted Dina was only playing one coin at a time and was about to tell her to play three when she screamed.

"I won! I won!" She jumped up and down as the machine spewed coins into the tray.

Russ looked at the three sevens lined up on the payoff line and shook his head.

"What's the matter?" Dina asked, looking at the scowl on his face. "I won, didn't I?"

"Yeah," he laughed. "But only a hundred dollars. If you had put in three coins you would have won a thousand. I was just about to tell you but you're too fast."

"But I won a hundred, didn't I?"

"Yes but . . ."

"Well, alright then," she kissed him and smiled. "I won."

"You sure did," Russ relented. "Now, you can buy dinner at Caesar's."

"Oh no," she shook her head negatively with a grin. "This is my gambling money. I'm going to use this to win more."

"Ha, famous last words. Anyway, play it one more time to pull the winner off. Who knows, maybe you'll get back to back jackpots but put in three coins please."

"Okay," she winked and played the coins with no luck. "Darn. Well what do I do with all these quarters?"

"Here you are, Miss. Too bad about the grand," said the change girl handing Dina a coin bucket big enough to hold all the quarters.

Russ grinned to himself and helped Dina load the quarters into the bucket. The change girl had hurried over when she heard the machine hit. They didn't miss a trick. She watched them empty the machine tray, probably thinking what a dumb shit Dina was not for having played three coins. Russ handed the girl a handful of coins and steered Dina towards a change booth.

"Thank you sir," the girl called after him. "Come back soon."

"Why did you give her that money?" Dina asked.

"It's all part of the game Honey. She told you what machine to play so you're supposed to be grateful. Hell, it was only five or six bucks anyway. It works the same way on the gaming tables. If you're winning you make a bet for the dealer. It's done all the time. Contrary to what a lot of beginners think the dealers really like to see a winner. They're looking for the tips or tokes as they call them."

"Well," she grinned. "I hope I'll be able to give the dealers a lot of tips."

"Maybe," he smiled. "With beginners luck you just might do all right."

"Hey," Dina laughed, counting the money for her quarters. "I've got over a hundred and thirty dollars. Not bad for starting with ten dollars, huh?"

"What can I say," Russ hugged her. "Beginners luck. Now let's get upstairs and change. We'd better make some reservations for dinner. Where and what do you want to eat?"

"I don't know," she said, stepping into the elevator. "But I want to be pampered. You know, something really elegant. How about . . . mmm, lobster?"

"Lobster it is. There's a terrific seafood restaurant here in the hotel. I'll make reservations as soon as we get to the room."

"All right," she kissed him fully on the mouth pulling him against her body.

Russ felt himself respond as her tongue probed his mouth. He pulled away quickly as the elevator stopped at their floor, grinning sheepishly at a man standing in the hall, waiting for the elevator.

Their room was actually a one bedroom mini-suite with the bedroom separate from the living room, or lounging room as the hotel preferred to call it. The suite was done entirely in tones of gold and white. Dina rushed through the rooms on a quick inspection, oohing and aahing at everything. Russ opened the double french doors leading onto the balcony and stepped out to look down on the busy strip. Dina joined him

"Oh Russ, it's beautiful. The bathroom is bigger than my old apartment. I bet it cost a fortune."

"No, not really" he said, putting his arm around her shoulders. "Besides, nothing is too good for you."

"Mmmm, you're sweet." She kissed his cheek.

155

"Anyway," he led her back inside and closed the doors. "Let's have a toast. I ordered champagne."

"You think of everything, don't you?"

"I try," he grinned.

A dozen yellow roses sat beside a chilled champagne bucket and a basket of fruit on the coffee table. They sat down on the massive sofa and Russ opened the champagne. He nodded to the roses indicating the card.

"Read it. They're for you."

"Really," she beamed. "I thought they came with the suite."

Russ watched her as she read the card. He poured the champagne and handed her a glass. She placed the card on the table and looked at him over the rim of the glass as they clinked lightly in a toast.

"Just plain and simple," he said, noting the moisture in the corner of her eyes. "To us."

He watched a look of softness come into her face that he'd never seen before as she sipped the champagne, her eyes never leaving his. Slowly, she lowered her glass and leaned forward, kissing him fully on the mouth. Her lips touched his, lightly at first, then harder with more pressure. Her free hand pressed against the back of his neck and her tongue probed his open lips. He held her for a long moment then slowly she pulled away. A tear trailed down her cheek and she lowered her eyes from him.

"Dina don't . . ." he started.

"No," she quickly touched his lips with her finger-tips. "Don't say anything. It's a beautiful moment. Besides," she smiled, gaining her composure. "Nobody ever bought me champagne and roses before. Thank you Russ. Thank you."

Russ smiled again and nodded. Touching their glasses, they emptied them and placed them on the table.

"More champagne?" he asked.

"No," she said, getting up and heading into the bedroom. "I'm going to take a hot bath. Why don't you call down for reservations. I want that lobster you promised me."

"You got it," he said after her.

Russ made the reservations and poured himself another glass of champagne. He sipped it and thought of Dina's moment of tenderness. It was unlike her. In the time he had known her, he had never seen her drop that hard mask of cynicism she held out to the world like a shield to hide behind. For a moment he had broken through that shield and it had caught her off guard. Maybe he was making progress after all.

Their relationship for the past few weeks had been pleasant enough but it was strictly on her terms. She refused to be questioned about herself or her activities. A couple of times after she had moved into his apartment she failed to come home from work until the next day. When he attempted to ask her about it she blew up, so he just dropped it. He knew she had spent the night with someone else but he never brought it up.

She willingly submitted to him during that period whenever he wanted but there was no passion in her lovemaking. She'd let him have her and, once, he went down on her but she wouldn't reciprocate. He felt she had probably given head to other guys and more than likely enjoyed it but she wouldn't come across with him. It irritated him but he guessed the way to her had to be patience and tenderness. He believed she had never been treated like anything but a tramp. He was going to change that and hopefully her attitude. As he thought about Dina he realized how little he knew about her. She never talked about her life before her marriage and he really knew very little about that period. Once, he had asked her about Ken and she'd only say he was a nice guy and she didn't want to discuss him, so Russ let it go.

Well, now that they were out of Boston and she was dependent on him, he could crack through the wall she had built around herself. For a moment there, she'd become vulnerable and he knew it had thrown her off guard. He glanced at his watch noting they had a couple of hours before dinner. She would probably be anxious to get back down to the casino. Beginners luck coupled with the excitement of the town, would fan the gambling fever she didn't even know she had.

Russ refilled his glass and walked into the bedroom. The door to the bathroom was open and he could hear her humming to herself. He sat down on the edge of the king size bed and slipped off his shoes. He'd wait for her to finish, then take a shower. He could see partially into the bathroom. The walls were totally mirrored and although the bathtub was not in his direct line of sight he could see her reflection. Only the top of her shoulders and head were in view as she lay back in the tub. White pillows of bubble bath coated her arms which rested on the edge of the tub. She had wrapped a towel around her head in turban style.

The tub itself looked king size from his view. It was raised and had small carpeted steps up its side. He saw a shower outlet above it and a round circular rod for the shower curtain which was pulled back. He knew it was not unusual for the suites to have oversize tubs that were in reality jacuzzis.

"Hey," he called out. "Don't fall asleep in there. We've got things to do, places to go."

"Oh wow," she said turning her head slightly and seeing him in the mirror. "I was almost asleep. Man, I can't believe this place. I mean, Russ, it's absolutely fantastic. Is that champagne you've got there?"

"Yeah," he held up the glass in a toast and sipped it. "Want some more?"

"Sure. Bring the bottle."

"You got it," he said and retrieved the iced bucket and her glass from the other room.

He returned to the bedroom and quickly shed his clothes except for his shorts. Might as well give it a shot he thought to himself as he walked into the bathroom. The top step of the tub was flush with the rim and he placed the bucket and glasses on it and sat on the middle step leaning towards her. He filled her glass and handed it to her.

"Madam's champagne," he grinned. "Will that be all?"

"Thank you Russell," she said in a high falsetto voice "You may stay and wash madam's back momentarily."

"Yes madam. I can dig it," he laughed.

She sipped the champagne. "Mmmm . . . that's good. Do you know this tub has a ledge around the inside to sit on and it must be about three feet deep. I've never seen such a big tub."

"What can I say," he winked. "This is Vegas. Everything is extravagant, especially in the suites. Hell, some of the other hotels have tubs that are damn near

159

mini-pools. Here, watch this," he turned one of the gold knobs in a recessed panel just about the edge of the tub and the water churned under the bubble bath.

"Hey . . ." Dina squealed jumping to her feet. "That's cold!"

"Oops. Sorry," he quickly adjusted the temperature. How's that," he said, eyeing her foam covered breasts as she slowly eased back down into the water until it was up to her neck.

"Wow!" she grinned. "There's a jet of water going right up my booty. It feels good . . ." Dina raised up, arching her back, using her elbows on the rim to support herself. She undulated her hips slowly against the stream of water. Her chest rose out of the subs and wobbled slightly as she closed her eyes and clenched her teeth. Russ stared at her breasts partially covered with subs. Her wet skin glistened in the soft light and he felt a surge flow into his loins. The dark tips of her full mounds poked through the puffy patches of suds as they arched even higher, then slowly she relaxed, letting her breath ease from her lungs. She opened her eyes settling back in the tub and looked at him. Their eyes locked and she moved towards him, rising easily to press her lips against his. Her mouth opened and her tongue probed his mouth. She wrapped her arms around his shoulders and pulled him towards her. He knew what she wanted and holding the kiss, eased his body up until he was sitting on the rim of the bath with his legs dangling in the water. She hungrily licked his lips and their tongues flicked at each other. She eased kisses down his neck and onto his chest nibbling slightly at his nipples. Her fingers curled into the waistband of his shorts and pulled them down.

Russ leaned back as she nestled his erection between her round slippery breasts and wrapped her wet arms around his waist. She hugged him and her face pressed into his stomach her teeth busily nibbling his taut skin. Dina knelt on the inside ledge of the tub with her legs spread apart. She felt the jet of warm water surging against her abdomen and raised herself slightly until she positioned the spot she wanted the water to hit. When the stream was just exactly right she hunched against it also causing her breasts to slide up and down his hardness. She heard the water being sucked into the overflow ports of the tub and it excited her even more.

"Oh god," she whispered, feeling the other water jets around the tub course against her lower body. Her tongue lapped his belly button and her hand snaked down to encircle his thickness. She looked up at him and licked her lips sensuously. He watched fascinated as she opened her mouth, her lips forming a circle and her head bowed slowly into his groin.

Chapter Fourteen

Jeff counted the notches he made on one of the support poles. Every day he added a notch and every day he counted them. He figured his calender was accurate to within at least ten days of their capture.

"How many Jeff?" Ted asked.

"One hundred and fifty-six counting today."

"One hundred and fifty-six," Mayhew mimicked him. "Man, you guys are so full of shit. You make my ass tired."

"Hey Ken, come on . . ."

"Come on my ass," Ken said disgustedly. "Man, you're just as bad as he is. Every morning he makes his little fuckin' mark and every morning you ask him how many. I mean, really. What fucking difference does it make? What are you guys going to do, have a fuckin' celebration when you get to a thousand? Man, you can make marks on every rotten pole in this stinking hut till you're blue in the face and it ain't going to do you a bit of good.''

"Man, I just want to know,'' Jeff said defensively.

"For what?''

"Because I do.''

"Bullshit. It don't make no difference if we've been here six months or six years cause nobody knows we are alive. You said yourself that Charlie switched our dog tags. So all we're going to do is rot in this camp. They'll keep us alive as long as we can load and unload their supplies and carry their shit. And man, when its over, they're going to throw us in the shit pit or dump us in the river for fish food because . . . get this. Nobody, not the Army or our families think we are alive. As far as anybody knows except Charlie, our asses are burnt crispy critters and that's the end of that.''

"You're wrong Ken. Sarge said we're gonna get out of here.''

"Ted. You're an asshole. You still believe that shit. The Sarge. The Sarge. Man, he ain't been a Sergeant in over six months. He's just like you and me. Three rats trapped in a hole. We're all the same. Rats! I don't care if he was a fuckin' general when he came in here because those guys out there with the guns have made us all equal. Yeah man,'' he laughed sarcastically. "We are all equal nothin's.''

"I don't care what you think,'' Ted said. "If I didn't believe we'd get out of here eventually, I'd give it up. I got to have that hope. I just don't believe this is the end of everything. Why do you always have to be so negative anyway?''

163

"Like the Army says man, I got an attitude problem. Damn, I can't believe you guys. Here I am sitting in a gook camp with a bum leg that never stops hurtin', eating shit and hauling shit, with two idiots that count the days till the cavalry comes charging over the hill to rescue us. Well dream on buddies cause it ain't gonna happen. Jam your hope up your ass."

"Look Ken," Jeff spoke up. "You just keep feeling sorry but keep it to yourself. Ted and I are getting out of here and so help me god, if I have to carry you every foot of the way, you're going with us. Now shut the fuck up."

Jeff stalked out of the hut and was joined by Ted. They squatted by the small charcoal pit a couple of paces from the hut. Jeff stirred the faint ashes, dropping some bits of wood on the barely lit coals. Their captors now allowed them a small cooking fire for their rice and tea. One of the village women brought their food and a few bits of charcoal twice a day. Early in the morning, then again in the evening. The embers were never allowed to go out.

Jeff fanned the little fire until it was burning then added the bigger pieces of wood. Ted hung the tin of rice soaking in water on the spit over the fire. Usually some bits of fish were mixed in with the rice. Most of the time they didn't bother to heat the tea. He figured they got about three pints of tea a day and a couple of handfulls of rice each. Sometimes Nhang would bring them a raw vegetable or fruit, usually bananas, or pieces of sugar cane.

His relationship with the young Vietnamese had improved over the months. He was constantly asking about the United States or France. Jeff knew Nhang was stealing the extra little things he gave them. He was taking a chance every time he smuggled something to them.

Jeff was playing a waiting game. Their physical condition had more or less stablized. They had all lost a great deal of weight. He guessed he had lost about forty pounds. They were all covered with sores and rashes. The only time they bathed was when it rained, then they were allowed to scrub themselves as they stood outside. They'd wash themselves with their clothing and hang it inside the hut to dry. The monsoon season had ended about four months ago, so now it rained about once or twice a month.

Ted sipped from the tea can and handed it to Jeff. "He's getting worse everyday," he said, nodding toward the hut. "But I didn't realize he'd gone that far."

"Yeah. I know. His leg really bothers him. Ted, we've got to convince him to hold on a little longer. I'm sure we can make a break pretty soon. I've just about got it all figured out only I'm afraid to tell him because if he snaps he just might tell somebody."

"Hell Sarge, you heard him. He's not far from that point now. I doubt if he'll last another month."

"I know. He's getting more and more depressed each day. He won't talk about his wife or family anymore. Except when he's on a work detail, he won't come out of the hut. I don't know Ted, you're going to have to reach him someway. I can't. He's very hostile towards me."

"Well, I'll try."

"Yeah. Here, take him some tea."

Ted took the tea and went into the hut. Jeff could hear them talking as he absently stirred the rice with a stick. He knew Ken was having constant pain with his leg. It would start to heal then reinfection would occur and the wounds would open up and fester. When it got bad enough, the nurse would wash it with disinfectant and rebandage it. That was the extent of the treatment until the bandage wore off and it would flare up again.

Ted had made a crutch for Ken out of a tree limb and he hobbled around on that, never really regaining the full use of his leg. Both Jeff's and Ted's wounds had healed completely. Jeff knew that Ken felt he was going to be a handicap to them if they tried to escape and that it was probably a hopeless situation. Their chances of escaping, even if all three of them were healthy, were slim at best.

After they had regained their strength, they were forced to work around the camp. Ken was used as an orderly in the field hospital. He performed mostly menial tasks. The one he hated most was emptying the human waste buckets. He had to carry several buckets at a time, stacked on a yoke, to the latrine pit, empty them, then take the buckets down to the river to wash them out, using his bare hands and sand. The first week he couldn't keep down his food after cleaning the buckets. Ken had refused to carry the buckets at first, going back to the hut, staying there the rest of the day. When Jeff and Ted returned to the hut after their detail, they learned they would not be fed until Ken worked. Jeff told Nhang he would take Ken's place but that was not allowed. Initially they agreed not to work at all but that only lasted two days. Jeff realized it was fruitless to resist because the Vietnamese were more than willing to let them starve to death. So on the third day they went to their details.

Jeff and Ted were unloading trucks arriving from the north and reloading trucks and sampans headed south. Jeff was amazed at the efficiency of the supply route the NVA had established. Supplies from the north were brought in by various means of transportation. Trucks, carts, bicycles and backpacks hauled in war material of every shape and form. It was sorted, neatly stacked and within twenty-four hours it was reloaded, again on any means of transportation to continue south.

Troops arriving from the north were camped overnight and marched south at daybreak. It took Jeff about two weeks to realize the pattern. This camp was merely a link in a giant supply chain. He figure the links must be about forty miles long. He noted the numbers on the trucks and that tipped him to the routine. Each truck arriving from the north stopped at the camp and was unloaded. The driver would be changed and the truck loaded with wounded or casualties to return north. He noticed the same truck would arrive back at the camp every two or three days. The trucks arriving from the south were loaded with supplies and returned south. The same procedure was used for the carts and bicycles. So, he concluded, the means of transportation were assigned to a certain link in the chain, continuing a round trip constantly in that particular link.

Small shops were set up in the camp to repair any vehicle arriving from the north or south. The exceptions were the sampans. They arrived from the south disguised to look like fishing boats. No more than four would be at the village at any given time. The trucks and sampans from the south transported bodies along with the wounded. The bodies were shipped north immediately. Jeff had to admire the NVA because considering what they were up against, the primitive system they were using seemed to be effective as hell.

Initially, the traffic in both directions was tremendous. In the past few weeks it had slowed to a snail's pace. Since the monsoon was over, he suspected the NVA were no longer on the offensive.

However, judging from the number of troops and supplies passing through this camp alone, the enemy's strength in the south must have been significant. Certainly, this wasn't the only route. The entire trail complex consisted of several main trails and hundreds of tributaries.

The camp hospital housed only the critical patients. The walking wounded were quartered in the huts nearest the hospital. All the arriving seriously wounded had some previous medical treatment, so Jeff guessed they were being relayed north up the trail. Since the NVA couldn't airlift like the Americans they were forced to shuttle their wounded from field hospital to field hospital allowing a day or so of rest between transportation.

The less seriously wounded were treated and remained in the camp until they were well enough to travel back south. Jeff had once mentioned to Nhang that the troops returning south were not fit for combat. Nhang grinned and said they were not going to the war right away but to a big rest camp in the mountains.

Jeff began to get the overall scope of the operation from watching combined with bits and pieces of information from Nhang. The supply depots were located at each end of the chain link, but field hospitals were about every fifth link. Each hospital treated the wounded for a specific combat area within its radius and was also used as a shuttle point for a particular trail. Yeah, primitive, he thought, but effective. He wondered if they had prisoners of war in the other camps.

Chapter Fifteen

"Edwin, I am tired of arguing about it. I've seldom taken a stand against you but on this issue I am firm. Now, are you going to drive me to the airport or must I drive myself. I'd really rather not leave my car parked there for several days."

Ed Hefley threw up his hands in frustration and looked at his wife. He knew the determined set of her jaw and the uselessness of further discussion. "I'll take you. Let me get my keys."

"Thank you," she said, pulling on her gloves.

The first few minutes of the drive were in silence as Ed maneuvered through the early morning suburban traffic, then finally onto the freeway. It would take another twenty minutes to get to the airport.

Kathy Chandler had telephoned Emily Hefley about a month ago, proposing she join a group of women for a protest march in Washington, D.C. Initially, Emily had politely declined, citing previous engagements and obligations. She had mentioned the call to her husband and he agreed she had no business marching in the streets with a bunch of radicals. Then, a week after the call, she announced she was going and had asked Kathy to coordinate the arrangements.

The following weeks had led to constant arguments with her husband. Emily stood firm offering no explanation other than it was her duty as a mother and time to take a stand. She secretly felt good about her decision and nothing her husband could say would talk her out of it.

"Emily," Ed said finally. "Just tell me why you're going? After all these months. Why now?"

She turned sideways, facing him, resting her back against the car door. She watched him as he glanced at her, then back to the road. He had aged since their son's death. Ted's loss had taken something out of both of them. They had avoided sharing the grief and each had suffered privately. Now, for some reason, she saw how much older he looked. She knew how proud he'd become of Ted. In his letters from Vietnam, he wrote of finishing college and getting married to Kathy, having a family of his own. Ted seemed to mature with each letter. The news of his death had devastated his father.

"I guess it's just a lot of little things Edwin. Remember, in his letters how he'd use, 'Dad or Mom' at the beginning of almost every paragraph."

"Yes."

"Well, I think . . ." she paused.

"What?"

"I don't know. Maybe, like he was reaching out to us. Trying to bring us closer together. Like he was

171

saying we shouldn't be afraid to show our love for one another. Several times he wrote about the Chandlers and what nice people they were and we should try to meet them. I believe he wanted us to see how they functioned as a family but he wouldn't come right out and say it. Am I making any sense?''

"Yes. You felt that too?''

"Then I was right! Yet, we never discussed it. We couldn't even share that. God, what kind of parents were we? All he ever wanted was a family. We gave him everything he wanted but ourselves, and that's what he wanted the most. So in answer to your question, I guess that's why I'm going to Washington. We've been selfish Edwin. You with your business and me with my various activities and busy social calender. Our only child, our son, had to die thousands of miles away from home in a worthless war and he was never sure we loved him.''

"Emily. Don't upset yourself. He knew we loved him. It won't change anything by . . .''

"How did he know?'' she interupted him, wiping her eyes with a tissue from her purse. "No,'' she held up her hand. "Let me finish. Just wait a minute.''

He remained silent as she regained her composure. She was right. He saw how Ted had used the Chandlers as role model parents. He wanted Emily and him to be like them.

"I know,'' she started again. "I can't change anything for Ted but this senseless war has got to stop. It's not only the mother's that have already lost sons and daughters in Vietnam. Kathy said it would be all women concerned about the war. Wives, fiancees, sisters, women from every walk of life, protesting to end it. To bring back the men, release the prisoners and stop sending them there to be killed or crippled. The women of this country hold a majority vote. It's up to us to show congress and the President that we've had enough of Vietnam. You know I never watch news films of Vietnam on television. Have you ever asked yourself why? What woman? What mother, wife or sweetheart could stand seeing her loved one being dragged from a battlefield. Don't those people who make the film think a soldier's family might be watching? I couldn't bear to see a film of Ted like that, or if it was even like that for him. I don't ever want to know how he died. Would you?''

"No."

"Edwin," she touched his arm. "I'm sorry we disagree but this is something I feel I must do. I have to be a part of this protest. I'll not ask to do anything like this again but this one time I am going to be part of it.''

"I understand Emily," he said touching her hand on his arm. "I understand. Just promise me you'll be careful and call me every night. We have a lot to talk about when you get back.''

"I know Edwin. I know.''

They arrived at the airport and he helped her check in for the flight. Before leaving he waited until the plane taxied from the boarding ramp. He stopped to place a long distance call before departing the terminal.

"Hello.''

"Hello, Mr. Chandler. This is Ed Hefley. Ted's father. How are you?''

"Oh. Fine Ed. how are you?''

"Very well. Say, Mr. Chandler. I just put my wife

on a plane for Washington. I believe she is meeting your daughter and . . ."

"Yes, she is. And my wife also."

"What? Your wife?"

"Yes. My wife and daughter both went."

"Oh. Well anyway. I'm calling to make a reservation at your motel, if it's available?"

"Sure. We've got plenty of room. What'd you have in mind?"

"I just thought it would be nice to visit your part of the country. You know we never had a chance to talk when you were out here for the funeral. Considering the circumstances, I guess I wasn't much of a host."

"Don't apologize Ed. I understand."

"Thank you. I would like to see you and I could have Mrs. Hefley join us after this Washington thing.'"

"That'll be nice Ed. When are you coming out?"

"Well, I've got to get some things in order here. I'll try to make arrangements for a flight tomorrow."

"Fine Ed. Call me later with the details and I'll meet you at the airport."

"Good. You'll be hearing from me this evening."

"I'm looking forward to it. Goodbye."

"Goodbye."

Chapter Sixteen

Valerie Spencer finished unpacking her suitcase and sat down on the bed of her hotel room. The sound of traffic from the busy Washington street below could barely be heard over the hum of the air conditioner. She stared absently around the room and her eyes came to rest on the colorful pamphlet next to the phone. She picked it up and glanced through it briefly, hardly paying attention to the wonderful sites and monuments it urged one to visit. She'd been to the capital years ago as a child on a trip with her parents. This trip would not be for sightseeing.

She really wasn't sure why she had come. Since Jeff's funeral her life seemed to pass each day with less and less meaning. Except for a week off, she had returned to work as if nothing had happened. The people around her were sympathetic at first but their pity diminished as the weeks went by. She did her job efficiently as ever and kept to herself.

Penny and Cal Banner hovered over her initially and had tried to get her to stay with them for a couple of weeks but when Val insisted she wanted to be alone and return to work they relented. They continued to have dinner or take in a movie occasionally but Val preferred to remain alone, mostly at home. She often took long drives into the country on the weekends. She had found a secluded spot in the Virginia hills with a small stream and went there frequently to be alone with her thoughts. The quiet tranquil beauty of it allowed her to relive her moments with Jeff.

The ringing of the telephone snapped her out of her reverie and she stared blankly at the instrument a moment before answering it.

"Hello," she said softly.

"Spencer? Is this Valerie Spencer?"

"Uh, Yes . . . Yes. I'm Valerie Spencer. Who's this?"

"Oh. Hi, this is Kathy Chandler. Is anything wrong Mrs. Spencer? You sound . . . Did I wake you?"

"Ah, no. No, I was just thinking of something."

"Well. I'm glad you came. For a while I wasn't sure you were going to make it."

"Yes, well I . . . ah, wasn't really sure myself until a couple of days ago."

"Anyway Mrs. Spencer. My mother and I are anxious to meet you. Right now she's helping Mrs. Hefley get settled in her room. Her son was on your husband's team. Ted, that's her son, and I were engaged. I'm afraid I didn't have much success with the relations of anyone else on the team except two other mothers and possibly one other lady, but I can fill you in on all of that later. The reason I called is to invite you to meet all of us in the hotel lounge. Would that be all right?''

"Yes. I suppose so."

"Good. Then let's say in thirty minutes?"

"Yes. That'll be fine."

"All right then. I'm looking forward to meeting you Val. Bye."

"Goodbye, ah . . . Kathy."

Val hung up the phone and decided to change clothes before going to meet the others. She selected a simple pants suit and slowly undressed as her thoughts returned to Kathy Chandler. She had the impression the young girl was sincere in her feeling about the Vietnam war. The entire country was getting tired of it. Kathy was a college student so she was probably in the mainstream of the protest movement. However, it wasn't Kathy that convinced Val to come to Washington. She had her own reasons for coming,

The media had played up the protest for several weeks. Women's groups from all over the country would be meeting this week for various seminars and discussions under the banner of Women of America. Val noticed when she checked in the lobby several tables had been set up and women from different groups were registering members and passing out literature. POW/ MIA's, DAR, League of Women, Women For Peace, Mothers For Peace, and a dozen others, all gathering under the leadership of Congresswoman Emily Hollingdale of New York. She had been a thorn in the President's side since being elected two years ago.

Congresswoman Hollingdale had been elected by the women's vote and she was confident that constituency, nationwide, could replace anyone in government. For weeks signatures had been collected and she was personally presenting the petitions to the President and later to the North Vietnamese delegation in Paris. She had arranged for prominent women from all fields including several celebrities to speak and moderate meetings throughout the week. It was all to be capped off by a massive march on the last day. The projecting by Hollingdale that a million women would come to Washington to represent the millions that couldn't come, clearly demonstrated the power of the American women.

Val finished dressing and touched up her make-up. She glanced at her watch and left the room. The hallway was busy with women coming and going and she joined a group waiting for the elevator. She eased into the elevator when it arrived, blocking out the chatter of the other occupants.

Evidently, Hollingdale's message had gotten through to Kathy Chandler. She had told Val during their first phone conversation that she was attempting to contact all the wives, mothers, or girlfriends of all the men of Jeff's team. Of the fourteen team members only three had come back alive. Jeff had mentioned some of the guys on his team in his letters but he never talked about his job in Vietnam. Val had reread some of his letters after Kathy's call and identified the names against a group picture Jeff had sent. Overall, she knew very little about the men on his team.

The elevator reached the ground floor and Val was swept out of it by the force of the crowd. The lobby was much more crowded now, as women of every description and dress moved among the various organizational tables. Bellhops hustled bags of luggage for new arrivals and tried to maneuver through the mass of people.

God, Val thought. Washington must be bursting at the seams with women.

Val thread her way through the crowd to the lounge. She stopped at the entrance peering into the slightly dim atmosphere. A hostess approached her.

"I'm sorry, Maam," she apologized smiling, indicating with a sweep of her hand, the throng of people within. "We are filled up."

"I see," Val smiled back. "Do you know if Miss Kathy Chandler has a table inside? She's expecting me."

"Oh yes. Let me see," she checked a notepad. "Are you Mrs. Spencer?"

"Yes. Valerie Spencer."

"Thank you Maam. Please follow me," she turned and led Val in a weaving route to a far corner of the lounge. The place was packed and the noise of chattering was deafening. The hostess stopped at a semi-round booth where five women were seated and spoke to the younger woman seated on the outside facing Val. The woman nodded to the hostess and rose to her feet extending her hand to Val.

"Hi," she smiled, taking Val's hand firmly in her own. "I'm Kathy Chandler. Welcome to Washington." She unexpectedly hugged Val, kissing her lightly on the cheek. "Oh," Kathy smiled, her eyes twinkling as she stepped back, her hand still clasping Val's warmly. "Please excuse me for being so forward but I'm just so happy to finally meet you. Here," she indicated the booth opposite her seat. "Sit down and let me introduce the other ladies."

"Thank you," Val grinned at the group as they scooted around to make room for her. She slid into the booth looking at Kathy as she sat down. Val clearly liked the girl. She displayed an immediate warmth and friendliness that Val felt was truly genuine.

"This is my mother," Kathy started next to her, going clockwise. "Bonnie Chandler. Next to her is, Mrs. Hefley. Next is, Mrs. Jarvis," indicating the lone black woman in the booth. "Then Mrs. Davis. Her son was the Lieutenant of their patrol."

"Hello," Val said and nodded to each woman as she was introduced. "I'm pleased to meet all of you."

"Mrs. Kenton should be joining us tomorrow," Kathy continued. "Her son was the medic on the patrol. And I'm afraid that's all that'll be coming. I managed to contact the other families except one wife and they all declined for one reason or another. Mrs. Mayhew, the wife I couldn't get a hold of, had left Boston and I didn't know where to reach her. Anyway, we are just trying to get to know one another here, so feel free to join in the conversation and tell us about yourself whenever you're ready."

"Please don't feel," Bonnie Chandler said, "that you must bare your heart dear. We understand you may still have some difficulty relating to your loss, so don't feel obligated. I myself haven't experienced the personal loss of a son or my husband, but I truly share your grief. I only knew Ted for a short time and his loss was heartbreaking to my daughter and me. However, I know I could never feel the pain Mrs. Hefley endured for her son, or you, for your husband." Mrs. Hefley patted Bonnie's hand affectionately.

"Nor I, Mrs. Spencer," said the black woman. "My son, Huey, has been back from Vietnam for several months now. He's having some difficulty adjusting and finding work, but he's alive and safe. I, ah . . . almost feel I don't belong here with you ladies.''

"Now Millie," Mrs. Davis said. "Don't you even think that. One of the reasons we are all here is to help young men like your son. Those that did their job over there and came back safely will need our support too. I think we all can share the fact that our young men lived and fought together on the same team. Maybe it was your son that helped one of ours at a time they may have needed it.''

"Yes. Maybe so Cora," Mrs. Jarvis said with a sigh. "Maybe so."

"Certainly she's right Cora," Bonnie said. "Now let's get a drink for Valerie. May I call you Valerie dear? We are all on a first name basis here.''

"Of course, ah . . . Bonnie isn't it?''

"Yes, and Kathy, Emily, Millie, and Cora," she waved around the table again. "What are you drinking Valerie?''

Val glanced around the table at their glasses. "Wine will be fine.''

For some reason Valerie was drawn to Bonnie Chandler. She could see where young Kathy got her values. Listening to Bonnie talking and asking questions of the other women, Val had the impression she was earnestly concerned with each situation. Her eyes displayed an inner warmth that seemed to reach out to each woman.

Val listened politely as the women talked without joining in the conversation. She felt reluctant to open up her heart to these strangers, although she knew they would be sincere and sympathetic. She liked them all and she politely related how she and Jeff met and fell in love but she didn't go into detail. None of the ladies attempted to pry information from her and she was grateful when Bonnie, evidently sensing Val's reluctance, skillfully directed the conversation to another subject.

"Have you ladies seen the schedule of meetings, lectures and seminars for this week?" Bonnie asked. "I believe there's an itinerary in every room."

They all nodded in agreement.

"I think," Bonnie continued. "Congressswoman Hollingdale has done a terrific job organizing all these notable speakers. I've already outlined the ones I'm attending."

"She certainly seems to have covered quite an array of topics in problem areas," Kathy added.

"Yes," Millie Jarvis cut in. "There are several discussions on helping the returnee readjust and cope with civilian life. I plan to attend as many as I can."

"I noticed there were some," Cora Davis said, "dealing with the emotional and psychological problems of a loss."

Val had learned that Lieutenant Davis had died in the hospital in DaNang. Only Private Gains, PFC Jarvis, and Corporal Kenton had returned to the United States. Kathy told them that Kenton, the medic, had lost both legs during a rocket attack on their base camp. He was awarded the Silver Star for treating the wounded during the attack when he was hit.

"I want to attend Dr. Brother's seminars," Val said.

"Me too, Val," Kathy smiled. "I went to one of her lectures on campus. She's great!"

"And I see the POW/MIA's wives will hold meetings on managing the family, maintaining a household, and the stress of being a lone parent," Emily Hefley said.

"I think I can sympathize with them the most. They are in limbo, not knowing if their men are alive or dead. At least I have resolved myself that my son is gone."

"I see what you mean, Emily," Bonnie agreed. "They must be going through their own personal hell by the uncertainty of it all."

"Well," Kathy cut in. "I believe we should all study the schedule and make a list of what we want to attend, then tonight at dinner we can compare notes. Possibly, we'll be able to go as a group or at least pair off. By the way, I made dinner reservations for all of us here at the hotel. Unless of course, you have other plans?"

Everyone agreed to meet for dinner at seven as Kathy looked around the table.

"My organizing daughter," Bonnie smiled, "appears to have matters well in hand. I, for one," she looked at her watch, "have had enough wine. In fact, I'm afraid it has made me a little sleepy, so I'm going to take a nap before dinner."

"That sounds like a good idea, Bonnie," Millie Jarvis said. "I'm plum worn out from this traveling."

"Amen," Cora Davis added.

"All right ladies," Kathy got up. "We'll all meet later in the dining room. I'm going shopping. Anyone care to join me? Val? Emily?"

"No," Emily begged off. "I need my nap also. You young girls go ahead."

"Val?" Kathy questioned again.

"No," she said. "I'm a little tired too, but I would like to go one of the days while we're here. Towards the end of the week perhaps?"

"Okay . . . Bye," Kathy said cheerfully.

"Bye," they all bid in unison as she left.

183

The remaining ladies got out of the booth. Emily Hefley insisted on paying the check she held clenched in her hand. After a few moments of protest and good natured bantering they all agreed to let Emily have her way. They separated at the elevators.

The reminder of the week passed quickly. Valerie attended several of the lectures. For the most part the women had arranged their attendance to coincide as a group. Val went to two seminars by herself because she wanted to ask questions she didn't want the others in the group to hear. She had been suprised by some of the answers, especially during one of Dr. Brother's lectures. During the question and answer discussion she found there were several other women experiencing the same problem as her.

Tomorrow was the last day of the convention and would end with the mass march past the White House. Congresswoman Hollingdale announced to the media that the protest week had been a major success. By last count, a million and a half women had gathered in Washington and had brought several million additional signatures of support on petitions. Her message to the President and Congress had been clearly established. STOP THE WAR! or face the consequences in the coming elections.

Val was returning from a shopping trip with Kathy and Millie. She left them in the elevator and returned to her room. Bonnie was coming to her room for a drink before dinner, so she ordered from room service and called Bonnie's room to let her know she was back.

The man from room service arrived the same time as Bonnie. Val signed the check and he departed. She made two drinks, handing Bonnie hers.

"'Well, how was the shopping?'' Bonnie asked, sitting down in one of the two easy chairs with her drink in her hand.

"Uh . . . Nice. I enjoyed it." Val moved the other chair so she could sit facing Bonnie. She sipped her drink, then set it on the table.

"Kathy is fun to be with. She seems to live life to the fullest."

"She does," Bonnie said proudly. "Her father and I have watched her mature into a young woman with great pleasure. Of course, she was the average adolescent with the usual problems but she never was a problem to us. That's something I've been grateful for. She always came to us when something was bothering her and we tried to be open and honest with her. She has a mind of her own and is determined once she makes up her mind but she's never been a disappointment to us."

"I sensed your relationship with her was more than Mother and daughter. More . . . friendly."

"Yes. We are friends. She had her own crowd in high school but it seems once she started college and got her independence, so to speak, we grew closer. I'm sure she has close friends at school but she's picked me to be her best friend. I honestly feel privileged to be her friend."

"You should be. I think it's very rare. I could never have that kind of relationship with my mother. If you know what I mean?"

"Yes. I do."

"Bonnie. I hope I'm not being too forward but I wanted to discuss something with you. It's very personal and I really don't think the other ladies would

185

understand. Besides, it involves Mrs. Hefley to a certain extent and . . . your daughter.''

"Well Valerie, I'm flattered you chose me. I hope I can be of some help. I had a feeling you were troubled. What is it dear?''

"I'll get to it in a moment. But first, could I ask you some questions about Kathy. They . . . uh . . . are personal, so if you don't want to answer, I'll understand.''

"Go ahead Val, and we'll see.''

"Okay. Here goes,'' she drained her glass as if to summon the courage. "Was Kathy ever engaged to anyone besides Ted?''

"No.''

"Do you know if she'd been in love before Ted?''

"Well, she's had some boyfriends. Of course, she went steady a couple of times. However, no. Ted was the first one. I watched it develop and it was a beautiful thing to see.''

"I bet it was,'' Val smiled. "You're certain they were truly in love? It wasn't just . . . ah . . .''

"Infatuation?''

"Yes.''

"I'm sure. I know Kathy wasn't a virgin before Ted. Their relationship wasn't one based on sex. They liked each other and had a lot in common. It's something that's hard to put into words. I think I knew they were in love before they realized it. Do you understand what I'm trying to say?''

"Yes. I do. Jeff and I are like that. We just enjoyed being with each other. I thought I was in love before. You didn't know I had been married and divorced before Jeff, did you?''

"No.''

186

"Yes. To a career Army officer. That was our problem. He wanted me to enhance his career by sleeping with his superiors. That's another story. Anyway, with Jeff I realized I hadn't been in love before and surprisingly, I knew I was in love with him from the start. Our relationship blossomed immediately. It's funny when I think about it because in retrospect, Jeff didn't realize immediately. Oh, he was infatuated with me. I believe because I am a couple years older than him, he was afraid of me. I admit I kept waiting for him to commit himself and when he didn't I made the advances. Actually, he was willing to love me from afar, so to speak. You know, like a teenager has a crush on a teacher."

"That's sweet."

"Yeah," Val smiled. "It was. Once our love got underway though, it was full speed ahead. Before he left for Nam, it had developed to the point where we were almost like one person. I don't know Bonnie. It's hard to explain. You know how some couples that have been married a long time seem to function as one person? Sometimes, they even begin to look like each other. Like brother and sister?"

"Yes. To a certain extent, Mr. Chandler and I are like that. We always seem to know how or what each other is thinking."

"Exactly."

"You and Jeff were unusual. Normally, it takes years for a marriage to get to that point, if it ever does."

"I know. That's what I was getting at about Kathy. You'd know if they were that close, wouldn't you? I mean . . . if she felt something about Ted, she would have probably confided in you."

"Yes. I'm sure she would but I'm not certain what

you're getting at. I don't think their relationship reached the point of yours and Jeff's, if that's what you're asking. And now, I believe she's resolved herself to Ted's death. She's not clinging to any notion he's alive. That's what you're getting at, isn't it?''

"Yes. I know Jeff is still alive. So are two other men from his team."

"I see. Ted?"

"Yes."

"I noticed you always talk of your husband in the present tense."

"You think I'm crazy."

"I think you have your reasons. I don't think you're crazy."

"Maybe you'll change your mind when you hear the rest of it. I'm not sure myself. One of the reasons I came to Washington was to see if there were any other women experiencing the same thing."

"And?"

"I didn't find any, or at least none that will admit it. I thought, just possibly, there may be others like me. You know several of the lectures I attended by myself was for the sole purpose of asking pointed questions in that area. I didn't commit myself but I asked Dr. Brothers if she had come across the problem or had heard of it."

"What did she say?"

"Evidently it's not uncommon. She had a fancy name for it. I believe she was trying to say it was just wishful thinking."

"And that people with these obsessions should seek professional help."

"Yes. How did you know?" Val looked surprised.

"I guessed," she grinned. "But I'm not surprised. I have the feeling you're basing your belief on something other than premonition. Right?"

Again Val looked surprised. Bonnie's perception amazed her.

"Yes. It is more than premonition. I know Jeff is alive. So is Ted, and another soldier named Mayhew. I, ah . . . more than know, I've seen them!" Val paused, waiting for her reaction, not knowing what to expect.

"I believe I could use another drink. Here," Bonnie said getting up. "I'll make us both one."

"Now you think I'm crazy?"

"Nope, not yet," she grinned. "But I'm dying to hear the rest of it. Like I said, I believe you have a good reason. I believe you're an intelligent woman and not taken to seeing ghosts. So take your time and get it off your chest."

"Thank you," Val took the fresh drink and Bonnie returned to her chair. "Well, here goes. When they told me Jeff was dead I didn't want to believe it. My mind was fighting the reality of it. I know that's common when one is unprepared for the death of a loved one. Also, there was the fact that Jeff's casket was closed. However, I gradually let my friends convince me Jeff was dead. Then, about a week after the funeral, I saw them."

Bonnie let her talk without interruption. The young woman's voice lowered in tone and quavered as tears formed in her eyes. She felt Val had never told anyone else what she was relating and it was difficult for her to bring it out. She searched for words but the sincerity of them was over whelming.

"I thought, no, I knew, I was only dreaming. I . . .

189

but it was so real. The first time I saw them, or, dreamed about them, they were in a ditch of some kind. They were sitting in the bottom of it. The three of them. Only, there was another man. A foreigner. A Vietnamese, I suppose. They seemed to be tied together. I could hear Jeff calling to me. He was hurt and calling to me. I woke up crying. I was terrified and couldn't go back to sleep. In fact, I was afraid to go back to sleep. I remembered the dream vividly. I can remember it in detail now. All of them. I'd never had a dream bother me so much. It was real. Too real!''

Val paused to wipe her eyes. She sensed Bonnie wanted her to continue without interruption. She took a deep breath and saw the understanding in her eyes.

''The second dream, or vision.'' There, she said it. Bonnie nodded knowingly. ''The second vision was about a week later. He was in a cage or pen of some kind. It was small, not big enough for him to stand up or lay down full length. He was alone and naked. His body was covered with bruises and scratches. He was sitting with his knees pulled up into his chest and his arms hugging his legs. His head was down, resting on his forearms and his body shook from the cold dampness.''

Bonnie shivered involuntarily and hugged her arms unconsciously as Val went on.

''I heard him cry out to me again but this time it was a message. 'Val I'm alive. I'll come back to you. Val, I'm alive. I'll come back to you.' Over and over he repeated it. I realized he wasn't saying it but thinking it. I remember waking up screaming his name. The dream repeated itself twice during that week. Each time it was exactly the same.''

Bonnie watched Val intensely as she absently pushed

a strand of hair from her face and wiped her eyes again. She paused, fighting to control herself.

"Take your time dear," Bonnie leaned forward and patted her hand.

"The last time," Val's voice was almost a whisper now. "Was about a month ago. The three of them were squatting by a cooking fire outside a small hut. They were dressed in black pajamas and eating from a can they passed to one another. This time there were no words or messages. They weren't even talking to one another. Just passing the can to eat, and drinking from another can. They looked wretched and worn out. I could see their faces clearly and even with several days growth of beard and their unkempt hair, I recognized the other two men from a picture Jeff had sent. They were all thinner and their features were ragged but I knew who they were. I didn't wake up violently from that dream and it lasted a long time. Then it just faded slowly as I opened my eyes and stared at the blank ceiling of my bedroom. I got out of bed and went to my dresser. I found the pictures in a drawer and checked them under the light. The vision was clear in my mind and I didn't have any trouble identifying the other two men as Ted and Ken."

Val was sobbing freely now and Bonnie came to her. She knelt on one knee and hugged her as her body shook. "Go ahead honey, get it out of your system. You've been holding it in too long. Go ahead."

After a few moments Val pulled away. She smiled weakly at Bonnie and excused herself going into the bathroom. Bonnie went to the window staring silently into the fading daylight. She was convinced Val believed in the dreams. Stranger things have happened.

Was it possible a mistake had been made? Could it be made? The military wasn't infalable by any means. Bonnie pondered the possibilities and decided it could happen. After all, combat led to violent death and horribly mutilated bodies. In fact, there were unknown soldiers tombs and graves.

Bonnie left the window and made fresh drinks. She returned to her chair as Val reentered the room. "Feeling better?" she asked.

"Yes," Val smiled thinly, taking her chair. "I'm sorry."

"Don't be silly. I think you've done yourself a world of good by telling someone. Val, did you ever ask anyone about your husband's death?"

"Yes. Officially, he was killed in combat and his remains were too disfigured to be viewed. Unofficially, I pestered Cal Banner, my girlfriend's husband, until he finally relented. He's a Sergeant and was a friend of Jeff's."

"What did he say?"

"He said Jeff's team was being picked up by helicopter and the one Jeff was on never got off the ground. When they went back in to get it, they recovered only bits and pieces. The wreckage was pretty well charred and none of the bodies recovered were whole. All identifications were made from the dog tags."

"Did you ever see Jeff's dog tags?"

'Yes. They were in his personal effects. They were melted together, I, ah, could only read one of them."

"Did they know or did they find all the tags to match the number of bodies?"

"I don't know but Cal did say that three members of the helicopter crew were missing. I don't know if he meant their bodies were missing from the wreck or they were POW's/MIA's, or what.''

"You think the Army has made a mistake?"

"I'm positive the Army's made a mistake! Jeff is alive and so are the other two. It sounds crazy but I know I'm right."

"I think you might be.''"

"See, one of the reasons I wanted to talk to you alone is because I didn't want to give anyone false hope! I know the three of them are alive, but what if I told Mrs. Hefley about this and her son didn't come back."

"I understand. What are your plans now?"

"Back home I guess. Back to work. I've got to live with my dreams and hopes. Maybe some good will come out of this week. The women of America are certainly with Congresswoman Hollingdale."

"Yes Val. I pray to God we can end this terrible war soon. I thank him I don't have a son of military age. I find it hard to express my feelings and compassion to you women that have men or sons over there, or have lost them. I see the hurt in your eyes and it overwhelms me. Perhaps we'll force a solution and they can come home. When are you leaving?"

"Tomorrow. I've got a one o'clock flight. Are you going to tell Kathy about this?"

"I'm not sure yet. Maybe, but not until we're back home."

"Bonnie. I just want you to know I appreciate you listening to me and thanks for understanding. I feel relieved now that I've told somebody. You don't know what this has meant to me."

"Val, I only hope you are right. It's too bad men like

your Jeff have to pay the price with their life and suffering because governments can't agree."

"I know. I was bitter about Jeff going to Vietnam but he said it was his job. He said it was what he was trained for and was proud to go. He wouldn't even think of questioning the validity of it. In fact, in his mind there wasn't any question of validity. He was a soldier and duty was duty. He has absolute faith in his government and the Army."

"That's the irony of it Val. I'm sure there are thousands that felt that way, and the government they proudly serve let them down. When this war is over they are going to have to add up the positives against the negatives. I hope it won't have all been for nothing."

"I hope so too, Bonnie."

Chapter Seventeen

Jeff watched Nhang cross the compound, heading for the hospital. He was pretty sure he had convinced the young Vietnamese to help them. He knew he was risking their lives by telling the boy of the escape but it was imparative Nhang go with them.

Things were starting to happen and Jeff realized they couldn't wait any longer. The camp was virtually deserted and nothing had moved up or down the trail in a couple of weeks. Their two guards, Nhang and the old man, plus three Viet Cong patients were the only soldier types left in the camp. Of course, the small hospital staff was still here but everyone else had left.

All the supplies had moved south about five weeks ago so there were no work details. Jeff and Ted took over Ken's duties in the hospital. Ken had developed a raging fever a month ago and had spent ten days in the hospital. Apparently, with so few patients, the doctor decided it was easier to treat him there instead of the hut. His leg still bothered him off and on and he needed the crutch to get around. After he was released from the hospital he returned to the hut but he didn't have to work. He spent most of the day sitting outside the hut lost in his own depressing thoughts. He bickered constantly with Jeff blaming him for their predicament.

This morning Nhang confirmed Jeff's fears that something was up. He had overheard the doctor talking to the camp Chief. A large force was moving down the trail from the north and would arrive within a couple of days. Evidently, a major offensive was being planned. The monsoons would start again in a month or so and the NVA and VC were sure to take advantage of it. Also, Nhang would be leaving the camp.

Apparently, every man would be needed for combat, so the old man was to lead Nhang and the three recuperating VC to the mountain rest camp. Later, they would join an operating VC unit. A truck with guards was supposed to arrive and transport the American prisoners north to a regular POW camp in North Vietnam.

So, there it was finally. The thing Jeff feared most. Once they were in a permanent prison camp any chance they had of escape was gone. Ten months, he mused, and they were finally going to move them. Well, it surprised him they had kept them here as long as they did.

Nhang was afraid. At first he didn't want to hear anything about escaping. The more Jeff talked, the more frightened he became. He still wasn't entirely convinced when he left. Jeff knew it was still touch and go with Nhang and time was running out. He'd have one more chance when Nhang brought Ted back to the hut from the hospital detail. He would have liked more time but it was too late now. They had to leave at night and this was their last night.

The captors had gotten complacent, so getting out of the camp was the easy part. Evading recapture was the tough part. Over the months Jeff had gone over the escape in his head a hundred times. He'd carefully think a plan out and try to invision every detail. For one reason or another he rejected plan after plan. There were just too many intangables.

He had no idea how the American forces were conducting operations in Vietnam. How was the war going? Was search and destroy still a method of operation? How well was the VC line of communication? A hundred questions more and he didn't have the answers. He knew they had to go south on the river. They could only travel at night and they'd have to live off the land. Mayhew was going to be a problem, not so much because of his leg but because of his mental state.

The VC would expect them to move south, then east, trying to make contact with U.S. forces. They would also expect them to use the river as much as possible. So to Jeff it all boiled down to making their escape and avoiding capture. They'd have to survive one day at a time. He figured they'd have twenty-four hours before every NVA and VC north of Saigon knew about them. They'd have to consider every village and hamlet as hostile to them and every Vietnamese as the enemy. Jeff wasn't a gambler but he knew the odds against them had to be phenomenal. Well, like he said, one day at a time.

Nhang returned with Ted. Jeff had started the fire and looked up wordlessly as Ted hooked the rice and tea cans on the spit over the glowing embers. Nhang glanced at Jeff uncertainly and joined the old man who was squatting near his cooking fire in front of the adjacent hut.

When the camp had thinned out several weeks ago the old man and Nhang had moved into the next hut. They alternated guarding the prisoners and one of them was always stationed by the fire at night when the prisoners were made to go into their hut. Jeff doubted if either of them remained on guard all night but one was always present when they entered the hut at night and one was there when they came out in the morning.

Dusk was settling on the camp as Ken joined them outside the hut to eat. The old man and Nhang were eating and talking in low tones about twenty-feet from them.

"We're going tonight," Jeff said in a hoarse whisper.

Ted and Ken stopped eating, looking at him with startled amazement.

"What?" Ted glanced nervously at the next hut.

"Don't stop!" Jeff cautioned. "Just act normally and listen. I said we're leaving tonight."

"You're crazy," Ken admonished lowly.

"Look Ken," Jeff leaned forward, toward the young man. "I'm sick of your bellyaching. If it hadn't been for Ted and me you'd be fishbait by now. We've carried you for ten months, so as far as I'm concerned your living on borrowed time. Well pal, we're busting out of here tonight. Tomorrow, a NVA escort is arriving to take us north to a regular POW camp. So it's now or never. I ain't going to no camp up north. I've heard about how they treat their prisoners in the Hanoi Hilton. Now, you've got a choice. Come with Ted and me and maybe, if you've got the guts to stick it out, you'll make it. Or sit on your butt here and wait for the taxi to North Vietnam. I really don't give a shit."

Jeff settled back and finished the rest of his rice, not looking at Ken.

"How do you know they are coming for us Sarge?" Ted asked.

"Nhang told me." Jeff repeated his conversation with Nhang as they listened quietly. He also told them of Nhang's reluctance and the importance of him coming along.

"Do you think he bought it?" Ted asked.

"Not completely. He's afraid, but I also think he's more afraid of being a VC in the field. He'll come, I just have to convince him a little more."

"I'll come too," Ken muttered finally. "I . . . if you guys will let me."

"Sure, Ken. Sure. Right Sarge?"

They both waited in silence as Jeff looked coldly at Ken, then nodded. They looked relieved and Jeff watched them clasp hands in 'Nam fashion' and grin at each other. He leaned back on his elbow glancing over his shoulder to the other hut. Nhang was squatting alone in front of the fire. The old man had gone into the hut for the night. Jeff smiled to himself. He had told Nhang it was important that he'd be on guard duty tonight. Maybe the young Vietnamese had already made up his mind.

Jeff felt a whiff of cool breeze blow across his face as darkness fell. He closed his eyes, listening to the sounds of the jungle. The camp and small village was settling down for the night. He looked across the compound to the hospital. He could see the lanterns burning at each end of the building. Since there were only three patients

199

in camp they had been allowed to stay in the hospital instead of one of the huts. The two nurses would be in there with them. The doctor would have gone to the main hooch, to his quarters. The camp administrator was the only other person in the hooch. The Chief, as Nhang called him, was a North Vietnamese responsible for the operation of the camp. Jeff knew he wasn't a soldier but he had authority over the soldiers that passed through the camp. He hadn't made any contact with the prisoners since taking over the camp, replacing the chief that died in the latrine pit.

"Let's get inside," he said to Ted and Ken, motioning toward their hut. He got up slowly and followed them into the hut, glancing once more at Nhang. The boy remained as he was before, squatting near the fire.

They settled quietly in the total darkness. Their eyes were used to the dimness but they could barely see each other. They sat in the middle of the hut, their legs crossed in indian fashion, except for Ken, his bad leg stretched straight out in front of him. They leaned forward, in a small huddle, keeping their voices low.

"How we gonna do it Sarge?" Ted asked.

"Basically it's simple," Jeff started. "We wait another two hours. Everyone should be asleep by then. We get Nhang, steal one of the village fishing boats and float south on the river until daybreak. We'll have to find a place along the bank to hide during daylight."

"That's it?" Ken asked. "Just walk out of here and sail happily down the river? Man, you're spaced. What about the Charlies, the old man, the three in the hospital? The Chief?"

"We waste 'em!"

"What?" Ted asked in disbelief.

"We waste everyone left in camp," Jeff continued. "The Doc, the nurses, all of them."

"Sarge," Ted said. "The three patients aren't exactly invalids. I mean, man, they're ready to march. They are one hundred percent VC, and they are healthy. One of them was cleaning an American carbine and he had at least two full mags of ammo next to him. He eyed me a couple of times like he might enjoy some target practice. The other two had ChiCom rifles next to them."

"Great!" Ken swore sarcastically. "Just fucking great!"

"Look," Jeff was getting pissed. "I didn't say it was going to be easy but you two sound like you're ready to give up. Now, do you want to hear the rest of this or not? We ain't got all night."

"Yeah. Okay." They nodded in agreement.

"But Sarge," Ted said. "Do we have to waste the Doc and the nurses? I think it's against the rules of war or something to do them in. What good would it do anyway?"

"Fuck it. Waste 'em," Ken quipped. "They're Charlies ain't they?"

"No Ken. I mean it. Hey, come on man. They saved your life didn't they? I mean, they're not going to come after us."

"Okay. Okay," Jeff hissed. "We hit the three Cong's, the old man and the Chief but, and listen to this, if any of the others get in the way or try anything cute, they get zapped. Right!"

He waited, giving each man a hard stare. Silently, they nodded affirmatively.

"Fine. Now here's what we have to do."

Jeff carefully outlined the plan. He went over each point making sure they understood. He stressed how surprise would be on their side. The VC thought they had the prisoners in a hopeless situation and they wouldn't dare try to escape. When Jeff was satisfied the two soldiers knew what he expected of them, he told them to get some rest. He eased back and closed his eyes feeling a big knot of apprehension in the pit of his stomach.

The VC had made a big mistake by not moving the Americans. The laxity of the guards over the months and allowing the prisoners to develop a daily routine contributed to the VC's false sense of security. The prisoners had followed orders as meekly as dogs, never causing any trouble, accepting their captivity as inevitable. True, the Americans were in poor condition and they would have hardly been able to overpower a proper guard force but the VC had let their guard down and that was their fatal mistake. Now, they'd pay for it.

The village wouldn't pose any problems. The old man guard was from the village and would come in handy when they were ready to leave. The women and children and the few elder fishermen wouldn't try to stop the armed Americans. A nagging doubt of Nhang still troubled Jeff. The boy was scared, there was no doubt of that but was he scared enough? They needed him and most of all they needed the rifle he had. The rifle was an old Chinese carbine with a fold over bayonet. It was shared by Nhang and the old man. Wouldn't it be funny, he thought, if they didn't have any bullets. The rifle had a built-in magazine and he had never seen the breech open. He sat up suddenly, shaking his head stupidly, glad Ted and Ken couldn't see the dumb grin on his face.

"I got to talk to Nhang," he whispered towards them, crawling out of the hut. "Just sit tight until I give you the word."

Jeff eased over to the fire pit, squatting before it. He motioned to Nhang to join him. The boy looked around cautiously, then slowly stood up and quietly joined him. Nhang squatted, facing him, holding the rifle propped between his knees. He looked at Jeff questioningly.

"Do you have any ammo in that damn thing?" Jeff pointed to the rifle.

"Ammo?" Nhang looked at him blankly.

"Yeah, ammo. Bullets! Do you have any bullets in the rifle?"

"Ah . . . For sure Sarge. See." Nhang worked the bolt action on the rifle, turning the breech opening toward Jeff, exposing a half chambered round. "Two bullets," he grinned proudly.

"Two! You mean . . ." Jeff almost shouted, then lowered his voice to a whispered hiss. "You mean, you and the old man been guarding us for almost a year with one beat up old rifle and all you have is two bullets? I don't believe it." He shook his head in dismay.

"For sure," Nhang looked hurt. "Chief say, one for you and one for Hefley. Don't need one for other man because he got bad leg."

"All right. Don't sweat it." Jeff reached out slowly with his right hand, taking hold of the upper stock of the rifle. "Let me have it Nhang." Jeff saw the fear come into his eyes and he quickly looked around, retaining his grip on the rifle. "Sarge. I . . ."

"Come on Nhang," Jeff coaxed lightly. "We need

203

you. You're the only one that can get us back to the Americans. You got to come with us. Nhang, listen, when the NVA come tomorrow and find out we escaped and you're still here, they are going to kill you. Remember, like I told you before, you are also a French citizen. When we leave Vietnam, you leave Vietnam. Now come on. Give me the rifle."

"For sure Sarge?" Nhang looked at him with pleading eyes. "You no bullshit me?"

"No Nhang." Jeff felt him release his hold on the rifle. "I'm not bullshitting you."

"Okay Sarge." Nhang let go of the rifle. "What we do now?"

"Now," Jeff smiled and inspected the rifle. "We *didi mau* the fuck out of here. Ted, Ken," he whispered toward the hut opening. "Come out here . . ."

Chapter Eighteen

Jeff watched Nhang creep silently up the steps of the command building and position himself next to the door. He was armed with a stout bamboo pole and was supposed to stop the Doctor or Chief if they came out. Jeff and Ted were crouched beside the steps leading into the hospital. Jeff had the rifle, with the bayonet extended. Ted held another bamboo rod. Ken hid just outside the opening of the old man's hut, armed with his crutch.

The hospital entrance didn't have a door. In its place hung mosquito netting from the top of the frame to the floor. Jeff eased up and peered into the hospital. The kerosene lamp at his end of the building had been turned down to let the patients sleep. At the far end of the building a lamp burned brightly in the netted operating room. The nurses had their sleeping mats in there, allowing them some privacy. He thought he detected someone moving in that area.

He nodded to Ted, affirming the three patients were where he said. They appeared to be sleeping as Jeff parted the bottom of the netting and craned his head for a better look. They were on the right side about three feet from the door. He was thankful they weren't at the far end of the hospital.

The VC closest to the door was supposed to have the American carbine. Jeff's eyes searched the darkness for the weapon. He finally saw it, propped against the wall near the man's head, within easy reach. He couldn't be sure if the ammo magazine was loaded into the weapon or not. All three men were laying on their backs approximately three feet apart.

Jeff pushed the netting out of the way as he positioned himself on the steps. He indicated to Ted to hold the netting and gave him a thumbs-up signal. Ted nodded and Jeff plunged into the hospital. In two steps Jeff was next to the first VC. He drove the rifle down squarely in the middle of the man's chest, hearing the bayonet break the breast bone, feeling it sink into softer flesh. His force drove the bayonet completely through the man and into the floor.

Ted lunged after Jeff and stumbled on the threshold. He uttered a curse as he spilled on his hands and knees at the foot of the third VC. Ted's bamboo rod slammed against the floor but he managed to keep it in his hands. Jeff tried to pull the bayonet free as the impaled man kicked wildly with his feet. His hands had reached up, clenching the rifle and actually pulled his upper body further up the bayonet.

Jeff released his hold on the rifle and reached for the

carbine as the other two VC sat up. The one nearest Ted screamed as Ted swung a sideways blow with the pole catching him on the side of the head with a loud whack. Ted had swung from the kneeling position so all his force was behind the blow. The VC in the middle reached for his rifle as Jeff found the carbine. He felt the ammo magazine in place and fought frantically to work the action, bringing the muzzle to bear on the VC. The carbine jumped in his hands as he sprayed the VC and the one Ted had cold cocked. The damn thing was on automatic!

Ted rolled to his left out of the line of fire as the resounding chatter of the carbine broke the still of the night. Jeff quickly released the trigger and watched the three bodies quiver and die.

One of the nurses burst from the netted area and screamed as she ran towards him. He swung the carbine to cover her, catching a glimpse of something shining in her hand.

"Stop!" he shouted in Vietnamese. "Stop!"

She was half way to them and still screaming as her arm raised up like she had a knife. Jeff thumbed back the selector of the carbine and squeezed the trigger. The bullet caught her in the upper chest knocking her down. Her momentum carried her forward a few more feet and she dropped about ten feet from Ted. She didn't move. Ted got to his feet and picked up the shiny object she'd dropped. It was a scapel.

"Here," Jeff handed Ted a rifle. "Check back there and . . ." He was interrupted by the sounds of gunfire.

"What the fuck . . ." Ted cursed, grabbed the rifle and crouched for cover against the wall.

"Stay down," Jeff shouted and jumped to the door.

He stepped half out, looking to the command building and saw Nhang leap over a body on the steps and scurry under the porch, out of sight. Another shot blasted the night as the Chief slammed through the door and stopped on the edge of the porch. He held a handgun aiming it at the floor of the porch, screaming after Nhang. The gun boomed in his hand and Jeff raised the carbine. He fired three quick shots and watched the Chief slam back against the wall, then stumble forward, falling over the railing to the ground in a crumpled heap.

Jeff stepped down and walked toward the command building, keeping the carbine ready. The camp was suddenly quiet. He nudged the dead Chief with his foot. The body on the steps moved slightly and groaned. It was the Doctor.

"Nhang," Jeff called. "Come out of there. Ted?"

"Yeah."

"Check out the rest of the hospital. There should be another nurse in the back."

"Right," Ted called back.

Nhang crawled out from under the porch as Jeff picked up the handgun. It was a Russian 9mm automatic.

"Nhang," Jeff asked. "What the hell happened? Are you hit?"

The boy brushed himself off. Jeff could see he was shook.

"No, Sarge, but the Chief," he pointed to the body. "He try to shoot me!"

"I told you to stay hidden and hit them with the pole."

"I know. I hid by the door and when shooting start the Doctor come out fast. I step forward away from

208

door to hit him and he fall on steps. Chief shoot at me from inside and hit door. I jump under hooch, and . . ."

"Okay. Okay," Jeff stopped him. "You did good." He handed the carbine to Nhang. "Here. Give this to Ken and bring the old man over here."

Nhang nodded and gave the Chief a fast look, then ran toward the hut. Jeff walked over to the Doc, who was trying to sit up. He was holding the side of his head and blood was trickling between his fingers. Jeff pulled him up to a sitting position on the steps and pointed the handgun at him. The Doc's eyes widened with fear as Jeff looked at him coldly.

The whole thing had taken less than a couple of minutes. Jeff heard someone calling from the village and a couple of kids crying. Ted came out of the hospital dragging the other nurse by her hair. She was crouched over but on her feet trying to keep up with Ted's long strides. He pushed her down next to the steps and looked at Jeff.

"She was back there. Hiding in a corner," Ted grinned. "She's scared shitless."

"Did you check those Charlies? Are they dead?"

"They're dead. Where's Nhang?"

"He's getting Ken and the old man. There they are now."

Ken marched the old man up to them. He was chattering away like there was no tomorrow. He looked funny as he tried to bow to Jeff with his hands held over his head.

"What's he saying, Nhang?" Jeff asked.

"He say please don't kill him. VC make him soldier but he is just a fisherman. He plenty scared now."

"Okay Nhang, listen," Jeff pointed to the village.

"You tell him if he wants to live to do exactly as I say."

Nhang spouted rapidly to the old man, who paused in the middle of his bowing to listen. When Nhang finished, the old man nodded quickly and started bowing again.

"He say okay. You number one boss."

"Ken. You take the old man and Nhang over to the village. He's to tell the villagers to stay in their huts and they won't be harmed. Have him find the best boat and get it ready for us. See if you can find some water jugs and food, or anything else you think we might need. Nhang, tell the Doc here that we're going to tie him and the nurse up here. We aren't going to kill them."

Nhang spoke to the Doc relaying what Jeff had said. Both the Doc and the nurse looked relieved and Nhang departed with Ken and the old man toward the village.

"Ted, watch them," Jeff started into the command building. "I'll see what I can find to tie them up with. Get them on the porch against the wall."

"Right Sarge."

Jeff entered the command building and searched it thoroughly. He found some rope and tossed it out to Ted, telling him to get any medical supplies they could use from the hospital after he secured the prisoners.

In the back of the command building Jeff found a small radio room. He smashed the transmitter and searched a desk, keeping several pouches of documents and maps. In another room he found a large box containing the Chief's personal things. Among them, he found ammo for the handgun and three American hand grenades. He picked a small cloth bag to put the grenades in and was surprised to find three sets of dog tags. He looked at the unfamilar names and dropped them in the bag along with the grenades and extra ammo.

He filled a backpack with rice, fruit and vegetables and left the building. Ted was waiting for him by the porch. He held up a pack and shook it.

"Man," he smiled. "These VC got a lot of American stuff in there. Where the hell do they get it?"

"Shit. Who knows . . . Probably stolen by zips working in our bases. Did you check the dead VC's packs?"

"Yeah. I got all the ammo and the other two rifles."

"How much ammo?"

"About ten rounds each for the rifles and one mag for the carbine. On yeah, I lifted their thongs. It's a lot better than this Goodyear shit we got. Their canvas boots were all too small for us. I found some new black pajamas. I grabbed the biggest ones I could find."

Jeff kicked off his old tire thongs and slipped on real ones. He helped Ted pack up all their goods and gave the Doc and nurse a last look. "Hey," Jeff remembered. "What about the other nurse?"

"She's dead, Man."

"Okay. Let's go."

They found Ken and Nhang waiting for them by a small boat. It was a typical river fishing boat. About ten feet long and three wide. It was open but was made so three curved poles could be fitted to form an arch frame amid-ships and covered with woven mats. Usually, one of this size was used by two fishermen. One in the bow and one in the stern. The man in the stern could lean back and row two oars with his feet that fit in thong straps on the oar handles. This allowed his hands free to cast and retrieve the fishing net. Jeff had always been

211

amazed how expertly they controlled the boat with their feet.

"Where's the old man?" Jeff asked.

"He's in that hut over there," Ken pointed. "Do you want him?"

"No. Forget it. Let's get moving. We got to put some distance between us and this village before daybreak. Ted, you take the bow. Watch for anything ahead of us. If you see any lights or hear any voices, just raise your hand. Ken, sit facing the left shore. I'll face the right. Same thing, if we see or hear anything, we give a silent signal. Nhang, you row, facing the back. I'll tap you on the shoulder if we sight anything. Stop rowing and steer us towards the closest shore if that happens. The current is south so just keep us in the middle of the river. You and I will take turns rowing."

They loaded the boat, everybody taking their positions. Jeff helped Nhang push off from shore and they drifted towards the middle before Nhang started rowing with slow even strokes.

"Remember," Jeff cautioned in a whisper, "no talking."

Jeff settled back and glanced upward. The brilliant night sky lit by a half moon and studded with stars filled his eyes. He realized he hadn't seen stars since they'd been in the camp because of the heavy jungle canopy. He had seen only small patches of the daylight sky. His eyes searched for the brightest star he could find and he made a silent wish.

Chapter Nineteen

The first night on the river was uneventful as they quietly drifted south. They feasted on fresh fruit and raw vegetables. For the first time in almost a year Jeff's stomach was full. In fact, he almost threw up. He and Nhang took turns on the oars, switching about every thirty minutes.

Jeff figured they had left about ten o'clock at night. Daybreak would come about five in the morning. They would have to be well concealed by then. The current seemed to be about two or three miles an hour and with their rowing maybe they'd pick up a couple of more miles. It was hard to tell at night and he wasn't much of a sailor anyway. Hopefully, they'd be ten or fifteen miles down river before they had to stop.

During the night they passed three villages. Two on the left bank and one on the right. As far as he could tell they seemed to be about an hour apart. When they sighted a village they'd stop rowing and drift past it, keeping the boat in the middle of the river. A dog started barking when they passed the last one and some-one with a flaming torch walked out toward the bank but they had drifted a couple of hundred yards beyond it and he doubted they had been spotted.

A pale moon rose over the river giving some visability but hidden now and then by scattered thin clouds. The beauty of the evening sky was breath-taking. I guess it's true about little insignificant things in life, Jeff thought. Such a simple sight as the bright stars, which he hadn't seen in ten months, appeared so majestic. Several shoot-ing stars flashed across the sky during the night and he was overwhelmed by their brilliance.

He suspected Ted and Ken were experiencing the same feeling. Each man lost in his own thoughts and probably touched deeply by the possibility they might make it. Was it too soon to hope they'd succeed? Jeff knew he'd never go back. No matter what happened from here on, he'd die fighting before being taken prisoner again.

Jeff saw the pale hint of daybreak far off to the east above the treeline on their left. He tapped Nhang on the shoulder and motioned for him to steer for the left bank. Nhang pulled both oars from the water and fit one of them into a slot on the stern, using the oar as a rudder now. In the smaller one man boats it was common to use one oar in this fashion, for steering and forward movement.

Looking for a thick overhang of foliage, Jeff scanned the bank. It was still a little hard to see but he knew they shouldn't have any trouble. The jungle along the river grew right to the banks. Various types of trees and bushes, names unknown to Jeff, sprouted out from the shore. These, along with numerous vines of all shapes and sizes combined to form a living canopy out over the bank for several feet.

The boat drifted into the vegetation and stopped dead. Ted and Jeff pulled along a wall of greenery searching for a spot that suited their need. Suddenly, a huge dark shape loomed in front of them blocking their course. They eased the boat toward the sinister mass and discovered that it was a thick tree. The river had evidently eroded the bank from under its roots causing the tree to lean out over the water in a precarious forty-five degree angle. It extended about forty feet over the river with part of its dense foliage touching the water. Vines and moss trailed in a tangled mass from the tree to other trees and vegetation on the bank. It was made to order for their purpose. Jeff knew it was a stroke of luck finding the tree in this position. As soon as the monsoons started up again the heavy rains and high winds would finally dump the tree into the river.

"Okay," he whispered. "In here. Ken, hand me that machete."

They positioned the prow of the boat against the overhang and chopped their way in. Slowly, they inched through it, tugging and pulling and cutting, trying not to cut away too much and leave an obvious path. It took about five minutes till they broke through. Nhang attempted to push some of the vegetation back into place as the stern passed through the opening but he needn't have bothered because most of it sprang back on its own.

"Damn," Ken muttered softly. "This shit is thick!"

"Man," Ted grinned. "It's almost like being in a cave."

"Yeah, but," Jeff admonished. "Let's wait till daylight and see how concealed we actually are before we all start patting ourselves on the back. Come on, we need to tie up so we don't drift."

They tied parallel to the shore using the ropes in the bow and the stern, affixing them to thick roots that covered the bank. They settled back waiting for daylight, talking in hushed whispers.

"As soon as it gets light," Jeff began. "We got to get organized. You know, like take stock of our supplies, ammo and things like that. Since we're going to be traveling at night, I suggest everyone try to get some sleep. However, I think it's important two of us stay awake at all times. We can watch each other to make sure we're not all sleeping at the same time. What do you think?"

"Yeah," Ken nodded. "Sounds good to me."

"Me too," Ted agreed.

Nhang nodded affirmative.

"Okay," Jeff continued. "Ted, you and Ken sleep while Nhang and I are awake. Maybe try to get three or four hours at a time, but for christ's sake, if you feel you can't stay awake, shake someone else. Understand?"

Again they all nodded agreement.

"Good."

Jeff looked straight up. There was a break in the overhead canopy that normally would have been filled by the fallen tree. He could see the graying touch of dawn through the twenty foot open patch almost directly over their boat. The bank was just about eye level but the thick underbrush growing right to the edge of the

216

river blocked their line of vision inland by at least three feet. He was satisfied they were well concealed. Anyone, either from the bank or the river would have to be almost on top of them to see them. Still he didn't want to take any chances.

"Nhang and I are going to scout inland for a couple of hundred meters. You guys put up the center shelter of the boat. Use some of the vegetation for camouflage so it will blend in with the rest of this place," Jeff directed.

"Okay Sarge," Ted said.

"Sarge, can we wash up and throw away these rags?" Ken asked.

"Yeah. Good idea," Jeff grinned. "You both smell like goats anyway but don't splash around and make a lot of noise."

"Come on Nhang," Jeff said, taking the machete and climbing up on the bank.

Hefley watched them disappear after only a few steps into the bush. "Damn," he swore. "That shit is thick. What do you want to do first Ken? The shelter or the bath?"

"Man, let's get the shelter first. Ain't no sense in getting cleaned up and sweating to put this shit together."

"Let's do it then. How's the leg?"

"Fuck man. Like always. Just aches whenever I move it."

"Hey, I got a bunch of bandages from the hospital, I'll rewrap it after you wash."

"Did ya cop any morph?" Ken quizzed expectantly.

"Uh . . . Yeah. I got a few vials. Why? I thought you said the leg wasn't that bad."

"Forget it," Ken turned away avoiding Ted's look.

"I mean . . . You know. I was just wondering if you had any, in case we might need it."

"Don't bullshit me Ken," he started to raise his voice, then lowered it quickly to a whisper. "You've been clean a long time. Now don't try to fuck up things by getting a rush on. Man, I don't believe you. We hop out of a VC prison camp and you want to get high."

"Man, I said forget it," Ken smiled weakly. "I was only asking. Don't get hot!"

"Okay, but listen Pal," Ted gave him a hard look. "We need each other to get out of this shit. I mean . . . Man, you got to realize where it's at. I ain't going back and I'll blast the sorry motherfucker that tries to take me back. Now dig it, Ken. I'm not fuckin' around. Charlie's gonna have to kill me this time. So you keep your ass straight and cover my butt and I'll cover yours, okay?"

"Got ya." Ken avoided his eyes again. "Let's get this shelter up."

They spent about ten minutes erecting the shelter. Three flexible wooden slats fit into notches on each side of the boat, bending to form a bow. They lashed the rice mats over the poles with attached thongs making the concave hut. Another mat tied to each end could be dropped to complete the enclosure.

Ted clambered up on the bank and gathered foliage to cover the small hut, handing the scrub to Ken. After a few minutes he stepped back to survey their work. The small shelter covered about six feet of the boat, leaving about two feet of open boat at each end. Ted pulled two more light branches with thick leaves and handed one to Ken.

"Here," he pointed. "Wedge this along the side to

218

cover the bow. I'll get this end." He crawled back in the boat and positioned the branch so it stuck up a couple of feet, further blocking the view from the river. They had left the ends tied up on the shelter so Ted crawled through it, noting there was enough room inside it for two men to lie down comfortably. He helped Ken finish putting the branch into place. "That should do it."

"Yeah," Ken said looking up at the opening. The sky was bright now and daylight flowed through the overhead clearing illuminating their alcove. "Charlie's gonna halfta be a goddamn paratrooper to see us in here. Now, can I take a bath, Mother?"

"Roger," Ted grinned. "But no splashing."

Ted helped Ken ease over the bow using the tangled roots along the bank as foot and handholds. He slipped into the water to his chest and found a gnarled submerged root to sit on. He leaned back against the bank letting his legs float out in front of him, his arms stretched out to the side, keeping a firm grip on a vine, feeling the slight tug of the current.

"Man," Ken sighed, his head back, closing his eyes. "This is almost as good as a hot bath in a tub. Did I ever tell you I used to dream of taking a bath?"

"No man. When?"

"You know," his eyes still closed and a grin on his face. "Back in the camp. Yeah, dig it. I was laying in this big white tub with the water so hot I could barely stand it. It was filled with this blue bubble bath so all you could see was my head. I had a tremendous hard on, so you could see the head of that too, just barely, above the suds. I mean hard!" Ken looked at him, gritting his teeth. "Hard my man! Like I could drive nails, you know?"

"I can dig it."

"Yeah. Anyway," he leaned back again, closing his eyes. "I'm just laid back, about half whacked and Dina, my old lady, eases in to the bathroom. Without a word she steps into the tub, straddling me, with her hands on her hips and a big shit-eatin' grin on her face. I look up at her. Man, what a fuckin' sight. Oh . . . I forgot to mention that she's buck ass naked, didn't I?"

"Yeah, you did."

"Well, she is," Ken continued, a dreamy look on his face. "I'm staring right at her bush and she's looking down at me between her big tits. Her nipples are hard and pointed."

"I thought you said you were staring at her bush?"

"Hey man, don't interrupt me. It's my fuckin' dream."

"Sorry. Go ahead."

"So I'm diggin her entire body. You know?" he peeked at Ted with one eye.

"Yeah. Yeah, I know," Ted said impatiently. "Come on."

"Well Dina eases down, slowly. Real slowww . . ." he dragged it out. "Her bush just touches the tip of my dork. She's still got this fuckin grin on her face as she rotates her hips and teases me with her hot box. I try to thrust up but she pulls away, so I just lay back and remain cool. Finally, she's positioned right over the target and she slips down over me and glides down my rod. She's hot and juicy but I remain calm. She has me all the way in her now and leans forward so her big boobs rub against my slippery chest. Her nipples feel like nails. She's using the muscles in her twat to massage me and she kisses me hard on the mouth. I grab her solid butt, ready to blow her fuckin' brains out. I pull back and . . ." he paused.

"And what? You fuck head."

"I kicked the plug thing," he laughed. "And all the water rushes out and sucks me down the drain."

Ken quickly dodged away as Ted swiped at him, trying to duck his head. He tried to quiet his laughter and finally had to duck underwater to regain his composure. When he surfaced Ted was holding his sides supressing his laughter.

It was several minutes before they had control of themselves. Ted gasped for breath thinking how long it had been since he had laughed. He raised up slowly from a rolled ball position and peered at Ken's grinning face over the bow. "You're a fuckhead."

"Oh man," Ken smiled. "I couldn't resist it. You should have seen the look on your face. You kept leaning over the boat as I was talking. Man, I thought you were going to fall into the river."

"I know, man. You had me going. Wow. My stomach hurts."

"Hey," Ken asked seriously. "Did you guys pack any soap from your shopping spree?"

"Yeah," Ted turned and picked up one of the packs. "I grabbed some in the hospital when I was throwing shit in the bag." He rummaged through the pack until he found the soap and handed it to Ken. "I grabbed a bunch of salve and bottles of stuff and a couple of tins of powder. We're going to have to get Nhang to identify some of this stuff for us."

"Speaking of Nhang," Ken lathered his hair. "Do you think we can trust the Zip?"

"Hell," Ted shrugged. "What other choice have we got?"

"Well, he is a Cong."

"Not anymore, he isn't. Don't forget, we left the old man plus the Doc and the nurse alive. They know that Nhang helped us, so he can't very well go back. I really think Jeff's using that as our insurance."

"I hope Nhang knows it. By the way, where the fuck are they? How long they been gone?"

" 'Bout twenty minutes I guess. That shit's pretty thick in there. Anyway, hurry up, I want to wash too."

"Hurry up. Hurry up," Ken mimicked. "I'm back in the fuckin' Army."

"Bet your ass, son. Now, shut up, wash up and let me check out what we got here."

"Aye, aye. Mon General." Ken snapped a stiff salute and sunk below the surface, holding the salute.

Ted busied himself emptying the packs they had stolen. He carefully placed the contents in neat rows near the center of the boat, separating and grouping the items: clothing, medicine, food and miscellaneous. In Jeff's pack from the main hooch, he discovered a cloth toilet article bag containing a straight razor, tin of soap, a lathering brush and a toothbrush. He tested the edge of the razor and found it extremely sharp. He picked up the toothbrush and thumbed the bristles. Man, how long had it been since he had brushed his teeth? Damn, he thought. It's funny how he missed the simple things in life but never realized it until he couldn't do them. The old man had cut their hair with scissors about four times during their captivity. Actually, all he'd done was chop at the length around their head. They were allowed to shave every couple of weeks, of course without the benefit of soap. So even that was a painful ordeal. Once, in the early months, Ken had refused to shave or get his hair cut until after a few weeks. By then he was scratching himself raw from the mites and lice.

Ted heard Ken humming lowly to himself and smiled, shaking his head. He shared the exhilaration Ken was feeling now. Their hopes were soaring and they were on a high. It wouldn't last because they had a long way to go and it was going to get tough, but for now, well, it was their first day of freedom. Their first fit of laughter in ten long months had eased the pressure of capture. Hell, he thought. I want to jump up and down and scream with joy. It had taken all his strength to keep from roaring with laughter at Ken. Damn, it felt good. He picked up a carrot and bit the end off it, munching it slowly, savoring the taste. Damn! Damn! Damn! He smiled to himself. He'd always hated carrot.

"Help me out, Ted." Ken pulled himself out of the water, extending his hand.

"What? Oh, sure."

Ken stepped gingerly into the boat carefully shifting his bad leg so not to put too much pressure on it. Ted looked at the leg. It was starting to discolor again around the old wounds on the thigh. For some reason, it would seem to get better for a while then it would suddenly flare up with infection. The Doc would lance and drain the festering pus sacks and put fresh dressings on it. Ken complained about it now and then but he'd never go to the Doc until it got real bad.

Ted pointed to the shaving gear. "There's a razor if you want to shave. Be careful, it's sharp. And there's a little pocket mirror, watch you don't flash it towards the river. What'd you do with your clothes and bandages?"

"I wedged them in the roots on the bank. Don't worry, they won't float out into the river. Man, those rags stunk!"

"Yeah," Ted grinned, slipping out of his tattered pajama tops and pants. "Mine're little ripe too. There's a pile of clean ones, grab a set."

Ted stepped carefully on the boat, using the bank to slip into the water. He found a place to sit and leaned back to relax after dunking his head under water a couple of times. Damn, it felt good! The coolness of the water and the gentle tug of the current rocked him slightly and he let his legs drift out from under him.

"Say Man," Ken grinned at him from the boat as he swished the lathering soap in the water. "Don't fall asleep. Oh yeah, keep your hand over your dong, there's a big horny fish down there."

"Did he bite, or suck?"

"He just nibbled a little bit when I was telling you that story. I almost got a nut and blew him away."

"Screw you."

"Right on," Ken laughed and disappeared from his view.

Ted lathered up his hair, then rinsed it thoroughly. He repeated the process twice, then washed his body. He touched the tender inflamed skin of his crotch and almost cried out. He, like the others, had a severe rash in that area. The rash appeared after the first couple of weeks of captivity. It itched like hell and never went away. The Viet Cong wouldn't treat them, so they learned to suffer with it. Eventually, the rash spread to their armpits, between their fingers and toes. In Ted's case, the rash between his legs was the worst. It extended from his genital area, down the insides of his thighs almost to his knees. Hopefully, one of the tins of powder he had taken would help heal it.

Ted heard movement in the bush and jerked around to see Jeff and Nhang come into view. Jeff was breathing heavily and drenched in sweat. He gave Ted a thumbs up sign and clambered onto the boat behind Nhang. The Vietnamese boy had a stalk of bananas slung over his shoulder.

Ted rubbed his body down one more time, then reluctantly left the water, joining Jeff in the bow. Ken had slipped back to the stern and was talking to Nhang. Jeff stripped off his ragged clothing and slipped over the bow into the water. Ted picked up the shaving gear, positioning himself forward on the bow so he could talk to Jeff.

"How'd it go!" Ted asked, lathering his face with the brush.

"That shit is thick out there," Jeff said exhaustedly. "There doesn't seem to be anyone in the immediate vicinity. We didn't find any trails or paths."

"How far out did you go?"

" 'Bout two hundred meters. We angled out to the right, cut across the top, then back in. Hell, if it weren't for Nhang I'd have gotten lost. Man, twenty feet from this bank, you can't even tell there's a river here."

"What took so long?" Ted asked, carefully guiding the razor over his rough beard.

"For one thing, it's so dense. For another, I'm so damn out of shape and weak. We had to stop every five minutes, so I could catch my breath. Nhang found some edible roots and nuts, so we stopped for that. He also got some bananas."

"Yeah. I saw them."

"How's our supplies?"

"We're in pretty good shape as far as food goes. Plenty of rice and vegetables. Some fruit. There's some smoked fish but that won't last long. We can probably make a fishing line and catch some. Oh, we got a casting net, maybe we can get some crabs or something. That is if any of us knows how to use it. Maybe Nhang, huh?"

"Yeah, but we're going to have to eat everything raw. We sure can't take a chance of a cooking fire. As for the rice, we'll just let it soak in water for a couple of hours under the sun. By the way, have you seen or heard any activity on the river?"

"No. Nothing." Ted scooped handfuls of water, splashing his smooth face. He'd nicked himself a couple of times but it was worth it. He almost felt human again.

Jeff climbed out of the water and into the boat. The sun was fully up now and their little alcove had brightened considerably. The overhead opening allowed the light in but it blended throughout the vegetation creating rays and shadows. It would be difficult to see into their hiding place.

"What kind of American medical supplies did you get?" Jeff asked as he picked up the lathering brush and applied it to his face.

"Well, not a lot really," Ted looked down at the packs. "Plenty of bandages, some morphine vials. A tube of burn salve and a can of sulpha. Let's see, a can of foot powder. No, two cans and . . . ah, that's about it for the GI stuff. The Vietnamese stuff, Nhang's gonna halfta identify."

"Okay. You and Ken go ahead and eat. Use whatever we got for the rash. Hell, use the foot powder. Get some sulpha on Ken's leg and bandage it up. Nhang and me will take the first watch. You guys can curl up under the shelter. It's going to get hot as hell in here pretty soon. Try to get some sleep and . . .'' Jeff tensed suddenly and quickly put down the razor and grabbed a rifle, staring through the thick foliage toward the river.

Ted heard them now and motioned to Ken and Nhang in the stern. He wrapped his hand around the stock of the carbine easing the bolt back and checking that it was loaded. Satisfied it was ready to fire, he took up a position next to Jeff.

Jeff cocked his head sideways and listened intently. He heard men talking in Vietnamese and the splash of water. They were moving closer, from up river. He snapped his fingers and motioned for Nhang to join him.

Nhang moved cautiously through the boat and stopped behind Jeff, peering over his shoulder.

The voices were louder now. They were chattering in Vietnamese and it seemed to Jeff that there were two distinct voices. He saw a flash of movement through a small break in the cover. The men were passing pretty close to the alcove on their side of the river.

"What are they saying Nhang," Jeff whispered, catching a continuing flow of movement now about thirty feet out from them. "Who are they?"

"Fishingmen," Nhang whispered back. "Two men. One man say to throw net in water by tree. Other man say, no good. He already lose one net under water in branches some days ago when fishing with his son. He say to go to middle of river, past tree."

They listened silently to the steady dips and strokes

of the oars as they passed from right to left and faded down river. They relaxed and Jeff was pleased with their hiding place. He had only caught tiny glimpses of the fishermen and they were on open water. He had no doubt they would be almost impossible to spot behind the vegetation, especially with the shadows the light created.

"I think," Jeff went back to his shaving, "that we can expect traffic to be going up and down the river all day. So don't worry about it unless someone tries to hack their way in here. Just make sure we are all quiet and don't move around when anyone's out there."

They all nodded in agreement.

"Okay. You guys sack out. Nhang," Jeff pointed to the comb and scissors. "Do you think you can cut my hair a little. In fact, cut it as short as you can. Maybe I can get rid of some of these bugs."

"For sure Sarge," Nhang grinned. "In Bien Hoa, I was number one barber."

"Christ! Is there anything you didn't do?"

"Not much Sarge, I pretty good businessman for GI."

"I bet."

They spent the rest of the day in the concealed cove. The sun filled it with heat and during the afternoon the humidity rose to an almost unbearable level. They took turns sleeping and during their waking hours, they took care of personal needs. Bathing again, cutting their hair, eating and just generally getting themselves together. The simple act of running a comb through their hair was refreshing and exhilerating. Nhang had showed them months ago how to use the fiber from inside a small bamboo stalk to brush their teeth. Ted was surprised how well it worked, although he couldn't say much for the taste. So now, to use a real brush, even without toothpaste, was a real treat.

The men were beginning to wind down. Each man was lost in his own thoughts of home now that they were actually free. The reality slowly sunk into each man as he dreamed of a past love or the promise of a new one. Questions plagued each of them. What had changed? What was this like? What was that like? Was so and so still alive? What would the homecoming be like? Each one fantasized the event. From arrival to the quiet moment alone with a loved one. The promise of renewing their lives filled their every thought.

Chapter Twenty

It was a bridge! Jeff couldn't believe it. A goddamn bridge out here in the middle of nowhere! It was crude, that's for sure, but spanned the river effectively and blocked their path. The dark form was barely visible a couple of hundred yards in front of them. If it hadn't been for the lanterns on poles every twenty feet or so, they might have run right into it.

They had come around a bend in the river and there it was, several hundred feet ahead. Jeff had been rowing and the current was stronger so they were moving pretty fast. Nhang had frantically tapped him on the shoulder and hissed for him to stop. Jeff quickly glanced over his shoulder and saw the lights. He was momentarily stunned and they drifted within a couple of hundred yards before he managed to swing the boat into the right shore. They fought along the bank to find a hold to stop the boat, trying to be as quiet as they could. When they finally got it secured, they could hear voices and see the dim movement of foot traffic on the bridge. They were too close. Much too close.

The span was approximately four hundred feet long and about three feet above the water. They would see people carrying bundles and packs in a steady stream from the right bank to the left. Figures moving in the opposite direction seemed to be empty-handed. Lanterns burned brightly in what seemed to be encampments at each approach to the bridge. They could clearly hear the voices, along with some shouting or loud command giving. The sound of vehicle traffic came distinctly from each approach area. However, no motorized vehicles moved across the bridge—only carts and bicycle traffic.

Damn, Jeff swore silently to himself as he watched the activity. He criticized himself for not being alert. Everything had been going so smoothly. They had left the cove a couple of hours after dark and made the second night's trip without any problems, managing to find a good hiding place for the second day. It had passed uneventfully and they set out for the third night on the river. Again, he and Nhang shared the rowing and he had just taken over for Nhang after about four hours on the river. He had noticed the swifter current and was pleased with the progress they were making. Lost in his thoughts of trying to figure out the time and distance they had covered, they'd come upon the bridge so fast it rattled him.

"What'll we do now Sarge?" Ted whispered.

"I don't know. Let me think a minute."

"Do you think they heard us?" Ken asked.

"No," Jeff sighed. "Thank God for that. Shit, listen

231

to the noise they're making. They're sure not worried about being discovered.''

"Yeah. And it also means there's no U.S. forces operating in this area,'' Ken added.

"I think you're right about that,'' Jeff agreed.

"Well,'' Ted said. ''We got our asses in a jam now. We sure can't go forward and we can't stay here. It's going to be light in a couple of hours and we're too damn close for my money.''

"Roger that,'' Ken whispered uneasily.,

"Damn!,'' Jeff shook his head. ''We've got to back off. We don't know what kind of activity there's going to be along this bank. Okay, listen. We pull the boat along the shore as best we can. We've got to get back to that bend we came around a couple a hundred yards back. I know it's going to be tough in the dark but we've got to put more distance between us and the bridge. Luckily, we're on the right bank and the river curves to the left, so there should be some erosion along that curve. There should be plenty of cover the way this jungle grows right to the river.''

"Okay,'' Ken whispered anxiously. ''Let's just get the fuck out of here.''

"All right,'' Jeff continued. ''Let's get the bow turned up river. Ted, you sit on the bank side with me and help pull us forward. Ken, you stay where you are and use one of the oars to keep us from drifting towards the middle of the river. If you can touch bottom with it, try to pole us along. Nhang, you do the same thing from the stern. Everybody understand?'' He waited. ''Okay, and be quiet!''

They struggled with the boat, fighting the current, slowly making their way back up river. Again, the heavy vegetation on the bank provided firm leverage and cover. They pushed into the brush of the bank and pulled the thick overhang around them. Hopefully, they would be completely concealed when daylight came.

Jeff eased apart the foliage so he could see the bridge. They were about three hundred yards from the structure, a hundred yards from the curve. He watched silently as the end stream of figures moved across the bridge, like a column of ants. After several moments he closed the gap he was looking through and settled down in the boat.

"What are we gonna do now Sarge?" Ted asked.

"Fuck, I don't know," Jeff said dejectedly. "We're stuck! Shit!"

"Do you know where we are?" Ken asked.

"Yeah," Jeff answered. "At least, I got a pretty good idea. There was a rough map in one of the pouches we took. Nhang and I were studying it while you two were sleeping yesterday. Figuring we've come about fifty miles down river, we should be about twenty miles south of the plantation where we were taken prisoner. We passed it during the second night. If we could have stayed on the river a couple of more nights, I was hoping to make Dak To, that's where the river intersects highway nineteen coming out of Cambodia. It should be pretty secure and controlled by friendly forces, but now, that's out of the question."

"So what's our option?" Ted asked.

"We've got to go inland," Jeff stated flatly. "Straight east and try to make contact with some friendly forces. As soon as it's light, I'll look at the map again, maybe I can pinpoint our location to within a couple of miles. I think we are within twenty-five miles of Pleiku or Kontum, but I'm not sure."

"Hey Sarge," Ted asked. "Aren't there a couple of fire support bases northwest of Kontum, just above Rocket Ridge?"

"There were, but we don't know if they are still there. Don't forget, we've been out of it for almost a year. Besides, we should be south of them already. We . . ." Jeff stopped as a heavy engine roared to life near the bridge. He turned and peered toward the bridge.

The sound was unmistakable . . . a tank! He listened as the driver gunned the big engine, then finally let it settle to an even idle. The area around the bridge was still dark but the sound had come from the right shore. Damn he thought, that bridge didn't look sturdy enough to hold a tank. He heard the grinding of gears in the distance, then the clanking of metal tracks as the vehicle moved. It was too hard to see but he knew the tank was moving forward toward the shore. Loud shouts and yelling traveled across the water towards them.

"Nhang," Jeff asked. "Can you hear what they are saying?"

"No Sarge. Too far away."

The tank engine roared, rising and falling, as the driver apparently maneuvered it near the bridge. It sounded like it was being positioned a few feet at a time. After several moments, it stopped. The yelling subsided and it was quiet again. Jeff peered into the darkness, his eyes straining at the bridge. Finally, he saw a dark shape partially blot out the figures on the bridge as it moved slowly from the right bank to the left.

"Son of a bitch," Jeff cursed lowly.

"What's happening Sarge?" Ken asked.

"They're floating a tank across the river!"

"Floating a tank?" Ted hissed. "How?"

"Shit," Jeff shrugged. "On some kind of damn barge. I can only make out the gun turret."

"Holy shit!' Ken said amazingly. "Charlie ain't never had no tanks."

"He's sure got 'em now," Jeff watched the steady movement. "They must be pulling the barge with ropes."

It took about ten minutes for the dark shape to cross the width of the river. The shouting and yelling started again and the tank engine bellowed as it started, then clanked up the left bank and faded into the jungle.

"Man," Jeff turned back to his companions in the boat. "Things must be shit hot in this area if the NVA are bringing in the heavy stuff. We never saw any tanks or track vehicles come down the trail through our camp. Nhang, is there another trail?"

"I don't know, maybe," Nhang answered. "One time I hear soldier from north say he was in wrong place. He supposed to be with big gun on same same trail."

"What the fuck is a *same same* trail?" Ted asked.

"You know," Nhang indicated with his hands making a straight out parallel motion. "Same same."

"You mean," Jeff asked, "two trails going in the same direction but separated by a couple of miles?"

"For sure," Nhang nodded. "Two trails."

"I'll be a son of a bitch," Ted grinned. "Those slick mothers run their heavy shit on an adjoining trial. Sorta, keeping all their eggs out of one basket."

"Man," Jeff shook his head. "The more I learn about these people, the more amazed I am."

"Fuck 'em," Ken said. "They're still gooks. Ah, I mean . . . the congs, Nhang. Not you."

"No sweat Ken," Nhang smiled.

"You just keep believing that shit Ken," Ted said. "And we'll be in this war for another ten years. Hell, you've seen how effective the trail is. These people aren't dummies. They may have to do things the hard way but they do it. Christ, a GI pisses and moans if he has to carry a box of ammo across the fuckin' street."

"Okay, you guys," Jeff interjected. "Don't get into a goddamn hassle. We got NVA a couple of hundred yards away. It's starting to get light, so lets settle down."

The sun rose, slowly lighting the river, and the normal traffic in the area came to life. Fishing boats appeared from both the north and south going about their business, regarding the war as a minor inconvenience. Jeff periodically checked the activity on the bridge after satisfying himself that they were well concealed.

The bridge, he soon saw in the better light, was constructed on heavy pilings, spaced about fifteen feet apart. It seemed to be made of individual spans of thick logs, tied together and fitted precisely on the supports. He was surprised to see the traffic allowed to proceed up and down the river as one of the middle spans was raised in drawbridge style. Approximately once every hour, beamed supports were quickly erected near the west base of the middle span. A number of ropes and pulleys were attached and manned by fifty or sixty peasants on each of the two main ropes. The east end of the span was raised, allowing the boats to proceed under the bridge. Of course, the traffic crossing the bridge was stopped, as was the barge transport, each time the

236

span was opened. Jeff suspected the peasants manning the span ropes were also used for the barge ropes.

The barge continued transporting tanks across the river at the rate of about three an hour. Jeff noted they were Soviet built T-54's and manned by NVA regular forces. Trucks pulling 130mm artillery and 37mm anti-aircraft guns were now regularly crossing the bridge. Two of the 37mm AAA guns were positioned in sandbagged emplacements, one at each end of the bridge. Jeff saw the firing crews in place and ready for action. The gun on the east bank covered the south approach and the gun on the west bank covered the north approach. He knew the guns were capable of traversing 360 degrees.

Damn, he thought, the NVA must hold this entire area. They were operating in full view of the local population without fear of reprisal. The setup here appeared to be a major thrust into the central highlands. Just how badly had the war gone in the past year? Sure, he had heard rumors before his capture, that the defense of this area, from Dak To to Pleiku, was being turned over to the South Vietnamese II Corp, as part of the Vietnamization program. Hell, the Vietnamese army, or ARVN as the GI's called them, were even supposed to bring in one of their crack Airborne Brigades to man Rocket Ridge. Were things really that bad for the ARVN? Bad enough, to allow the NVA to operate this openly? Shit, this must be at least a division size force crossing the river.

Jeff turned from his peephole in the foilage and settled back in the boat. It was well into mid-morning. Nhang was watching the river's north approach from the bow end of the boat. Ken was curled up on a mat amid-ship and appeared to be sleeping. Ted was sitting cross-legged in the stern, a couple of feet from Jeff. He was fileting a fish they'd netted during the night.

"Looks bad, huh?" he handed Jeff a piece of fish.

"Uh huh," Jeff nodded, popping the raw bit into his mouth, chewing the coarse flesh quickly as he fought back the urge to gag. "Damn bad pal. They're running troops and equipment across that bridge like there's no tomorrow. I'll tell you Ted," he took another piece of fish. "I never expected this. Man, don't let anybody shit you. Charlie's got his shit together here."

"Man," Ted nodded towards the distant rumbling to the east. "Sounds like somebody is popping some heavy artillery or making an air strike."

Since daylight, they had heard the sounds of battle far off to the east. Twice, aircraft, high overhead, had overflown their position a little to the south. They were on a west to east course, probably out of Thailand. The activity on the bridge had suddenly ceased with the sounds of the aircraft but Jeff doubted the bridge had been spotted. The planes were far too high. Several minutes after they passed they heard the heavier, whump, whump, of the bomb strikes.

"That's artillery now," Jeff acknowledged. "Listen how even and regular it is. Air strikes are more sporadic."

"Yeah, but whose?"

"From the looks of what they're hauling across the bridge, it could very well be NVA. Those are Soviet tanks and guns."

"Dig it. Fuck, it was bad enough when Charlie had just mortars and rockets. Now he's able to lay down some really heavy shit. I used to almost feel sorry for those poor bastards out there, when our big 155mm artillery would pop harassment fire on their asses all

238

night long. I remember thinking . . . Man, how can they keep their sanity with those rounds coming in on them. Shit, it damn near knocks you off your feet if you're within a mile of the gun when it fires. Just think what it sounds like coming in. Must be like a freight train coming at you.''

"I'd almost bet these troops moving through here must be some kind of re-enforcement for that battle that's going on out there."

"What are we gonna do, Sarge?"

"Hell, the only thing we can do. We got to go straight east, bypassing the battle zone. We should be about twenty-five miles from Highway 14. It's the major highway between Kontum and Pleiku, and our best bet. If I'm right, we should intersect it about ten miles north of Pleiku.''

"That's a lot of rugged uphill country between here and there. Do you think Ken can make it?"

"With our help, he's going to have to make it. We just might have one thing working for us, though.''

"What's that?"

"Well, it looks like Charlie owns all the real estate in this area. If he's pushing east on a big thrust, like it appears, then he's staying on this trail and not bothering the countryside.''

"You're thinking he won't have any patrols out in the bush?"

"Right. At least, that's that I'm hoping."

"Then, depending on what kind of battle they're fighting, and how big an engagement it is, we might be able to hit the highway in about two days."

"Yeah. I can't see how Charlie could control and secure the highway. He might have it bottled up at night but it's just too important to let him have twenty-four hours a day."

"So what's the plan, Sarge?"

"We sit tight, when it gets dark, we cross the river and cut out for the boonies."

"Sounds easy," Ted grinned. "I don't suppose you'd like me to ask you what you think our chances are?"

"Not really, man."

Chapter
Twenty-one

"Sarge! Sarge, wake up!" Ken shook him.

"Huh?" Jeff sat up quickly. "What's going on?"

"Patrol boat," Ken whispered. "Comin down the east bank. Real slow, like he's looking for something."

"Where?" Jeff scrambled to the bow, joining Ted, who was peering intently across the river.

"Straight across," Ted whispered. "Four NVA, they're checking the bank real close. You think they are looking for us?"

"Shit man," Jeff cursed as he saw the twenty foot motorized launch. "What else?"

The boat moved slowly along the east bank. One of the soldiers held a long bamboo pole, probing the thick vegetation when necessary, to get a clear view of the bank. Two soldiers, armed with assault rifles, scanned the shoreline and a fourth ran the boat. They were thorough, slowing the launch to check a heavy patch of foliage, then moving on.

Jeff quickly looked up river toward the west bank and his heart jumped into his throat. A second boat, about three hundred yards away, was using the same procedure along the west bank. It too held four soldiers. They had about five minutes before the NVA discovered them.

"They got us nailed," Jeff said, turning to face the others.

"Maybe they'll miss us," Ken said nervously. "We're pretty well hid, Sarge."

"No way, Ken," Jeff shook his head negatively. "They're beating the bush. We got to take 'em!"

"How?" Ken whimpered, almost at the point of tears. His hands were shaking. "Christ sake, Sarge. They're hardcore NVA."

"Shit, Ken. I don't know," Jeff snapped harshly. "Maybe we can surprise them. Look guys, we don't know how long they've been searching for us. It's just possible they've been beating the bank all the way from the camp. They've got to be pretty disgusted by now and maybe they won't expect us to be this close to the bridge. Come on, Ken. We need you on this, pull yourself together. Do we give up? Do you want to go back, and probably this time to a regular POW camp?"

Ken looked hesitantly from Jeff to Ted, then back to Jeff. "No," he whispered lowly.

"All right," Jeff glanced upriver. The boat was a couple of hundred yards away. The boat near the east bank was within fifty yards of the bridge. "We haven't got much time. We've got to waste 'em quick. Our only chance is to blast 'em and grab their boat, then make a run for it up river. The other boat is still on the far side of the river near the bridge. We've got to out run him.''

"Then what?" Ted asked.

"Let's take one thing at a time," Jeff continued. "Ted. You and Nhang get everything into the two packs. Ken, I want you on the bank, right there," he indicated a spot just above the middle of their boat, next to a big tree. "Take one of the rifles and use the tree trunk to brace yourself. I want you to take out the guy running the boat. Concentrate on him. Man, I'm counting on you to zap him. He's your target! Understand?"

Ken nodded wordlessly and pulled himself up a couple of feet onto the lip of the bank. Nhang handed him the rifle. The approaching boat was within a hundred yards of them as Ken propped himself against the tree and silently eased the bolt of the rifle.

"Ted. Stay where you are, there in the middle. Take the carbine. The guy in the bow with the AK-47 is yours. Nhang, you stay here next to me. Use the other rifle, I'll take the pistol. We get the other one with the AK, then I'll take out the guy with the pole. Ted, we got to grab the boat. They're only going to be a couple of feet from us. If you have to, get into the water after you zap your man. We can't let it drift away from us. Nhang, same for you. When your man goes down, reach for the boat. If it drifts out, swim for it and bring it back. If you guys got to go in the water, drop your rifles here. Ken and I will cover you and finish off anyone still kicking. Ken, when I signal you, slide into our boat and throw the rifles and packs into the launch. I'll pull the launch in as close as possible, get on board fast. I'll help you, okay?"

243

Again Ken nodded.

All right,'' Jeff breathed excitedly, his heart pounding in his chest as he took one last look. The launch was within a hundred feet, they could hear the steady put-put of the motor. The launch on the east shore had stopped at the barge site clearing. The ropes tightened as another tank started across the river from the west bank. "Get down," he whispered and positioned himself low in the boat, laying the barrel of the pistol on the side of the boat and peering across the sights. "Don't fire till I do."

Covey-21, a forward air controller out of Pleiku, checked his fuel load as he listened to the radio chatter from the strikes around Plei Mrong. Damn, he thought, they must be having a ball. A NVA division had engaged troops from ARVN II Corps and were almost to the point of overrunning the South Vietnamese Army. Traffic on the radio was almost unintelligible due to the vast number of air support being called in. The ferocity of the attack, along with the tanks and heavy guns had surprised the ARVN troops.

Captain Ron Blazedale checked his map and noted the time as his light O-2 zipped a hundred feet above the Ya Krong river. 1340 hours, he'd been in the air a little over thirty minutes. Well, he thought silently as he pulled the plane up several hundred feet, another fifteen minutes on the river and he could join the rest of his squadron over Plei Mrong. He looked to the east and saw smoke rising from the battle area ten miles to his right. He sighed and let the plane settle back down to his original altitude, flying just below the treeline above the river. He glanced casually at the smoke rockets hanging on the wings figuring he wouldn't need them until he completed his sweep of the river and joined the battle zone. Yeah, he itched to pull away from the river and call in a couple of strikes.

"Just a few more minutes baby," he whispered to the plane. "We'll punch out some smoke, do in a few Charlies and be in the Officer's club by suppertime."

He fought to control his boredom as he scanned the innocent river traffic below him. He hadn't seen a suspicious thing since takeoff. He had flown west from Pleiku along Highway 19 to Cambodia, then turning north to follow the river on its northeast course toward Dak To. He was allowed to break off northwest of Kontum and rejoin his squadron.

He shot through a curve in the river and suddenly sat straight up in the small cockpit. The river stretched before him in a straight line of three or four miles. He leaned forward, his body tensing as his eyes strained to identify the barrier across the river. He blinked several times and brought the object into focus as he rushed towards it. His hands tingled and the hair on the back of his neck bristled. The gap between him and the target closed to two miles, his mind started identifying smaller objects on and around the bridge as he fingered his mike button.

"Task Alpha," he toned evenly. "This is Covey-21. I have a target."

Captain Blazedale ignored the familiar spurt of anti-aircraft tracer rounds that suddenly shot out at him from the east end of the bridge. The rounds were low and to the left.

"Roger, Covey-21. This is Task Alpha," a voice crackled in his headset. "Go ahead with your ID and vector."

He dropped his eyes to his map pad, checking the coordinates of the target. His eyes swung back to the bridge as the tracer fire corrected into his path. He snapped the plane up and to the right, over the treeline and out of the gunner's sights.

"Task Alpha, Covey-21," he said calmly. "I have a bridge in sector niner at Delta one one. Heavy movement of NVA troops, trucks, and artillery. Appears to be a wooden bridge crossing for the trail over the Ya Krong river. Oh, oh . . ." he caught the muzzle flash of the 37mm. AAA, on the west bank as he crossed the trail, east of the bridge. The little Cessna shuddered slightly as he took a hit in the tail section. He jammed hard right, skimming the trees in a tight turn, away from the bridge. The light plane bucked and bounced slightly as he slipped left, then right, testing the controls.

"Covey-21. You still with us?"

"Roger, Task Alpha. I've taken a minor hit aft but no sweat." he said, heading due east from the bridge. "There's triple A's on each end of the bridge, and guess what?"

"Go, Covey-21."

"They're rafting a tank across the river! Along side the bridge. Got any bridge wreckers nearby?"

"Roger, Covey-21. I'm vectoring two Fox Fours to orbit your coordinates. They'll be on station in four minutes."

"Roger, Task Alpha. I'll run east of target for another minute and see if the trail comes out of the woods."

"Roger, Covey-21. Your Fox Fours will be Wham 68 and 69."

"Roger, Task Alpha," he acknowledged, smiling to himself smugly. He knew Wham 68 and 69, two F-4 Phantoms would have a variety of ordinance on board. In less than five minutes, Charlie was going to be minus one bridge.

Blazedale saw the clearing and the end of the jungle cover. He pulled the O-2 hard left as he whizzed past the end of the thick cover and over the now visible trail. He saw some small arms fire flashing at him and he laughed, swooping low over some paddies, straight away from the startled troops.

"Task Alpha, Covey-21 here."

"Go, Covey-21."

"I have a secondary target for you. The trail breaks into the open about two miles east of the bridge. Open fields on the right going up to the foothills. Terraced rice paddies off to the left for three or four miles. The trail is full of NVA in an armored column heading for Plei Mrong. I'm going back to mark the bridge. Send help!"

"Roger, Covey-21. I'm bringing up Covey-9, and a flight of VNAF A-1's, for the trail. Wham 68 and 69 are on your frequency. What's your favorite color?"

"How about titty pink?"

"Roger, Covey-21. Go get 'em!"

"Roger, Task Alpha." Blazedale grinned as he skimmed the rice fields causing several water buffaloes to scatter away from some farmers plowing their paddies. No sign of troops out here, he thought to himself, making a turn to the west. He planned to intersect the river north of the bridge, coming in low over the water and around the curve, that way, he'd eliminate a lot of firing time from the anti-aircraft artillery. He'd smoke the tank on the barge first, then the west gun emplacement. He knew he'd have to make another pass to smoke the east gun. The 0-2 responded a bit sluggishly as he pulled the plane up to clear the jungle. He was a half mile from the river and two miles north of the bridge. He eased back the throttle, lessening the buzz of his engine. No sense in making a lot of noise, he smiled to himself as the river came into view.

Jeff watched the prow of the open launch slide slowly past the veil of foliage. It was about five feet from them. The bow guard was watching the other boat as it floated among several fishing boats waiting for the bridge to open. Evidently, the other patrol was searching some of the enclosed boats. Just a few more feet, Jeff whispered to himself as he saw the operator of the launch come into view. He was sitting on the wooden motor housing, his hands on the wheel and control stand that was center and forward in the launch.

Agonizingly, the pole man amid-ships eased past their peephole. The tip of the bamboo pole probed the small opening, then thrust forward directly at Jeff's head. The pole hit the top of their boat with a heavy thunk and slid past his head. He grabbed the pole instinctively and pulled as the forward motion of the launch caused the pole to tear a bigger gap in their cover.

"Now!" Jeff shouted and fired through the opening with a clear view of the soldier in the stern. He watched fascinated as the man's head exploded and he dropped his rifle. Nhang's rifle boomed next to his ear, deafening him. Nhang's shot caught the soldier in the middle of the chest, knocking him backwards out of the boat. Ken's carbine chattered rapidly, ripping into the operator and spraying wooden chips from the console and motor housing. Son of a bitch, Jeff thought, he's got the damn thing on automatic!

Ted's rifle roared twice in quick succession and one of the soldiers screamed. Jeff heard a Vietnamese voice shouting and felt a tug on the pole. He yanked on the pole as he swung the muzzle of the pistol, aiming straight up the pole, he pulled the trigger twice. What seemed like slow motion in his mind, he watched the terrified look on the poleman's face as he saw Jeff. He had clamped both hands on the pole and was straining to get it away from Jeff. He was leaning forward as Jeff's first round nicked the pole near the man's hands and whined out harmlessly over the river. The second round caught him in the left arm and he yelped as he fell forward into the water, his right hand still clutching the pole. Jeff felt a sickening feeling in his gut as the man's forward motion caused the launch to buck away from them. He screamed over his shoulder for Ken to stop shooting. The rounds were blasting close over their heads, chewing up the launch. Ken's carbine must have jammed or he ran out of ammo because he suddenly stopped firing. Jeff knew Ken hadn't heard him yell.

"Get the fuckin boat," he shouted at Ted and Nhang. They hit the water and Jeff felt a tug on the pole. Christ, he thought, as the man in the water surfaced, still clutching the bamboo. Jeff aimed the pistol, raising to one knee. He pulled the trigger, feeling the jerk of recoil against his hand and the man slumped face down in the water, a gaping hole in the back of his skull. The entire sequence from his first shot to the last had taken less than ten seconds.

"Come on Ken," he snapped as he watched Ted reach the bow of the launch. His hand grabbed a rope trailing over the side and he turned back towards Jeff pulling the boat after him. Nhang splashed around getting himself in position behind the launch as it turned inward. Jeff looked across the river and the other launch was trying to thread its way among the tangle of fishing boats. Two soldiers were kneeling in the bow firing. The rounds were falling short but in a minute they'd be in range.

"What the fuck?" Jeff questioned as he turned to Ken and heard his weird laughter. "Ken, come on!"

Ken was sitting on the bank with his legs hanging over the lip. The carbine was tucked into his right side as his finger worked the trigger and the barrel swayed slightly from left to right as if he were spraying the enemy. A high pitched combination of laughter and giggling escaped his open mouth and a dribble of saliva ran down his chin. His eyes were glazed and bugged from his head.

"Ken," Jeff screamed as he leaped up, grabbing the upper stock of the carbine with one hand and Ken's leg with the other, he yanked, toppling the young soldier into the boat, pulling the carbine from his grasp.

"Sarge," he heard Ted from the water. "Catch the rope."

Jeff snagged the rope in his free hand. Ken layed curled at his feet, sobbing uncontrollably now. Jeff pulled the rope until the bow of the launch crunched against the side of their boat. Nhang hauled himself over the stern and into the launch and Ted pulled himself into the smaller boat, falling over Ken.

"What's with him?" Ted asked excitedly. "He hit?"

"No. He's flipped out. Toss your guns and gear into the launch." Jeff struggled to bring the launch along side the smaller boat. "Nhang, dump the two bodies over the side."

Chapter
Twenty-two

Jeff looked across the river. Their cover was gone, thanks to the firefight. The other patrol boat was still jammed among the fishing boats. Small boats bumped and banged into each other as they tried to clear a path. Three soldiers were in the bow of the patrol launch, popping rounds across the river. Jeff saw them splatter some fifty or sixty feet short. He almost laughed. Talk about a Vietnamese fire drill. He heard the splash as Nhang dumped the bodies. Traffic on the bridge had stopped to watch the spectacle. He lost all desire to laugh when he saw the 37mm. gun crew take their positions.

"Damn," he swore, knowing that gun could blow them out of the water in two seconds.

"Grab him, Ted," Jeff ordered. "We just ran out of time."

Ted picked up Ken by the waist and leapt into the

launch. Jeff jumped and pushed in the same motion causing the launch to drift back, away from the bank. He heard the dreaded steady report of the AAA gun and tightened instinctively, waiting for the rounds to shred the launch. He was sprawled face down in the bottom of the boat, eye to eye with Ted. Ken was under him. They waited, motionless for several seconds, as the gun continued to fire. Shit, Jeff thought, he should at least have been able to hear the near misses hitting the water or the bank. The whine of a light engine airplane mingled with the chaos of gunfire from the launch, the rapid bang of the anti-aircraft gun and the yelling and shouting from the bridge area.

Jeff jumped up and looked to the far shore and the AAA gun. In an instant he understood what was happening. He saw the bright flash of a spotter plane coming toward the bridge from the south. He glanced quickly to the west AAA gun and saw the crew swinging the barrel to intercept the little plane.

"Ted," Jeff shouted, as he picked up one of the discarded assault rifles. "Get this thing started."

Ted sprang for the control console as Jeff blasted a few rounds in the vicinity of the tangled mass blocking the other launch. The engine of the small plane sang and Jeff watched it spin up and over the east treeline, blocking a clear line of sight from the east gun. He watched it skim the tall trees knowing the west gun would open up soon.

"Nhang," Ted cried. "Help me!"

Nhang joined Ted at the simple console. For a terrifying few seconds he studied the panel, then pulled a small lever, unlocking the gearbox. Ted realized he'd been trying to start the boat with the gear engaged. The small engine sputtered to life as Ted pressed the start button again.

"Forward," Nhang pointed to the notch above the lever. "And back," he indicated the notch below the lever.

"Is this the throttle?" he pushed forward on another lever and felt the motor race, answering his own question. He slapped it into reverse and gunned the throttle. The launch started to back up slowly, then stopped. Something was holding them. Ted looked up and saw the trouble. Jeff had dropped the forward line when he jumped into the boat. Somehow, it had snagged in the vines and was holding them firmly.

"Nhang," Ted pointed. "We're caught. Get the line."

Jeff flinched as the west AAA gun started firing. He thought the spotter plane was a goner but the pilot snapped it right, away from the bridge and the gun. Jeff was sure he saw a tracer round go through one of the twin tails. He heard the plane buzz off to the east, fading away as the gun stopped firing.

"Come on," he screamed. "Let's get the fuck out of here."

Nhang tugged on the rope to no avail. It was caught fast. Ted looked around frantically for the machette. He knew he had thrown it on board with the guns. "There. Nhang." He pointed. Ken was lying on it. "There, the machette, under Ken. Cut the fuckin' rope."

Nhang understood and scrambled towards Ken as he rolled over and sat up. Nhang reached for the handle to pick it up.

"Fuckin' VC," Ken screamed and grabbed Nhang pulling him down on top of him. They wrestled in the boat.

"No VC, Ken!" Ted heard Nhang's muffled cry. "No VC."

"Oh shit," Ted muttered and slapped the boat in neutral. He leaped forward as Ken rolled on top of Nhang raising the machette. He grabbed Ken's arm stopping the downward slash. "Sarge, help!"

Jeff was right behind Ted. He had looked around to see what was holding them up when Ken yelled. Ted pulled Ken to his feet and was holding him from behind. Jeff forced the machette out of Ken's hand and dropped it next to Nhang. Ken had the face of a madman.

"Ken," Jeff screamed and slapped him hard. "Ken!" He slapped him again. "Damnit Ken, get yourself together. It's me, Jeff!"

Ken's eyes rolled and he blinked several times. His mouth opened and closed but no words came out. He stared at Jeff and the light of recognition flooded his face. Jeff nodded and Ted released his hold.

"You okay now?" Ted asked. "Man, you flipped out. Tried to kill Nhang. Thought he was a VC."

"Uh . . . Yeah," Ken wiped his face with the back of his hand.

Nhang slashed the rope and the launch swung free. He crouched in the bow watching Ken warily. Ted stepped back to the controls and swung the boat up river as the other patrol boat started firing at them again.

"Come on." Jeff grabbed Ken by the arm and half dragged him to the stern. He saw the boat was now free of the fishing traffic and headed for them. "Here," he pushed Ken down to a kneeling position and handed him an AK-47. "There's Charlie. Fire short bursts," he pointed to the approaching launch about two hundred and fifty yards away as he knelt and picked up the carbine, slapping a full magazine in it.

Ted had the throttle wide open, yet it appeared the patrol boat was gaining on them. He was running close to the west shore trying to eliminate a field of fire from one of the AAA guns. He planned to cut across the river at the bend, knowing that for a few seconds they would be completely exposed to both guns. Rounds from the patrol boat gunners were now dangerously close.

Jeff fired several bursts at the closing patrol boat and ducked instinctively as something whooshed close overhead. He blinked as a smoke rocket detonated on the left side of the tank of the barge. Again, a rocket shot by and slammed into the west clearing near the AAA gun. Twin pillars of white smoke rapidly rose from the impact area of the rockets as the spotter plane zipped low over their boat.

The east bank AAA gun fought to track the little plane. The gun had been lining up to fire at Jeff's boat when the plane appeared. The gun crews hesitation because of target choices allowed the O-2 to make his pass unscathed. The plane shot over the west treeline heading away from the rash of small arms fire on the bridge and the pursuing patrol boat.

Ted swung the boat for the east shore, fifty yards from the curve. "Man," he shouted excitedly at Jeff. "What the hell was that?"

"I do believe," Jeff grinned. "The Air Force has found this bridge. It's going to get pretty hot around here in a minute."

"Wow!" Ted beamed. "If I ever meet that pilot, I'll kiss his bare ass in a public place of his choosing."

"Listen," Nhang pointed. "He come back."

Nhang was right. The plane's engine buzzed as it circled back from the west. He was making another pass. Jeff glanced at the AAA guns. They heard it too and were setting up for a crossfire. His attention was diverted by the thuds of bullets hitting their boat. The pursuing patrol boat was within a hundred yards of them and the soldiers were starting to get accurate.

"Nhang," Jeff called. "Get back here with a rifle. We need more firepower. Come on Ken, let's make them keep their heads down."

Ted watched his angle into the bend. They started into the curve. He picked up a discarded AK-47 and checked the load as Nhang joined Jeff and Ken kneeling in the stern. He half turned and fired over their heads, joining the deadly hail of his companion's guns. He saw wood splinters fly from the bow of the other boat and one of the soldiers drop out of sight.

"I got one!" Ken screamed, leaping to his feet. "I got one!"

"Get down!" Ted swung his gun to the right and stopped firing as his last burst came deadly close to Ken. "You dumb shit. I almost nailed you."

Jeff pulled Ken down again and watched the AAA guns as the plane dropped over the west treeline a couple hundred yards south of the bridge. It swooped low over the water and fired a rocket. The east AAA gun opened fire, getting off several rounds before the rocket exploded at the base of the sandbagged emplacement starting another column of white smoke. Jeff couldn't tell if the plane had been hit or not, although it appeared some of the tracer rounds went right through it.

The entire river crossing was now covered in a cloud

of thick white smoke. The bridge was barely visible as the 0-2 hurtled toward the cloud and its protection. The west gun opened fire placing a lethal curtain blindly in the path of the plane. Jeff heard the whine of the plane's engine cough and sputter as it rushed through the smoke and suddenly appeared, coming straight at them. The engine was silent and black smoke trailed behind it in a thick stream. The plane tilted in a crazy angle with the right wingtip pointing down, just several feet above the water. It was within fifty feet of crashing into them when the pilot flipped it into level flight and zoomed twenty feet above their heads.

Jeff watched the glide angle of the plane as the pilot fought to keep it level. The left wing dipped as it started into the bend of the river, now several feet above the water. The pilot over corrected and the right wing knifed into the water causing the plane to cartwheel around the curve and momentarily out of their sight. He heard the loud smack as it hit the water.

"Get to the plane, Ted," he shouted, "we got to get the pilot out."

Jeff swung his attention back to the bridge and the pursuing patrol coat. The scene was complete mayhem. The white smoke was rising in three distinct columns. He could see figures on the bridge running frantically to clear the structure, knowing what was coming. The boats that had been waiting on the north side of the bridge were scrambling to get away from it. The patrol boat had closed to fifty yards and Jeff fired a quick burst at it as they pulled around the curve and lost sight of it.

"Reload," Jeff directed Nhang and Ken. "Get set.

As soon as they come around the curve blast 'em. Ken, you alright?''

"Yes," he mumbled as he grabbed one of the packs and dumped the contents. "This is what I need," he grinned, picking up two hand grenades.

Jeff turned forward and saw the wreckage of the plane twenty yards ahead. It had come to rest intact against the east bank. The twin tails had slammed into the bank and were a crumpled mass in the twisted vines. The fuselage was partially submerged with the left wing slanting down into the water. Part of the right wing was gone. The remaining stub of the wing pointed up in a 45 degree angle. The windshield was shattered and he could see the helmeted head of the pilot slumped forward over the controls. The plane had apparently cartwheeled around the curve and as it pancaked right side up, it slid backwards into the bank. Black smoke was still billowing out of the engine compartment.

"Get the bow in under the right wing," Jeff said, rushing past Ted. "There, next to the right door."

"You think he's still alive?" Ted called after Jeff.

"Ain't but one way to find," Jeff started but was drowned out by the resounding thunder of an F-4 Phantom as it pulled out of it's attack dive on the bridge. Simultaneously, two explosions rocked the jungle. Ted gritted his teeth as the concussions sucked the air around them.

"Jesus," he cried, hunching over from the force as the second F-4 screamed by overhead. This time the explosion wasn't as severe but when he heard the loud whoosh, Ted understood why. The second plane had dropped napalm.

"Hold it. Hold it," Jeff yelled.

Ted grabbed at the throttle and snapped the gear into reverse, trying to slow the boat as the bow slipped under the right wing with a couple of feet clearance. Jeff grabbed the wing and stopped the forward motion of the boat. He quickly slipped over the bow and into water that came up to his waist. He snatched the door handle and struggled to get it opened. Finally, he braced his knee against the fuselage and yanked. It came open and he pushed it aside, climbing half into the small cabin.

Nhang heard Ken muttering something to himself as he turned to watch the two F-4's make their climb-out. He was crouching next to Ken, peering over the stern when the jets made their pass. The roaring planes had jarred every bone in his body and as soon as he had recovered from the initial shock, he twisted, looking over his shoulder at them. He squinted, watching the smoke trails of the two planes as they started to fade high above them to the north. He saw the sun flash on their wings as they rolled and turned, losing them momentarily. He blinked and the tiny dots grew bigger. They were coming back!

Ted saw them too as he glanced back and forth from Jeff to the planes. "Oh shit," he whispered, and unconsciously braced himself. The images grew clearer as the Phantoms screamed in on a deadly track. Ted thought they were dangerously low as they swooped past the treeline behind him. Again, the earth-shattering detonations and sucking air blasted his entire body. He worked his jaw and shook his head trying to regain his senses and finally heard the rolling thunder as they pulled away.

"Help me, Ted," Jeff called from the water. He'd

pulled the pilot from the plane and was trying to push the unconscious man into the launch. Ted leaped forward, grabbing the pilot under the arms and pulled him into the boat. He turned and grabbed Jeff's outreaching hand and helped him in.

"Get us out of here! Quick," Jeff said, out of breath as he collapsed next to the pilot. "Stay along the east bank," he pointed north.

Ted pushed against the wing of the plane and scrambled for the controls of the boat. He swung the wheel, slipping the throttle forward as the prop slowly churned against the muddy bottom. Gunfire erupted behind him as the boat pulled free and swung past the wrecked plane. He looked over his shoulder as the patrol boat slid around the curve, fifteen yards behind them. Two soldiers were squatting low in the bow. The unexpected appearance of the Americans startled them briefly. Ted saw Nhang's rifle recoil and one of the soldiers dropped from view. The other soldier fired wildly and Ted felt a tug in the back of his left arm. He ducked and snatched the rifle at his feet. As he turned to fire, Ken stood up, blocking his target. Ted couldn't believe what happened next.

"Here, motherfucker," Ken screamed. He pulled the pin of a grenade and flipped it almost casually into the NVA boat.

"Ken get down!" Ted heard himself shout. "Nhang, grab him!"

"Here's another . . . You bastards!" Ken screamed again and tossed the second grenade.

The soldier in the bow managed to fire a quick burst before the grenade went off. The force of the bullets knocked Ken backwards, spinning him around. He flopped in the bottom of the boat, his right leg a bloody mess, twisted awkwardly under him. Ted saw the NVA boat heave with the two consecutive blasts. Metal fragments whizzed hotly through the air as the boat erupted in flames and smoke. It sank immediately as they pulled away from it.

"What was that," Jeff asked dumbly, crawling on his hands and knees past Ted.

"Man," Ted moaned. "Ken's hit. He stood up to toss a grenade and they zapped him. Help him Sarge . . . Help him!"

"All right . . . all right." Jeff reached Ken and ripped the leg of his pants away. He almost threw up. The bullets must have smashed through his right kneecap and lower leg bone. Chunks of flesh were missing from each hit. Splinters of bone protruded from the lower leg wound. The kneecap and half the joint was missing from the upper wound. Tendrils of flesh and stringy white tendons hung limply from what was left of the leg. Blood streamed into the bottom of the boat mixing with the bilge water.

"Son of a bitch," Jeff swore. "Nhang. Give me the pack with the medical stuff."

Nhang handed Jeff the pack. "Is he dead, Sarge?" he asked. "I try to pull him down but he like crazy man. I sorry, Sarge. I sorry . . ."

"Don't worry about it," Jeff tore open some bandage and gauze packs. "Shit, it ain't your fault. We got to stop this bleeding or he will be dead." Jeff stuffed gauze around the wounds filling the gaps of missing tissue. Nhang helped him wrap bandages over the guaze and tie them off. Jeff pried two wooden slats off the motor cover with the machette to use as splints and

Ken screamed when they straightened the leg to position them, but slumped into unconsciousness almost immediately. Jeff made a tourniquet and tightened it. "Nhang, stay here with him. About every five minutes loosen this for a half a minute, then tighten it up again. Understand?"

"Okay, Sarge. I understand."

"Good. I'm going to check on the pilot." Jeff stood up and moved to Ted. He looked around. They were a quarter of a mile north of the bridge. Heavy black smoke rose past the curve of the river. The wreckage of the boat and plane were still visible, then as if on cue, the plane exploded. Jeff saw a flash of movement in the sky and saw the F-4's making a tight low turn over the bridge and the crash site of the spotter plane.

"How bad is he?" Ted asked. "Is he going to make it?"

"I don't know," Jeff leaped to the pilot and searched his body frantically. "If we can stop the bleeding and get a Med Evac chopper in here, he might make it."

"How the hell are we going to get a chopper?"

"Ahhh . . ." Jeff grinned, holding up the pilot's survival radio. "With this!" He scanned the radio and thumbed the emergency 'beeper' switch, knowing it was now sending an audible continuous beeping signal on emergency frequencies. He noted the transmit button on the radio and decided to wait a few minutes before attempting to use it. He realized his unfamiliar voice and ignorance of proper call signs and codes would cause suspicion. He had to revive the pilot.

Jeff removed the pilot's helmet. He was bleeding from a cut on his lip and a gash on his chin. Jeff placed the handgun from the pilot's shoulder holster next to the helmet and searched his flightsuit. He noted the man's nametag as he probed for other wounds. The pilot's left wrist was swollen and Jeff touched the thick area, knowing it was broken. He removed the map pad strapped above the pilot's right knee and studied it after his examination. The man didn't seem to have any other wounds or broken bones and his breathing was steady and even. Jeff looked at the map pad again, eyeing the notation 'Covey-21' penciled on the bottom.

"Task Alpha to Wham-68 . . ."

"Wham-68. Go ahead, Task Alpha."

"Task Alpha to Wham-68, I'm getting a 'beeper' on emergency channel from your target vector. Have you spotted Covey-21?"

"Roger, Task Alpha. He's down on the east bank, four hundred yards north of target. Wreckage is on fire. If he's still in it, he's bought it."

"Roger, Wham-68. Beeper signal appears to be moving north, following the river. Get on that frequency and see if you can make contact."

"Roger, Task Alpha. We can only give you about five minutes. Our juice is pretty low."

"Check, Wham-68. I'm bringing in Search and Rescue."

"Roger, Task Alpha . . ."

"Covey-21, this is Wham-68," the radio crackled in Jeff's hand. He hesitated, staring at it.

"Covey-21, this is Wham-68. Do you read me?" the voice came from the radio again, saying each word clearly and distinctly.

Jeff slowly raised the radio near his lips and spoke. "Wham-68, this is . . . ah . . . this is Covey-21."

"Negative, Wham-68. Repeat, Negative," interrupted Task Alpha. "You have a negative signal . . ."

Jeff heard the transmission and his heart pounded in his chest. They knew it wasn't the pilot making the transmission. "Ted," he shouted.

"Let Nhang take the controls. Try to revive the pilot. Shit, throw some water on him or something . . ."

Ted left the controls and moved quickly to the unconscious pilot. He grabbed a water can scooping it over the side and splashing it in the pilots face. Nothing. He filled the can again, repeating the procedure, this time, patting the man's cheek. Still nothing.

"Wham-68," Jeff pressed the radio button. "This is Covey-21, I . . . mean . . . I'm not Covey-21 . . . aahhh . . . I mean, ah, I'm using the radio. He's unconscious!"

"Wham-68, to caller," the voice answered after a slight pause. "Identify yourself. Repeat. Identify yourself and give location."

"Roger, Wham-68. This is . . ." Jeff's voice was much calmer now as he relayed his rank, name, serial number and unit. "We are in a boat, proceeding north of the bridge you blew up. We pulled the pilot out of his plane. He is unconscious. We are trying to revive him. Do you read?"

"Roger, Sgt. Spencer. Standby . . ."

"We got 'em, Ted," Jeff shouted. "We got 'em!"

"Wowie!" Ted exclaimed. "Wowie!"

"Mmmm," the pilot moaned. His eyes fluttered and his right hand came to his face, rubbing his brow.

"He's coming around," Jeff nodded to Ted. "Give him some more water."

"Wham-68 to Sgt. Spencer," the radio came alive again.

"Sgt. Spencer to Wham-68. Go ahead . . ."

"Spencer, we have no knowledge of your unit in this area. Who are you?"

"Wham-68, please listen," Jeff's voice pleaded, his heart pounding desperately. "We are escaped POW's. Three GI's, Spencer, Hefley and Mayhew. One Vietnamese, Nhang. We've been prisoners for almost a year."

"Roger, Spencer," the voice acknowledged. "Is the 'Nammie' friendly?"

Jeff glanced at Nhang's grinning face. "Roger, Wham-68," Jeff said as he saw the two F-4's approaching from behind them. The Phantoms were low over the river and slowed to almost stalling speed. He knew they were taking a risk because if it was a trap, anti-aircraft guns along either bank could easily blast them. He grinned as one of the Phantom's peeled off quickly and climbed with a sudden burst of speed, as if he had read Jeff's mind. The remaining aircraft dropped even lower, passing left of them about fifty yards away. Jeff stood up and waved his arms frantically as the pilot tilted the plane slightly to get a good look at the boat. Jeff saw their helmeted heads in the forward and rear cockpits as the plane roared by, then made a tight turn to the right.

"Ohhh," Ron Blazedale moaned, sitting up and looking around with a blank stare on his face.

"Easy Captain," Ted cautioned, putting his arm around the pilot's shoulder and raising the cup of water to his lips. "Take it easy. We're friends. GI's. Here, take another sip of water."

"Oh man. My head . . ." Blazedale moaned, pushing the cup away. "Where am . . . Ouch! Damn . . ." he swore as he tried to move his hand. "My hand . . . What happened?"

"You crashed!" Ted started. "Charlie's AAA on the bridge got you. We, that is, Sergeant Spencer, pulled you out and . . ."

"Wham-68 to Sgt. Spencer . . ."

"Spencer to Wham-68. Was that you that just passed?"

"Roger, Spencer, I'm coming around again. What's the status of the pilot you picked up? Is he badly injured?"

"Spencer to Wham-68. He's conscious now. He has a few cuts and a broken wrist. He's a little shaky but he should be able to talk to you in a few minutes."

"Good show, Spencer. We're coming around again."

"Roger, Wham-68 . . ."

"Hey! What are you doing with my radio?" Blazedale asked and felt his empty holster with his good hand. "And where's my gun?"

"Right there," Jeff pointed to the gun, next to the helmet. "Pick it up if you want. As to the radio, I'm trying to get us rescued but your pals are being somewhat cautious."

"Man," Blazedale holstered his gun with his good hand and looked at them suspiciously. "Who the hell are you guys?"

"Tell him Ted," Jeff handed the radio to the Captain. "I'll check on Ken." He got up and patted Nhang on the shoulder. "Just keep it nice and easy along the bank Nhang. Those flyboys want to look us over again and if you see any Charlie's, head for the shore."

"Okay Sarge," Nhang grinned. "But no VC, they busy on bridge and trail. Sounds like big fight."

"Yeah," Jeff nodded, checking Ken as he heard the sounds of an air strike a mile or so to the east. "Ted," he looked at the bloody bandages on Ken's leg. "We need that Med-Evac pretty fast."

"Right," Ted shouted as he finished a quick explanation to Blazedale. "You heard him Captain. My buddie's leg is damn near blown off. Do you still think we are VC or deserters?"

"No," Blazedale said sincerely. "And thanks."

"Just get us a chopper, Captain," Ted grinned.

"Wham-68, this is Covey-21. Captain Ron Blazedale. Titty Pink . . ."

"Roger . . . Covey-21 . . . Welcome back."

Chapter
Twenty-three

Jeff read the mileage sign over the highway as he sped towards it, TUCSON 51 MILES. Another hour, he thought, trying to move his cramped legs without disturbing Valerie. Her head rested on his right thigh as she lay curled up, napping on the seat next to him.

"Jeff?" she asked lightly.

"Yeah, Hon," he touched her silky hair with the fingertips of his free hand.

"Are we getting close?"

"Another hour. Go back to sleep."

"Okay," she sighed dreamily, patting the inside of his thigh.

Jeff glanced at his watch and carefully passed a car. Almost two o'clock. Well, they should be pulling into the Chandler's motel by three. He eased the new Thunderbird back into the middle lane smiling with satisfaction at its performance. Since leaving Fort Campbell two days ago, it had run with perfection. Of course, they were taking their time, not pushing it. They had stopped the past two nights at nice motels, enjoying themselves and each other. It had really been the first time they'd spent an entire forty-eight hours alone, since his return from Vietnam.

Christ, he thought. His life! What a mess it had been for the past three months. The Army debriefings, press reporters, television interviews. The phone ringing constantly with friends and strangers wishing him well; some accusing him of being a murderer and baby killer.

Jeff tried to push the last three months of turmoil from his mind and smiled in anticipation, feeling the hot afternoon sun beating down on his forearm. It was turning red from the constant exposure out of the driver's window but he wouldn't roll it up and turn on the air conditioner. He still couldn't stand to be in a small enclosed place, even a car. As long as a window was open, he was okay.

Again he smiled, thinking of Ted, Ken, and Nhang. Especially Nhang, Ted had met his flight from Vietnam to Travis Air Base, California this morning. Nhang, Ted, and Ted's parents were flying to Tucson to meet him and Val. In fact, they should have arrived from San Francisco an hour ago. Damn, he grinned even broader, they were already at the Chandler place. He unconsciously pressed a little harder on the accelerator, then caught himself and eased back.

This would be their first reunion since leaving Vietnam. Ted would be marrying Kathy Chandler in the next two days. Mr. Chandler invited Jeff and Val along with Ken and his wife to stay at the motel as long as they liked, or in Jeff's case, for his long awaited thirty day leave. Nhang was arriving in the United States under Jeff's sponsorship until he could be legally adopted by him. Val had readily agreed to the adoption and was as eager as he to greet Nhang. He silently remembered the commotion he'd caused when he was told he was being medically evacuated from the hospital at Cam Ranh Bay, Vietnam to Clark Air Base in the Phillipines, then on to a stateside hospital of his choice. He promised Nhang he could go with them and had run into a wall of red tape. Hell, it even took a few threats to get Nhang to the hospital at Cam Ranh Bay.

Initially, after their pickup near the river by Search and Rescue, they were flown to the medical unit at Pleiku. They were treated and scheduled for another Med-Evacuation to the more elaborate facilities at Cam Rahn Bay but Nhang was going to the Vietnamese Army hospital in Saigon. Ted joined Jeff in his protest and screamed for the American base commander. Ken would have probably protested also but he was unconscious and full of morphine. Consequently, the base commander relented after several calls to Military Assistance Command Headquarters in Saigon.

So from the start, Jeff realized what he was up against in his fight to keep his promise to Nhang. They were kept together at Cam Rahn Bay for the first two days, except for Ken. His right leg had to be amputated so he was in a different ward and finally joined them on the third day. An endless stream of debriefings started, by Army and Air Force intelligence personnel and their counterparts from the Vietnamese Air Force and Army. Representatives from the American Embassy and one guy who didn't identify himself, Jeff knew he was from the CIA, were flown in from Saigon. The Army assigned a Major from the Office of Information to them exclusively. After all, they were considered heroes and the Army wasn't about to miss a chance for some positive publicity from a war that was lost. The Major briefed them on what they could and could not talk about due to security reasons. A formal press conference was called for the fifth day, just prior to their departure for Clark Field. Some reporters and camera crews had been allowed to see them but their questions were severely limited. They were to get film footage of the returned POW's smiling and eating steak and ice cream and apple pie, or posing with the prettiest nurses.

On the fourth day Nhang was interviewed by a Vietnamese Army Captain and some jerk in civilian clothes from the Saigon government. Nhang kept getting excited and his voice rose hysterically as they questioned him. He kept shooting worried looks at Jeff during the talk and when Jeff tried to ask Nhang what was going on the American Major told him to leave it alone. Jeff reluctantly complied and when the interview was over, he could see that Nhang was shook. He asked Nhang what was going on and he said they accused him of still being a Viet Cong and he was going to a VC retaining camp near Bien Hoa.

Jeff blew his stack! He told the Major from public relations and the dude from the embassy to start calling generals, the Ambassador, or the President, but he refused to leave Vietnam without Nhang. Further more, he'd raise so much hell at the press conference and any future ones, that the Major and the Embassy guy couldn't get a job selling free pussy. That hit them where it hurt and they knew it. Jeff stated his wish to adopt Nhang, pointing out that he was also a French citizen and that should make their jobs easier. Ted and Ken threatened to back Jeff all the way, so the Major and his pal departed to hastily start cutting red tape.

On the morning of the fifth day the two men returned and started a line of bullshit about facts having to be verified and records checked. Jeff kept up his insistence until the Embassy official agreed to take Nhang under his wing. He would stay with him in Saigon, without any harassment until the entire matter could be worked out. Being a person with dual nationality would work in Nhang's favor, the official assured him. Jeff relented after the official promised to allow Nhang to call Jeff on a weekly basis, keeping him informed of the situation. He also gave the personal assurances that the American Ambassador and Commanding General, Vietnam would do everything in their power to expedite Nhang's return to Jeff's custody.

The Major helped Jeff prepare a statement for the press conference elaborating on Nhang's help in their escape and outlining plans for his adoption by Jeff. Ted stated that if it hadn't been for Nhang's help they would have died in prison camp and never escaped, also pointing out that his knowledge of enemy activity and their location had enabled the Vietnamese Army to destroy a North Vietnamese Army division. Thus, he was a hero to the South Vietnamese government. The world press ate it up and Jeff figured it would be smooth sailing from then on.

They all placed calls to the states just before the press meeting. Val cried all during the time Jeff was trying to talk to her. He explained Nhang's situation and hoped Val would accept this decision. She happily cried yes, and kept saying how she knew he wasn't dead. He promised to call her every day from the Phillipines and not to worry if she saw pictures of them on the news, he was feeling a lot better than he looked. He told her they would be at Clark field for three days, then he would be shipped to the hospital at Fort Campbell, Kentucky. She was still repeating she loved him, over and over, as he hung up the phone.

Ted called his parents in California first, then Kathy Chandler in Arizona. He proposed over the phone and she accepted. She and her parents would meet him in California and they could make their plans. Ted told her his parents would contact hers, inviting them to visit while Ted was in the hospital at Travis Air Base, California.

Ken was unsuccessful in trying to contact his wife, Dina, in Boston. He reached his parents in New Hampshire and talked to them. He was disappointed to learn that they hadn't had any contact with Dina since the funeral. He told them he wanted to go to the Navy hospital in Boston and they were to meet him there. Evidently, one of them asked about his leg but Ken cut them off saying he would see them soon. He knew Dina must have heard of the escape. A reporter told him they were the lead story on very newscast. In fact, the phone calls had been set up by a major network and had been filmed and recorded for broadcast after some editing.

Jeff noticed Ken's depression and sullen attitude even on their departure from Cam Ranh Bay. He smiled only briefly at Nhang from his stretcher as they said goodbye on the boarding ramp of the Air Force transport jet. Nhang shook hands and hugged all of them with tears in his eyes as the cameras clicked and whirled. Jeff turned and walked up the ramp with a promise they'd be together soon.

The days at Clark Field were filled with more press conferences and interviews. The Army issued them new uniforms and processed them for their return to the States. Everywhere they went, he and Ted, Ken was confined to the hospital, they were followed by the press. People stopped them on their shopping trips to the PX to shake their hands and greet them. Gifts and cards arrived daily at their hospital rooms. Jeff knew people were only trying to be warm and friendly but it was starting to get to them all.

Ted and Jeff would go into Ken's room at night and try to get him out of his depression. Ken still couldn't reach his wife despite all the efforts of the Major and some of the press. They savored those few sessions alone at night, confiding in one another and relating their future plans. It was during one of those sessions that Ted brought up the idea that they have a reunion the same time he got married. He would plan it to coincide with Nhang's arrival in the States. They all agreed and it was set.

They were airlifted from Clark field to Travis Air Base. Jeff and Ken had a couple of hours delay before their individual flights, so they were able to meet Ted's and Kathy's parents. It was a tearful meeting for all of them except Ken. He was polite but quiet and distant. Mrs. Chandler told Jeff about her meeting Valerie in Washington, D.C., and Jeff was totally warmed by her open friendliness. He knew Val must have instantly liked her and shared her confidence with her. When Ted informed them all of the wedding and reunion plans,

Mr. Chandler insisted everyone would be his guest. It was agreed and they parted tearfully.

Jeff nervously checked his watch for the third or fourth time in the past ten minutes. Just a few more miles, he thought, fighting the urge to speed up. He shifted his weight uncomfortably on the seat, waking Val again. She sat up, brushing her hair back with her hands and leaned over, kissing him on the cheek.

"Getting anxious, huh?" she smiled, watching him.

"Yeah, I guess. Hell, they probably won't recognize me," he said thinking of the weight he'd gained since being home. He had lost over sixty pounds in the camp and Val hadn't wasted any time in helping him gain half of that back. His body had healed quickly.

"Oh," she laughed. "I'm sure you'll recognize each other. Did Ted mention if he'd heard from Ken?"

"Just that he talked to him a week ago and that was the last time. Ken supposedly knew his wife's address in Los Angeles and was going to see her."

"I guess getting those divorce papers from her really shook him up."

"I know," Jeff agreed. "Damn, you'd think after all that poor bastard has been through, she would have shown a little more consideration. The last time I called him in Boston at the hospital, I could tell he was still depressed. He must have taken off for Los Angeles right after I called him. Man, I hope he's alright."

"Hey," Val coaxed. "He'll be okay. Just wait and see, he'll show up just like he promised."

"I hope so," he said. "Anyway, if the directions Ted gave me are correct, the motel should be here on the right side."

"There's something, coming up ahead," she pointed.

"Yeah," he slowed down, reading the sign at the front of the motel complex. "This is it."

Jeff pulled the car into the parking lot. It was deserted except for two cars. He parked near the office and noticed a group of people sitting by the pool. He got out of the car and went around to Val's door. His hands were shaking and his stomach was doing flips. Val was already out and he took her hand and turned toward the group at the pool. Nhang was running towards them.

"Sergeant Jeff! Sergeant Jeff!" Nhang leaped at him.

"Nhang," Jeff choked in a whisper as they embraced. He felt the hot tears run down his cheeks. Ted rushed up behind Nhang and threw his arms around both of them. Jeff saw the wetness in his eyes. Val stood silently near them. Finally, they parted and looked at each other embarrassed as they wiped their eyes.

"Hey Nhang. You look great. Come on," he put his arm around Nhang's shoulders and turned to face Valerie. "This is my wife, Valerie."

"I'm very honored to meet you, Valerie," Nhang carefully articulated, sticking out his hand.

"And I'm very honored to meet you, Nhang," Val smiled warmly as she shook his hand, then pulled him into a friendly hug. "Thank you," she whispered into his ear. "For helping my husband come back to me."

"You know," Ted laughed. "He's had me coaching him on that greeting ever since we left San Francisco. Hi Val. I'm Ted Hefley."

"I'm sorry Ted," Jeff beamed, putting his arm around Nhang again as Val released him. "My head is spinning. This is Valerie."

"Hi Ted," Val smiled as she kissed Ted on the cheek and hugged him.

"Well," Ted grinned when they parted. "You're even more beautiful than Jeff said. Come on," he took her arm. "I'll introduce you to the folks."

Introductions and greetings were made by Ted to the group at the pool. Everyone was laughing and crying at the same time and finally Mr. Chandler poured champagne for everyone and proposed a toast. They all drank and tried to settle down in conversation.

"Ted," Jeff said.

"Yeah Jeff," Ted looked up.

"When is Ken arriving?"

Ted looked at him in disbelief. A stunned silence fell over the group as they all looked at Jeff.

"What's wrong?" Val asked.

"You haven't heard," Ted picked up a folded newspaper from a table and handed it to him, holding open the front page. "He's dead!"

"Oh no," Val cried, moving to Jeff's side, her hands clenched before her mouth.

Jeff read the bold headline *EX NAM POW KILLS TWO, THEN SELF IN L.A.*

"I'm sorry Jeff," Ted said slowly. "I thought you knew. It's been on all the news. Ken found his wife and her boyfriend. Some ex-Army Captain. It happened yesterday."

"Oh my God," Jeff shook his head. "No!"

CRITIC'S CHOICE

Espionage and Suspense Thrillers

THE ADVERSARY A. M. Kabal	$3.50
THE CITY OF FADING LIGHT Jon Cleary	$3.95
THE CHINESE FIRE DRILL Michael Wolfe	$3.50
DECISION IN BERLIN Robert Dege	$3.95
THE DEVIL'S VOYAGE Jack L. Chalker	$3.95
THE FACTORY Jack Lynn	$3.95
FATAL MEMORY Bruce Forrester	$3.95
THE FORTRESS AT ONE DALLAS CENTER R. Lawrence	$3.50
FREEZE William Raynor & Myles Wilder	$3.95
THE HOUR OF THE LILY John Kruse	$3.95
KENYA John Halkin	$3.95
THE LAST PRESIDENT Michael Kurland & S.W. Bart	$3.95
THE PALACE OF ENCHANTMENTS Hurd & Lamport	$3.95
THE TERRORIST KILLERS Geoffrey Metcalf	$3.95
THE TWO-TEN CONSPIRACY Leon LeGrand	$3.95
THE VON KESSEL DOSSIER Leon LeGrand	$3.95

Please send your check or money order (no cash) to:

Critic's Choice Paperbacks
31 East 28th Street
New York, N.Y. 10016

Please include $1.50 for the first book and 50¢ for each additional book to cover the cost of postage and handling.

Name_____

Street Address_____

City_____ State_____ Zip Code_____

Write for a free catalog at the above address.
Canadian orders must be accompanied by a U.S. money order.

CRITIC'S CHOICE
The finest in Occult & Horror

BLOODWORM by John Halkin	$3.50
BLOODTHIRST by Mark Ronson	$2.95
THE BRASS HALO by James Nugent	$3.95
THE GHOUL by Mark Ronson	$2.95
HALLOWEEN IV by Nicholas Grabowsky	$3.50
OGRE by Mark Ronson	$2.95
PLAGUE PIT by Mark Ronson	$2.95
PRAY SERPENTS PREY by Nicholas Randers	$3.95
THE SECRET by Adriane Malone	$3.95
SLIME by John Halkin	$3.50
SQUELCH by John Halkin	$3.50
WHEN SPIRITS WALK by Christine Gentry	$3.95

CRITIC'S CHOICE
The greatest mysteries
being published today.

CRITIC'S CHOICE

Captivating historical romances

THE CASTLE OF THE WINDS Jeanne Montague	$3.95
CHASE THE HEART Maggie Osborne	$3.95
COPPER KINGDOM Iris Gower	$3.95
CROSS CURRENTS Barbara Whitnell	$3.95
THE EMERALD VALLEY Janet Tanner	$3.95
FIDDLER'S FERRY Iris Gower	$3.95
HAWKSMOOR by Aileen Armitage	$3.95
MORGAN'S WOMAN by Iris Gower	$3.95
PROUD MARY Iris Gower	$3.95
SPINNER'S WHARF Iris Gower	$3.95
SWANDSDOWNE Daniel Farson	$3.95
THE TAVENER'S PLACE Joanna Trollope	$4.50
TREASURES ON EARTH by Jessica Stirling	$3.95
VIRGINSONG Frances DeTalavera Berger	$4.50